SAVED BY MAGIC

AN URBAN FANTASY NOVEL

JASMINE WALT

DYNAMO PRESS

Cover illustration by Judah Dobin. Cover typography by Rebecca Frank. Edited by Mary Burnett.

MINA

"**O**h!" I cried as I felt a mighty tug on the end of my line that made me overbalance and slide forward on the slippery deck. "I think I've got one!"

"It seems that you have—whoa!" Fenris dropped the flounder he'd just caught into the bucket, then lunged forward to grab me by the waist as I was nearly yanked overboard. I cried out as my knees slammed against the railing of the fishing boat we'd rented and nearly lost my grip on my fishing pole.

"By the Lady," I hissed as Fenris hauled me back into the center of the boat, very thankful for his shifter strength. I tightened my grip on the pole and gave another tug, and whatever was on the line yanked back so hard, I was nearly torn from Fenris's grip. "What did I catch, a whale?"

Fenris chuckled in my ear and reached around to grasp my hands atop the pole. "We're about to find out."

With Fenris's considerable shifter strength, combined with mine, the two of us managed to haul the fish into the boat. It thrashed viciously the whole time, all five feet of it, and Fenris was forced to sever its head with a machete lest it accidentally capsize us.

"We need a bigger boat," I panted as we laid the giant fish down on the bottom. Even if we cut it into pieces, it would never fit in the bucket we'd brought to hold our catches. "What in Recca did we catch?"

"A giant sea bass, I believe," Fenris said, staring down at the fish in amazement. "Quite the accomplishment, considering this is your first fishing trip. I've never caught anything so big myself."

I laughed a little. "I think it's safe to say that we're done for the day." I looked out onto the sparkling blue waters of the Western Sea and smiled. It was a gorgeous day to be out on the water, and I'd readily agreed to Fenris's suggestion that we spend our first morning in Canalo here. But now that our boat was filled with fish, and my skin was beginning to turn pink despite the protective cream I'd slathered on and the hat I wore, I was ready to turn back.

Fenris steered the boat back to the marina, where the dock staff exclaimed over our catch. They were very impressed when Fenris told them that I had wrangled the beast, and they took the fish back to the hotel restaurant, where it would be cooked and served for dinner. I grinned when one of them asked if he could take me out on his next fishing trip since I clearly brought good luck, and laughed when Fenris hooked his arm neatly around my waist and dragged me back to the hotel for a much-needed shower and change of clothes.

"Blast it," Fenris muttered when I walked back into the bedroom, one towel wrapped around my waist and another over my wet hair. "I still haven't been able to reach Iannis."

"I'm sure he'll turn up soon," I assured him as I sat down on the bed next to him. We'd tried contacting Iannis several times before leaving for Canalo, and again when we'd arrived, but each time the secretary Fenris spoke to told him that he and Sunaya had to leave on an urgent matter and would be back soon. "His wedding is within a fortnight—he can't very well miss it after inviting the entire government, and half the world besides."

Fenris sighed. "I hope you're right. When Iannis and Sunaya get called away on an 'urgent' matter, it usually means they've involved themselves in something dangerous and life-threatening. And this time I'm not with them."

I bit my lip. I could understand Fenris's worry—if Barrla, my own best friend, had gone off somewhere without notice and there was a strong chance that she was in danger, I would be figuring out how to track her down and get to her. But no one would say where Iannis and Sunaya had gone. Since they had been missing for days, from a crowded city, even Fenris's shifter nose would hardly be able to track them. The safest thing to do was wait until they returned—especially since the trouble we'd come to warn Iannis about was happening right here in Canalo.

"From everything you've told me about your friends, I'm sure they'll be fine," I assured Fenris. "They seem perfectly capable of taking care of themselves. You should put it out of your mind for now and go take a shower to wash off all that sea salt." I pressed a gentle kiss to his cheek. "I've really enjoyed what I've seen of Canalo so far, and we may as well continue to enjoy it while things are still peaceful."

Fenris smiled. "You're right," he said, turning his head to kiss me back. He rose from the bed and shucked off his clothes. "I'll see you in a bit."

Alone in our suite, I dressed for the day in a peach-colored dress, then brushed out my blonde hair and left it loose on my shoulders. Our hotel room was beautiful, decorated in shades of sea green and sea-shell white, which was fitting considering we were at the Marwale. We were pretending to be already married, Mr. and Mrs. Shelton, and if I had anything to do with it, this would be true before much longer. I had never cared for the mage custom of year-long engagements, and since Fenris was now technically a shifter, there didn't seem to be a good reason to abide by it.

Fenris and I had settled on this beachside hotel an hour away from Solantha because every room and couch within the capital was booked solid. We would have preferred to be closer, but we couldn't very well stay in the Palace in disguise without an invitation from Iannis and Sunaya. Besides, the guest rooms there were doubtless filled by all the officials who were coming for not just the wedding, but also the Convention. For Fenris's safety, it was best to keep as far away from his former colleagues as possible.

I expected Fenris to be finished with his shower by the time I was dressed, but the water was still running. I imagined Fenris was using the time to think, as I also liked to do sometimes. Not wanting to disturb him, I left a note on the desk, then wandered out to the lounge for some much-needed tea.

The lounge was a gorgeous outdoor area located on the hotel rooftop. Dozens of charming seating areas were grouped around fire pits that would light up every night, and beyond them was a spectacular view of the ocean. In the center of the rooftop lounge was a bar and café, and as I approached, I noticed with delight that they had a selection of mini cakes behind a glass display case. My stomach grumbled—it was only mid-morning, but Fenris and I had risen very early for our fishing expedition, which had been surprisingly exhausting. A cup of tea and some cake sounded like just the thing.

"An excellent choice," the cashier said with a smile as she rang up my selections—a small pot of chai and a slice of lemon cake, which would be brought to the table of my choice. I was just about to settle in one of the seating areas when a staff member appeared at my elbow, seemingly out of thin air.

"I'm sorry to disturb you, Mrs. Shelton, but there is a man

here to see you," she said. "He claims to be an acquaintance of yours?"

The way the woman's eyebrows rose, and the hint of censure in her tone, told me that the "man" in question was not the usual caliber of person who frequented the Marwale, and that if I didn't vouch for him, he would be thrown out.

"Did he give his name?" I asked, curiosity winning out over my need for tea and cake.

"No, he only said that he knows you and must speak to you urgently."

I frowned. "Well bring him up here, then." I wasn't sure who could be calling on me, but if I had to accept a visit from a stranger without Fenris around, I'd rather do it out here in the open, with witnesses.

The staff member nodded, and I found a seat to enjoy my tea and cake while I waited. A few minutes later, she reappeared, this time accompanied by a sandy-haired young man wearing travel-worn clothes and a knapsack slung over his broad shoulder.

"Marris!" I cried, jumping out of my chair so I could hug him. He smelled like sweat and dirt, and I quickly pulled him over to sit down next to me. "Please, get my cousin some refreshments, and book a room for him—you may put it on our account." I placed a silver coin in her hand.

The employee went off, shooting a dubious glance over her shoulder at my guest, and Marris let out a deep sigh as he sank into the chair cushions. "This place is lush," he said, looking around, and there was awe glimmering through the exhaustion in his eyes. "Where are you staying, in the basement?"

I snorted. "Of course not," I told him, then took another sip of tea. "We have a room, and so do you, now that you're here. Why *are* you here, exactly?"

Marris ran a hand through his already-disheveled hair. "I

meant to stay home, I really did," he said, sounding apologetic. "But the constable warned me shortly after you and Fenris left that the mages were still sniffing around, pestering him about my whereabouts. It was too dangerous for me to stay, and my presence was putting him in a difficult position. So I thought I'd come out here and try to make myself useful."

I raised an eyebrow. "Does Barrla know you're here? And how did you manage to track us down?" We hadn't told anyone in Abbsville which hotel we were staying at.

Marris gave me a sheepish smile. "Barrla's the one who told me. A friend of hers overheard Fenris on the phone at the inn, when he was booking your trip. She wanted to come along, but I told her it was much too dangerous. I left before she could get me to change my mind."

I winced. "She's going to skin you alive if you ever go back to Abbsville," I warned. Barrla would be furious—she hated being left out of anything, and would feel especially slighted considering her closest friends were the ones leaving her behind. It had been one thing for Fenris and me to go, since we were a couple, but for Marris, the man she was dating, to leave her in the dust? No way was she going to stand for that.

Marris grimaced. "I'll have to make it up to her somehow. But if there is going to be bloodshed and mayhem in Solantha, I can't have Barrla here. She doesn't know the first thing about protecting herself."

I opened my mouth to answer, then closed it again at the sight of Fenris weaving his way between the tables toward us. "There you are," he said as he came up from behind Marris. "Making friends already?"

"Fenris?" Marris turned in his chair to greet Fenris, then froze, his mouth agape. I cringed at the shocked look on his face—Fenris had used his magic to change his appearance slightly. He was a few inches taller, his hair was a shade of honey-brown, and his shifter eyes were now human-blue. Different enough that he would not instantly be recognized as Iannis's friend...but close enough that Marris could see plainly who he was, and what he'd done.

"Marris?" Fenris stared back at Marris, equally astonished. "What in Recca are you doing here?"

"What...you..." Marris spluttered. Knowing that the game was up, I took Marris by the elbow and led him to the other side of the rooftop, which was practically deserted. Fenris snapped his fingers and engaged the privacy bubble around us for good measure, and Marris's eyes narrowed as he watched the air around us shimmer with magic.

"You're a mage," he said flatly.

"We both are," I said before Fenris could respond. "Fenris has been hiding his magic because shifters aren't allowed to have any, and I've been hiding mine because I've been passing myself off as a human, for different reasons."

Marris looked at me as though I were insane. "Why in Recca would you want to do that? Everyone knows that mages live in wealth and comfort. You'd have to be crazy to want to live in Abbsville and work every day like ordinary people."

"I was running away from my family, and the easiest way to keep them from finding me was to pretend I was a human." I sighed at the skeptical look on Marris's face. It was clear he felt betrayed, but at least he was still listening. "If you would please sit down, I'll tell you all about it."

Marris warily did as I asked, and I explained to him about my sordid family history, and how I'd been forced to flee Haralis, my hometown, in order to escape my abusive relatives. "It's only these past weeks that I've finally been able to wrest my inheritance back from them and use my legal name without fear," I explained. "And why I can afford to stay at this 'lush place,' as you call it," I added dryly.

Marris shook his head. "Then why did you come back to Abbsville, if that was all handled? How do I know that you both aren't secretly spying on us for the mages?"

Fenris scoffed. "If I had been, don't you think I would have turned you, Cobil, and Roth in the moment I found out about the counterfeiting? I risked my life to keep you all safe, and you know it."

"I do," Marris said, looking chagrined. "But still...this is..."

"I know it's a shock," I said. "Believe me, I was shocked too when I learned that Fenris was a mage as well as a shifter, but he does have mages in his family, so it isn't that strange that he can use magic too. If the law allowed it, he would probably be living openly as one."

Marris blew out a long breath. "That must be awful, having to hide your true nature all your life," he finally said. "Something else we can thank the mage regime for, eh?"

"Yes, but that still does not mean I hold ill will against all mages," Fenris said sternly, reading the expression on Marris's face perfectly. "The Chief Mage of Solantha and his bride are close friends of mine, and we have come to Canalo to ensure that nobody harms them at their wedding. If you are here to join up with your ex-Resistance buddies and cause trouble, we will be on opposite sides."

"Opposite sides?" Marris echoed bleakly. "I thought we were all part of the League of Justice."

"Yes," Fenris said, "and the League of Justice should not be involved in what amounts to a terror attack."

"This is unbelievable." Marris shot to his feet. "You...you..." He pointed at Fenris, then me, then whirled on his heel. "I need some time to think about this."

Fenris and I exchanged worried looks as Marris stomped off, drawing expressions of censure and annoyance from the staff. "I hope he doesn't go off and tell anyone about this," I said, then bit my lip. Fenris and I were posing as humans at this hotel—since Fenris was a shifter, and I wasn't a fully trained mage, we hoped this would prevent awkward questions. Our role as rich humans should also make it easier to infiltrate the plot we were investigating, if we ever got that far. "Marris may not know that you're wanted by the Federation, but if he tells the wrong person he might still cause harm."

"I believe Marris's good heart will ultimately prevail," Fenris said, but he looked concerned. "We'll let him think on it the rest of the day, and if he doesn't come to us then, we'll just have to seek him out and talk some sense into him."

TWO

True to my word, I did not attempt to hunt Marris down after his abrupt departure from the lounge, though I could have. His scent was distinctive and easy to follow—he was probably out on the beach somewhere or in the room Mina had rented for him. But talking to him now would not be productive. He needed space and time to sort out his feelings, to come to grips with the revelation we'd blindsided him with.

Instead, Mina and I spent the afternoon at the beach, and I did my best to put Marris and my other troubles out of my thoughts. It wasn't hard—Mina was absolutely ravishing in yet another one of her bikinis, and her carefree mood as she splashed through the ocean water was infectious. We rode the waves, made sand castles, buried each other, and indulged in other fun things that I remembered doing as a small child, back when I was not Polar ar'Tollis, Chief Mage of Nebara, but simply Polar, my parents' beloved only son.

Later, we showered and changed back into our clothes, then had dinner on the open-air terrace of the hotel restaurant. Mina was delighted when they served us portions of her catch—perfectly grilled, with a side of baby carrots and roast potatoes.

"Mmm," she said around a mouthful of sea bass. "This is delicious. We should catch these more often."

I chuckled. "You'll have to get a bit stronger if you can hope to reel in another one of those beasts." Even I'd had trouble, though that was mostly because the fish had been thrashing about so fiercely. It was a strong animal...and tasted divine, especially with a squeeze of lemon.

We finished our main course and, as we waited for dessert to arrive, relaxed in our chairs, sipping at the wine. "It's the end of the day," Mina said as she stared out at the glorious sunset. The sun was more than halfway below the horizon, streaking the glittering water with gold and pink, and the colorful rays gilded Mina's troubled face. "Do you think he's left?"

"It's very possible," I admitted, setting down my glass of wine. "We cannot force Marris to side with us on this, just as he cannot force us to abandon Iannis and Sunaya. I should have been more careful."

Mina frowned. "More careful? With what? You couldn't have known he would track us here."

I shook my head. "I mean I should have been more alert to my surroundings. If I'd been paying attention, I would have scented it was Marris long before I'd approached. But I was still thinking about Iannis, and it didn't occur to me to be cautious. I may have overestimated how safe we are here."

"What, do you think there are enemies lurking around every corner?" Mina asked, sounding skeptical. "This isn't Haralis; nobody knows us here. Aside from this incident with Marris, we've yet to come across anyone truly troubling."

"Give it time," I said dryly, then took another sip of wine. Luxurious establishments like this hotel were frequented by the dangerous as well as the rich. More often than not, they were the same people.

I'd chosen this spot not just because the capital was over-booked, but also because I wanted to get the lay of the land from a safe distance. Despite Mina's insistence that we come in person to warn Iannis, I had chosen to write a letter first. Iannis's lack of reply had galvanized me into coming out here, and his disappearance was even more disturbing. I'd sent several ether pigeons to Iannis since crossing into Canalo territory, but Iannis had not sent one back, and I had to wonder if they'd ever arrived. It was possible that wherever he'd traveled was beyond their reach. Ether pigeons didn't confirm delivery or return once they were sent off. It was in part why they had fallen out of use, along with the invention of the telephone—they were much less reliable than a phone and were only used now on the rare occasions when making a call wasn't possible.

"Even if Marris does tell someone that we're mages, it won't make much of a difference," Mina said, trying to console me. "Half the guests at this hotel are mages, and we likely aren't the first ones to pass ourselves off as humans. It is not illegal. Mostly I'm just worried what Barrla will think when Marris tells her about this."

I smiled as I pictured her reaction. "Barrla will be just as excited as she will be angry, I suspect. She seems to have a penchant for the extraordinary."

Mina smiled too, though it was tinged with worry. "True," she said, then changed the subject. "I've been leafing through the newspapers and society magazines in the reading room, and all I've found was a lot of gushing about the wedding dress, the planned festivities, and the guest list." She lowered her voice a little. "Every Chief Mage in the Federation is attending, and many important dignitaries from abroad. How in Recca will I fit in with such a crowd?"

Chuckling, I reached across the table to take her hand. "I would not worry about the guest list," I told her, pressing a kiss to her knuckles. "The fact that you are my intended will make you more important in Iannis and Sunaya's eyes than even the richest emperor. The actual ceremony will be short and fairly private, and my friends will be thrilled to meet you. The main thing is to keep everyone safe."

Mina blushed a little. "We aren't the only ones concerned with keeping things safe," she said. "Perhaps the mages themselves will uncover this plot in time. I read an article about how Federal Director Garrett Toring was in charge of the Convention's security and has already arrived in Solantha with a large team of agents. He's supposed to be very thorough and intelligent. With all the resources at his disposal, is it likely we can do better?"

I grimaced, then snapped my fingers to engage the privacy bubble. "Garrett is indeed very clever—he's the reason I had to flee Solantha last year after the quake," I told her. "He nearly exposed the truth about my past, despite my shifter body and completely different looks, merely because I continued to study the same kind of esoteric books as I did before the transformation. We need to avoid him as much as possible."

"That will be difficult, if we are close to the Chief Mage and his bride," Mina said. "Although before we worry about that problem, we really need to figure out how to get lodgings in Solantha. Driving back and forth an hour every day will become tedious."

"I sent an ether pigeon to Comenius, a friend, who is the only other person aside from Sunaya and Iannis that I can trust with the knowledge of my presence," I told her. "He will tell us what he knows, and might even be able to help us find a place to stay."

Mina frowned. "Is he a mage?"

I shook my head. "He is a hedge witch, which means he will not be able to send a reply except by normal mail. The Convention is still ten days away, but I don't think waiting that long is wise."

"I agree," Mina said. "We should go visit him tomorrow."

"Leaving so soon?" Marris asked, appearing by Mina's elbow. She started, nearly dropping her spoon, and Marris gave her a sheepish look. "Sorry about that. Didn't mean to scare you."

"Are you done being angry with us, then?" I asked mildly.

Marris nodded. "I don't have any wish for bloodshed," he told me sincerely. "I will do whatever I can to help you, so long as you promise not to do anything that will harm humans or strengthen the mage regime."

"I have no wish to empower the Minister and his cohorts any further," I assured Marris. "I have never liked the man, and he is not very good at his job." Of course, long ago my vote had helped elect him to the position, but since then my idea of what a good Minister should be had drastically changed.

The waiter arrived with our dessert, and I asked him to bring a chair and a menu for Marris, so he could order something to eat.

"I can't read half of this," Marris muttered as he stared at the pages. "What the hell is sauce acks morilles?"

"It is pronounced *sauce aux morilles*," the waiter corrected him, a supercilious look on his face. "It means 'morrel sauce' in Forrane."

"And what the hell is morrel sauce?"

Sighing, I plucked the menu from Marris's hands. "Get him the filet *de bœuf grillé*, medium rare," I told the waiter. "Don't worry about it," I said to Marris in an undertone. "Foreign restaurants like these have a tendency to be pretentious."

"I'll say." Shaking his head, Marris leaned back in his chair.

"I have to admit this place makes me pretty uncomfortable. I stick out like a sore thumb dressed in these clothes while you two are sitting here looking like..." He trailed off, gesturing to Mina, who had donned the same yellow dress she wore earlier, paired with citrine-colored stones that dangled from her ears and throat.

"We're still the same people we've always been, Marris," Mina said softly. "What we wear and where we stay doesn't change that."

"No, but I'm getting real tired of everyone else around here looking at me like I belong out back with the dumpsters," Marris said, folding his arms across his chest. "If it's all the same to you, I think I'd be better off finding another place to stay."

"And where would that be?" I asked, genuinely curious. "Everything is booked up in Solantha, and you don't look like you have two coppers to rub together. If you need a loan..."

Marris huffed. "No thanks. I have a *few* coppers," he said. "And I've got contacts in Solantha who I'd bet are involved with whatever plan you guys are here to stop. I can go join up with them and find out what they're up to, and if it's something bad, I'll give you guys whatever useful intel I find."

"That would be quite helpful," I said, feeling very pleased, not to mention astonished, with the offer. "I should have thought of asking you myself."

Marris grinned. "You can't have all the good ideas, or there would be no one around to keep you humble."

Marris's steak arrived, and as he ate, we discussed our plans a bit more. He would infiltrate the ex-Resistance members lurking about Solantha and meet us at Comenius's shop in two days around closing time to tell us what he'd found. If we weren't there, he would leave an encoded message, and if the plot involved the killing of innocents, Marris would make every effort to ensure we were informed no matter what.

"I'll be off, then," Marris said once we were finished. "Better get to my friends before they turn in for the night."

"Safe travels," I said, clasping him in a brief hug.

"If things look like they're turning south, promise me that you'll get out of there," Mina said when Marris hugged her, too. "The last thing I need is to bring news of your death to Barrla."

"I have every intention of returning home safe to my girl," Marris said with a wink. And with that, he strolled off the terrace and out into the night.

THREE

After Marris left, Fenris went off to see to a few matters, amongst them arranging for a hired steamcar to drive us to Solantha in the morning. With little to do but twiddle my thumbs, I decided to go walk on the balustrade and enjoy the evening air.

It's beautiful out here, I thought as I skimmed a hand along the railing, watching the ocean crash against the shore. The moonlight limned the frothy waves in silver, and the stars twinkling brightly above my head were so numerous that the sky held almost more light than darkness. I'd thought that there would be fewer stars out here than in Abbsville because of the light pollution, but we were far enough away from Solantha that their splendor was not dimmed by the city.

A comet streaked across the sky, and I gasped and then quickly made a wish. *I wish that we soon will* really *be Mr. and Mrs. Shelton*, I thought fiercely as I gazed up at the fiery meteor that blazed past. I knew that Fenris's last name wasn't *actually* Shelton, but since he didn't go by a last name that would do as well as any.

Unless we went by my last name, I thought, with some

amusement. I wondered what my parents would think if they knew I was continuing the Marton line through a shifter. I liked to think that they would be happy for me, but I knew the truth—though they had loved me, they would not have been able to accept Fenris. What kind of children we might have would be anyone's guess—they might be mages, they might be shifters, or they might be hybrids, like the Chief Mage's bride. So few children had ever been born of a mage-shifter coupling that it was impossible to say, and Fenris was no ordinary shifter. He might not have the body of Polar ar'Tollis anymore, but mage blood still ran in his veins, or he wouldn't be able to use magic at all.

As I walked further along the balustrade and away from the lights spilling from the hotel windows, I saw the outlines of statues further up the path. Wanting to see them better, I conjured a glowlight—a ball of soft, yellow light that illuminated the way. As I held it up to look upon the face of a woman carved in white marble, I heard something rustle behind me.

"I had not realized you were a mage, too," a heavily accented female voice said, and I spun around. Standing behind me was a tall, elegant woman. She wore a fitted gown of some dark purple fabric with silver brocade, and her silver hair was scooped back from a beautiful face. "You are not wearing any robes."

"Neither are you," I said as I met her keen gaze. "And who might you be?"

The woman gave me a small smile. She had an ageless look about her, and I had a feeling it was not the product of glamour—she simply aged very well. "My name is Mirrine ar'Torat, and I am from Forrane," she said in that flowing accent. "The *Magicien Moderne* has asked me to report on the wedding."

"A mage reporter?" My eyebrows rose. "That is the last thing I would have guessed." More like the owner of the paper, or some kind of celebrity, from her appearance and manner.

"What, because I have good taste in clothing?" Mirrine

laughed as she moved closer. Her perfume wafted through the warm evening air, teasing my nose with its rich floral scent. "I assure you, there is more to enjoying a long life than merely spending money. A profession keeps boredom at bay and can always be changed for another if it gets stale."

I laughed. "True enough," I agreed, then introduced myself under my assumed name. The Marton family had not been noble but had amassed a fortune all the same. It was very possible this woman had come from money and simply worked as a reporter for fun. It was an unusual career for a mage, but not unheard of, and perhaps things were done differently in Forrane anyway.

"If you came to report on the wedding," I asked, "then why stay here instead of within the city? Surely you would want to be as close to the festivities as possible."

Mirrine sighed, tucking a wisp of silver hair behind her ear. "The city is dusty and full of construction workers—you can hardly move about without inhaling sweat and dirt. I much prefer this seaside hotel. Everything in Solantha is overbooked and too crowded just now."

I nodded. "That's why my husband and I are staying here, too," I told her. "Though it is only happenstance that we arrived just before the Chief Mage's wedding and the Convention. Mr. Shelton and I are recently married, and we are spending our honeymoon touring the Federation."

"You picked a poor time," Mirrine said, looking out across the water. "I have been to Solantha before, and it is quite a charming city under normal circumstances."

"Perhaps we'll return and experience it in its renewed splendor," I said, though I wasn't sure if that would happen. Fenris was only coming back to Solantha because his friends were in danger—it might not be safe for him to do so again.

"What do you think of the government?" Mirrine asked, turning to face me. "Specifically, your Minister Graning."

"He is not popular, especially amongst non-mages," I said baldly. "Given that humans tried to murder him not so long ago, I think it's safe to say that they hate him. I would not want to trade places with him, I know that much."

And I certainly wouldn't want to meet him in person, I added silently. The Minister had not even bothered to speak to Fenris personally when he'd decided to have him executed, even though Fenris had been a Chief Mage at the time. Any leader willing to discard one of his people so coldly was not worth speaking to in my eyes.

"Yes, I have heard all about that nasty business with the Resistance," Mirrine said. Her eyes glittered, and I got the distinct feeling that I was being measured. "Do you have any idea where the Minister might be staying?"

I frowned a little, wondering at her line of questioning. "According to the society magazines, he has elected to rent a large mansion in the Mages Quarter, rather than stay in Solantha Palace as he has in the past. The papers are speculating that there is tension between the Minister and Lord Iannis and wondering whether or not that will affect his decision on who to nominate as his successor."

Mirrine huffed. "If Lord Iannis and the Minister are on the outs, it seems very strange to hold this year's Convention in Solantha."

I shrugged. "There's no proof there is a rift at all, and if there is one, it might have occurred after it was too late to change the location. Personally, I think the Minister just wants more space and independence than he could have as anyone's guest."

Mirrine looked like she was about to say something else, but she stopped at the sound of footsteps on the pavement. Turning, I saw Fenris coming down the path, a small lantern in his hand.

"There you are," he said warmly, coming over to press a kiss to my cheek. "And who is your new friend?" he asked, turning to Mirrine.

"My husband, Mr. Shelton," I said to Mirrine. "Fenris, this is Mirrine ar'Torat. She is a reporter from the *Magicien Moderne*."

"Ah, a Forranian, then?" Fenris inclined his head, then said something in Forrane. The woman smiled wide, and they exchanged a few brief sentences.

"It is always a delight to meet someone in the Federation who can speak my mother tongue fluently," Mirrine said. She patted Fenris on the arm, then added, "I can see that you want to be alone with your pretty young wife, so I will leave you two to enjoy the gardens."

She walked off, and Fenris and I watched her go, impossibly graceful in her tall heels. "She knows I am a mage," I murmured as Fenris slipped his arm through mine. "She saw me conjure the glowlight."

"I wouldn't worry about it," Fenris said as he drew me close. "We probably will not meet again, and even if we do, she will not think it strange that you chose to pose as a human. Many mages do in mixed settings."

I opened my mouth to ask him another question, something niggling at the back of my mind. But Fenris took my face in his hands and kissed me, and I forgot all about the elegant Forrane woman and her probing questions.

FOUR

MINA

The next morning, Fenris and I headed for Solantha in our rented steamcar. It had an open roof, so I was forced to tie down my wide-brimmed straw hat with a scarf to keep it from flying away as the winds whipped around us. I wore a deep pink dress with white flowers that matched the band of my hat, and Fenris was dressed in jeans and a button-up shirt, a pair of mirror sunglasses perched on his strong nose. He'd added the sunglasses to his human disguise as an extra precaution—between that, his added height, and his adjusted features, nobody would recognize him. Especially not when everyone was intent on preparing for the wedding and Convention, two huge events within the same stretch of time.

Within an hour, the city of Solantha came into view, and with it, the sparkling waters of Solantha Bay. Leaning out the window, I took in the sight of the famous Firegate Bridge, gleaming red in the morning sun, and the sprawling city beyond it.

Solantha was a beautiful sight from afar, but as we crossed the bridge and made our way into the city, I was greeted by honking horns and dusty air. Many of the buildings were covered in scaffolding as workers toiled to repair them, and numerous streets were shut off due to quake damage that still had not been fixed, forcing us to take alternate routes that were even more congested than they normally would have been, according to Fenris.

"I knew the city was badly damaged," he said quietly as we drove, "but I didn't think there would still be this much construction going on."

Sensing the melancholy mood that had swept over him, I placed my hand atop his on the gear shift. "It wouldn't have gone any faster if you'd stayed behind," I told him. "None of this is your fault. From what you have told me, you helped with the emergency preparations and are very lucky to have survived at all."

Making our way through snarled traffic and steep inclines, I noted that beneath the scaffolding, dust, and noise, Solantha retained a certain charm, a special flair. While many buildings were still being repaired, even more had either survived or were newly constructed, and these were lovely—the architects had mixed old and new styles together into pleasing designs. As we approached the port, gulls wheeled overhead, and a cooling wind swept my hair back, banishing some of the dust.

Fenris and I found a guarded parking lot and walked the last few blocks to Witches End, the pier where his friend Comenius had his shop. The port sprawled alongside us, endless piers jutting out into Solantha Bay, and I saw many gaily-colored buildings, carts selling wares, and street performers. A female contortionist in a striped pantsuit bent her body into all manner of unnatural positions to my left, while a small boy offered me caramel corn on my right. I bought a small bag from him, then stopped at a cart to inspect the wares of a jeweler.

"This one would suit you well, ma'am," the woman said,

holding up a silver necklace with purple gemstones that matched the dress I was wearing.

I smiled. "I'm afraid I don't care for silver," I told her. "Let me try those pearl earrings instead."

"You can still buy silver if you like," Fenris said once we continued on, a small bag in my hand. "You don't need to avoid it on my account."

"I want nothing to come between us," I said, slipping my free hand into his. "I would never wear something that prevents you from being able to touch any part of me."

"Keep talking like that," he murmured, leaning in to brush his lips against my cheek, "and we'll never make it to Comenius's shop."

Heat flashed in my core, and I could feel the blush rising in my cheeks at the thought of making love to Fenris again. But I was quickly distracted as we finally turned onto Witches End. Like several other piers along the port, this one was lined with shops, but unlike the others, these were of a magical nature. Delighted, I released Fenris's hand and flitted from window to window. Here, there was a fortune teller's shop, offering devices for scrying as well as more personalized services. There, an apothecary, selling all manner of cosmetics, potions, and remedies.

"Gulayas, New and Recharged?" I asked, reading the sign on a shop halfway up the pier. The painted letters looked to be brand-new, and through the sparkling glass windows I could peek at a display of metallic ornaments of varying shapes and styles, the biggest roughly the size of my palm. "What is this?"

"A new shop," Fenris said, regarding the place with interest. "Gulayas are devices that can be used to transport a person from one place to another instantly. They had fallen quite out of use until Iannis discovered a way to recharge them that didn't involve a highly illegal ingredient. This may very well be the first shop of its kind to exist in the Federation, or perhaps all of Recca."

"Really? These objects can teleport you to another location? No matter the distance?"

Fenris smiled. "In theory, though I imagine the further the distance, the pricier the gulaya. The first charge has to take place at the destination, and the gulaya is forever keyed to that place."

"And they are very expensive to start with," I murmured, glancing down at the prices marked on the displays. Only a single customer was inside, and I doubted that the shop got many customers since they charged such an exorbitant amount. "Even so, we can afford it. I think we should each have one, in case of emergency." Had Fenris possessed a charged gulaya when he'd had to flee from his home state, things might have gone a lot easier for him.

As we continued on, I made a mental note to come back to the gulaya store later. At the end of the pier, we finally reached Comenius's shop—a charming two-story building called Over the Hedge. As we opened the door, a bell tinkled, signaling our arrival. The place was empty at the moment, allowing me an uninterrupted view of the fresh, simple décor and the herbal remedies, soaps, charms, and other varied merchandise on the shelves and tables. The air was laced with herbal and floral scents, and as I inhaled, I immediately relaxed.

"One moment please!" a male voice with a strong Pernian accent called from the back. The curtain behind the counter was pushed aside, and a tall man with ash-blond hair dressed in a brown and green tunic came forward. "Welcome," he said with a friendly smile.

"Comenius." Fenris smiled, taking off his shades and dropping his disguise. "It's been a long time."

"Fenris!" Comenius's bright blue eyes went wide. He

hurried from behind the counter and caught Fenris up in a quick, hard hug. "I got your pigeon, but I hadn't expected you to come this soon. Please, head upstairs."

Comenius locked the front door and flipped the OPEN sign to CLOSED, then herded us through the back of his shop and up the stairs into what turned out to be a second-floor apartment. He sat us down on the small couch in the living area, then brought us tea and cookies from the kitchen.

"I can't thank you enough for what you did for Rusalia," Comenius said as he sat down across from us, his voice full of emotion. His blue eyes burned bright as he met Fenris's gaze. "You nearly gave your life for her."

Fenris smiled. "There is no need for thanks," he assured Comenius. "I have lived a long life already—your daughter deserves to have a happy one of her own. Where is she now?"

"At school," Comenius said. "She is doing quite well now that she's finally settled down. She was heartbroken when she thought you were dead, you know," he chided Fenris. "You could have sent a note to let us know you were safe. Sunaya told us that you were probably alive, but without proof it's been hard to believe until you sent me that ether pigeon."

"I'm sorry," Fenris said. "I thought it would be safer if you didn't know where I was, and messages can be easily intercepted."

"True. Now, who is your lovely friend?" Comenius asked, turning to me with a smile. "I don't think we've met before."

"This is Tamina Marton of Haralis," Fenris introduced me, hooking his arm through mine. "And my fiancée."

"Fiancée!" Comenius exclaimed, looking astounded. "Why, Fenris, I never imagined, of all the things that might have happened when you left, that you would settle down with a woman." He looked me up and down again, his frank blue gaze assessing now. "You're a mage, aren't you?"

I nodded. "An untrained one. I was in hiding until very recently, in the same small town Fenris moved to, and I haven't completed my apprenticeship yet. That's how Fenris and I found each other."

"Well I'm very happy for you both," Comenius said, smiling. "Elania and I finally tied the knot this spring, you know."

"Congratulations," Fenris said. "I am happy to hear that the quake did not rob you of your nuptials."

"We did have to reschedule a few things, but we are very happily married now," Comenius said.

"Has anything else of note happened while I've been gone?" Fenris asked, settling back in his chair. I'd expected him to launch straight into the reason for our visit, but it seemed he was more interested in hearing how his friends had fared. Not that I could blame him.

"Rylan Baine is a free man now," Comenius told him after taking a sip of tea. "I remember that you became friends, especially while Iannis and Sunaya were on their travels. After the quake Iannis granted him a full pardon, and Rylan is now living with the Baine Clan once again."

"The Baine Clan?" I asked. "Isn't Sunaya's last name Baine?"

Fenris nodded. "Sunaya is a daughter of the Baine Clan, though she had strained relations with them for many years due to her half-mage heritage. I hope that has changed?"

"It has," Comenius confirmed. "Her aunt's attitude transformed overnight, and she's been very cooperative with the Canalo government ever since Rylan was freed. I hear that he's been clashing with his mother, though, so I'm not sure if that will last." His lips twitched.

Fenris smiled wryly. "Rylan has always been a free spirit, very much like Sunaya. His sense of adventure will demand to be sated sooner or later, and I expect it is driving him crazy to have to live with the clan again." His expression turned serious again. "And what of Annia?"

"She and Noria are both gone," Comenius said, his eyes dimming with sadness. "The mines where Noria was serving her sentence collapsed during the quake, and Annia went to look for her sister. Noria was missing when she arrived, and Annia has been searching for her since."

"Noria?" I asked. Fenris had told me a little bit about his friends on the trip here but hadn't mentioned Noria. Since it had been many months since the quake and she was still missing, I guessed she probably did not want to be found. I wouldn't either, if all I had to go back to was breaking stones in a penal mine.

"Noria Melcott," Fenris explained. "She used to work in the shop downstairs while she was a student. She is Annia's younger sister, and a technological genius. She defected to the Resistance and was sent to the mines as punishment once she was apprehended."

"Oh." My stomach sank a little. Fenris had told me that Annia was an enforcer. I couldn't imagine how it must have felt to learn that your sister was a criminal. I wondered if Annia would bring her back, or if she would join her in exile. It seemed like an impossible choice to make.

"I do hope that Annia returns safely, hopefully with Noria in tow," Fenris said. "I know how much you cared for Noria. If only she would see reason, Iannis would pardon her in a heartbeat."

Comenius nodded gravely. "I know. But you didn't come here to talk about Noria," he said. "You mentioned in your ether pigeon that Solantha is in danger?"

"I'm afraid so," Fenris said. "A trusted friend has told me that someone is assembling former Resistance soldiers for something big. Since both the wedding and the Convention are happening here in Solantha, this is the ideal moment for the Resistance to stage a comeback. I have sent a coded letter to Iannis, as well as a veritable flock of ether pigeons, but I have not heard from him, which is very strange considering the urgency of my warning."

Comenius winced. "Yes, well, that is because Iannis and Sunaya are not here."

Fenris frowned. "I learned as much from the secretary when I called, but she assured me they would be back soon. And that still does not explain why Iannis has not answered any of my ether pigeons."

"I'm afraid I don't know much," Comenius said, "but Kardanor, who is now Secretary of City Planning and Director Chen's beau, told me that she believes Iannis and Sunaya have traveled to Manuc to deal with a family matter."

"Manuc!" Fenris exclaimed. That was all the way across the Eastern Sea, near the Central Continent. "No wonder my ether pigeons have not been able to reach him. Is there no address I can send a letter to?"

Comenius grimaced. "No one knows exactly where he went, and Iannis never shared any details about his early life in Manuc. If anyone knows more, surely it would be you."

Fenris shook his head. "I know that his father has passed, and he mentioned once that he was an only child. But now that I think about it, Iannis was pretty close-mouthed about his origins. I have no idea what other family he might still have over there."

"We could send someone out there to find him, but I fear it would be a waste of resources," Comenius said, "especially since he is expected back any day. Kardanor said that Iannis took a double-strength gulaya with him, one that is anchored to the Palace, so he'll be able to return the moment he's finished whatever business has called him away."

"I certainly hope so," Fenris muttered. "The last thing we all need is for Iannis to miss his own wedding. It would be too humiliating for words, the scandal of the decade."

"You aren't the only one who is wishing for his swift return," Comenius remarked. "Kardanor told me that Director Chen is at her wits' end trying to downplay Iannis's disappearance in the face of increasing media curiosity, with Garrett sniffing about and making a general nuisance of himself. She has her hands full—half the venues are still being plastered and painted, dignitaries are complaining about the accommodations, and so on. I do not envy her job right now."

"Venues?" I asked. "Just how many are there going to be?"

"The actual wedding will take place at the temple on Hawk Hill, of course," Comenius told me. "That is restricted to close friends and family. But for everyone else there will be a huge banquet and fireworks at the Palace right afterward. And there will be daily receptions during the week before the wedding, hosted by various officials and high members of society who are vying with one another to demonstrate their wealth and importance. The Minister himself is hosting one, in one of the city's biggest halls."

"Well, at least this is good for the city," Fenris remarked. "Solantha can do with the income after all the damage it has suffered. I am glad to see everyone is busy."

Comenius nodded. "Busy people are less likely to engage in a revolt, so there is that. Hopefully the numbers that the Resistance are gathering are not too great, in light of the recently booming economy."

"We can hope, but we certainly can't count on that," I said. "Sunaya and Iannis may be gone, but surely there is someone else we can speak to about this. We can't just sit by and do nothing."

"Agreed," Comenius said. "I will send an anonymous warning to Director Chen, and to Garrett Toring as well."

"I wish we did not have to involve Toring at all," Fenris muttered. "But since he is the Federal Director of Security, it would be stupid not to make use of his resources."

"I shall make absolutely certain he gets no wind of your presence here," Comenius assured Fenris. "We will alert Sunaya and Iannis the moment they get back, but in the meantime, we need to tell Toring. It is his job to root out Resistance operatives, after all, and I see no reason to do it for him."

FIVE

FENRIS

After we finished up at Com's place, I took Mina on a little sightseeing tour of the city, starting with a cable car ride to Firegate Park. It was a delight to see the look on Mina's face as I walked with her to the botanical gardens, then strolled along the nearby streets, eating ice cream cones while we window-shopped. Everything looked so placid and cheerful that it was hard to believe that fighting and mayhem might be just days away.

We even spent a bit of time walking along Firegate Bridge, and I pointed out Hawk Hill, the location of the hidden temple where Sunaya and Iannis would get married—if they made it back in time.

"We should get married there too," Mina said, leaning her head against my shoulder as we walked arm in arm. "It wouldn't be a grand affair like the Chief Mage's wedding, but it would be beautiful, and we would have all your friends with us."

I smiled. "I like that idea very much," I said softly, though I didn't know how realistic it was. It was one thing to visit Comenius in secret, quite another to get married in Resinah's temple, in full view of the mage community. It was sacrilege to put a false name in the book when you signed the temple registry, and I would feel even worse about doing it in the temple of a city that I loved.

Still, I didn't want to crush Mina's hopes, so I didn't trouble her with my doubts. And despite the fact that I had to wear human clothes and hide my face with mirrored sunglasses, I greatly enjoyed walking about Solantha and seeing the fair city that I had begun to think of as mine.

Hungry from all the walking, Mina and I stopped at a restaurant for lunch and ordered soup and sandwiches. "As much as I've enjoyed the sightseeing," Mina said over her bowl of chowder, "I have a feeling you're antsy to get something productive done."

I smiled. "Am I that transparent?" I asked as I crumbled some salted crackers into my own soup.

"Not to anyone else, perhaps, but I'm learning to read you better every day." Mina smiled briefly. "It will be at least another day until we hear from Marris, and we don't know if he'll find out anything useful."

"We are putting him in a difficult position, forcing him to spy on his comrades," I murmured as I stirred my soup. "Marris was never a highly ranked member of the Resistance, so I doubt he will be told anything too important. But still, he may furnish some useful clue to follow up on, tell us something we might not otherwise learn."

"Who do you think is behind all this?" Mina asked, her silver-gray eyes narrowed in thought. "The Benefactor is dead. Or is she, really? Could it be that her death was faked, like your own?"

"She did fake it when she escaped from the prison in Dara, and dozens of other people were killed in the fire her accomplices set," I said. "I was already gone from Solantha when her body was discovered, but from the media reports, I was under the impression that she was definitely confirmed dead. Iannis and Sunaya would have made sure of it. Sunaya knew Thorgana before she was unmasked, and her shifter nose could not be fooled."

"Then is there anyone else with the resources and intelligence to muster the Resistance again, reunite it for a big attack?"

"There are probably several in the human community who could rally them again," I said, "but I am not well-versed enough in human circles to guess who. The Benefactor was very good at weaving her web of deceit and lies—she had many wealthy businessmen and politicians as her friends and supporters. Any one of them could have decided to take up the cause in the wake of her death."

"Hmm." Mina chewed on her lip. "Did she have any family? Any sons or daughters?"

"No children, but she did have a husband, a millionaire businessman in his own right. He was fat and boring, not really a revolutionary type—but then the same could be said of Thorgana, who fooled everyone with her bird-witted socialite act. He fled the continent when Thorgana was caught, taking some of his fortune with him. I doubt he'll be risking his neck by returning anytime soon, when he's still on the most wanted list." I drummed my fingers on the table. "I think I'll pay a visit to Rylan, Sunaya's cousin, to see if he has heard anything about the plot through his former Resistance contacts."

"That seems like a long shot," Mina said. "Didn't you say that he'd turned on the Resistance after he was captured?"

"Yes." I smiled wryly. "I myself convinced him to help Sunaya in exchange for a reduced sentence. He saved thousands of lives in doing so, but many in the Resistance will have branded him a traitor. Still, he might know something. We know from Marris that former Resistance soldiers still stick together and exchange information. It would be foolish not to ask."

"Do you want me to come with you? He sounds like an interesting guy."

"I'm not sure you'd want to," I admitted. "Rylan is a charmer, but his mother, Clan Chieftain Mafiela Baine, is something of a battle-axe, and probably still suspicious of mages." I hoped I would not run into her—she might be reconciled with Sunaya now, but I had yet to forgive her for the cruel treatment she had meted out to her niece when she'd been an orphaned cub. "She would quickly realize your true nature, since you have been using magic recently. As you are not wearing robes, she might suspect we are trying to fool her."

Mina snorted. "Never mind, then. I'll do some more exploring in the meantime—I wasn't quite done looking around Witches End when we left. I'll meet you back at the parking lot at six o'clock."

We finished lunch, and I kissed Mina goodbye before hailing a cab to Shiftertown. Unfortunately, it turned out that Rylan was away on business. The butler asked, rather snootily, if I wanted to present myself to the Clan Chieftainess, but I opted to make my excuses and leave.

Remembering that I had other contacts in the area, I walked over to Shiftertown Inspector Book Lakin's house, only six blocks from the Baine household. Lakin was at home, and very surprised to see me when I knocked on the door in my normal guise.

"By Magorah," he exclaimed as he let me inside the house. "I never thought I'd see you again! Aren't you supposed to be dead?"

I raised an eyebrow. "Didn't Sunaya tell you that I was alive?" I asked as I followed him into his living room. He didn't look at me as if I was a wanted man, to my relief. "I talked to her and Iannis on the phone only a few weeks ago."

Lakin huffed. "Sunaya and I haven't spoken much in the

past six months. She's got her hands full with all her new responsibilities, and I've moved on with my life."

"I'm very happy to hear that," I said, pleased at the sincerity in his tone. Lakin had been infatuated with Sunaya once, and I'd been worried that he might not be able to let her go. "Who's the lucky lady?" The scent of female shifter was all over the house. There also were some very feminine touches, including a woven rug on the floor that I suspected was handmade and some charming figurines on the mantel that I couldn't imagine Lakin buying himself.

Lakin laughed. "No one you would know," he said. "But I am the lucky one, not her. I'm very glad I accepted the offer to move to Solantha. But enough of that—why don't you stop stalling and tell me why you're really here?"

"I've learned of a plot to gather ex-Resistance members here in Solantha for a major operation," I told him. "I'm not sure if the attack is going to target the wedding reception, or the Convention, or something else entirely, but the news came from a trusted source. I've already sent warnings to Iannis and Director Chen. I originally came down here to see if Rylan knew anything about it, but he's out of town. Then I thought that perhaps you might have heard something."

"I'm afraid not," Lakin said, frowning. "If I had, I would have gone to the Mages Guild right away. And so would Rylan, these days. He wouldn't let anyone harm Sunaya. In fact, his close association with her is pretty much a guarantee that nobody would have told him about a plot like that. You think Sunaya is in danger?"

"She was one of Thorgana's main enemies," I reminded him. "If someone is out to take up the Benefactor's cause, or avenge her, Sunaya and Iannis would be prime targets. But even if they aren't directly targeted, they are in danger anyway—whatever these fellows are planning, Iannis and Sunaya will be in the thick of the action." If they came back home in time. I almost wished they would stay away, but that would mean they were dealing with even worse problems wherever they had gone.

"I'll definitely keep my nose to the ground and let you know if I hear anything," Lakin promised. "Most of the shifters have no love for the Resistance after they learned that Thorgana planned to turn on us, but there might be one or two morons who still support the cause. I'll sniff around."

"Thank you." I stood. "I should get going—no need to take up too much of your time. If you do learn something, send a message to Comenius's shop and he'll forward it. I'm trying to keep a low profile, in case I get a chance to infiltrate these plotters."

"Yes, I won't be discussing your visit with anyone but Sunaya, if I get the chance," he assured me. "And Rylan."

"Thanks." I rose to take my leave.

"Oh, wait!" Lakin raised a hand, stopping me. "I knew there was something I should tell you, and I've just remembered. An elderly mage came by here a couple of weeks ago asking about you."

My heart jumped. "About *me?*" Was it someone from Garrett's office, looking to apprehend me? But no, his agents were all young and keen. It would be most unlike him to employ anyone older than himself or encourage his people to disguise themselves as elderly.

"Yes. He was anxious to find you—or rather, your grave, since he'd heard that you'd died. Thought that I might know where it is, since you were a shifter." A sad expression crossed Lakin's face. "He seemed pretty dejected, and very disappointed when I couldn't help. From the way he reacted, I assumed he must be a good friend."

I frowned. "I don't know any elderly mages who would have

been deeply affected by my passing. Do you know what the man's name was?"

"He left me a card," Lakin said, patting his jacket pockets. "Let me see if I can find it."

Unfortunately, Lakin was unable to find the mage's calling card, but he promised to send word to me at Com's shop if he did find it, or if the mage came to visit again. As I left, I puzzled over the small mystery. Mostly, though, I was thankful that Lakin had received me as an old acquaintance rather than an enemy. He was smart and discreet, a good ally to have, though he clearly did not know anything about the gathering plot in his own city.

I'd better be careful not to show my face in front of Garrett Toring or the Minister, though, I thought as I took my leave. I had no doubt that they would be far less lenient if they discovered I was back in town.

SIX

MINA

After Fenris and I separated, I took a cable car back to the pier and returned to the gulaya shop that had caught my eye earlier. This time, there were no customers at all when I walked in just a bored-looking salesman standing behind the counter and the gleaming wares displayed on tables and shelves all around the premises.

"I'm sorry, Miss, but this establishment caters exclusively to mages," the man, who looked no older than thirty, said in a patronizing tone. "If you've taken a wrong turn, I am more than happy to help you find where you are going."

"*I am exactly where I want to be,*" I told the man in fluent Loranian, and he frowned.

"I...I'm afraid I don't recognize that language," he said, and I laughed.

"So you're not a mage yourself, then," I said. "Is there someone else in this 'establishment' that is?"

"That would be me, the owner," a young man said cheerily as he stepped through the door behind the counter. Unlike the salesman, he wore robes of deep blue, and I was taken aback by how fresh-faced he was, with a mop of curly hair and freckles on his pale skin. He couldn't be much older than me—in fact, I strongly suspected he was younger. His blue eyes twinkled behind his spectacles with good humor as he extended a hand to me. "Elnos Ragga, at your service."

"Mina Shelton," I said, shaking his hand with a firm grip. "Are you more willing to sell me a gulaya than this gentleman here?" I gave a pointed look to the salesman, who blushed.

"Zarin, why don't you go and catalogue the stores in the back," Elnos said. The salesman inclined his head, then hurried into the back of the store. "Sorry about him—working in a magical shop seems to have given him a bit of an inflated head. He doesn't realize that not all female mages like to wear robes. I wouldn't do so either if I could wear a pretty dress like that." He winked at me.

I laughed. "You seem very adult despite your youthful looks," I said. "If I didn't know better I'd say you're flirting with me."

Elnos smiled. "Recent events have forced me to grow up a bit more quickly than I would have liked," he said, and a shadow briefly flitted through his eyes. "Now, what sort of gulaya were you hoping to purchase today?"

"Have you been creating gulayas very long?" I asked as I let my eyes wander along the shelves. "I've heard they've only recently become legal."

"No, gulayas themselves have always been legal," Ragga explained, "but until recently, they could not be charged—or recharged—without using a highly illegal substance that was also used in death magic. That's why they had gradually fallen out of use, despite their obvious advantages. Even if you obtained the substance on the black market for exorbitant prices, and at considerable risk, it was only good for one trip. Plus, the ritual of recharging took several hours, and it was all too easy to make some mistake. That meant the whole thing had to be started over, using up more of the expensive ingredients."

"I see." What he told me matched up with what Fenris had said earlier. "But you got around those limitations?"

"Yes, although I cannot personally take the credit for this innovation," Elnos told me. "I am friends with Lord Iannis, our Chief Mage, who came across this new and easier way to recharge gulayas in an old diary. Apart from being a great Chief Mage and warrior, he is also interested in magical history, and unlike most other mages understands the scientific method. I'm the first one to license the process from him, and the only one with a specialized gulaya shop, as far as I know. We've only been open for about four months."

"Well, that explains why they're so expensive."

Elnos smiled. "Supply and demand, Miss Shelton. To be honest, this is somewhat of a side venture to me—I'm really an inventor, and I spend most of my time in my workshop in the back, tinkering with various ways to bring magic and technology together. That is why I hired a salesman," he said wryly, and I laughed again. "Though for the right kind of customer, my gulayas tend to sell themselves."

"Is it Lord Iannis's decree that the gulayas only be sold to mages, or yours?" I wondered aloud.

"A bit of both," Elnos said. "The initiating spell requires a small amount of magic from the user, and unless we modify that feature, humans cannot use them. The Chief Mage does not want them to fall into the hands of criminals, which limits the sales potential somewhat. Even so, I am doing quite well, and I have a variety of gulayas that suit most needs."

I asked Elnos more questions about his merchandise, and he explained to me that the gulayas on display in the storefront were simple, pre-keyed ones that were tied to various landmarks in Solantha. There were also double-strength ones that could transport two people if they were holding onto each other. The first three recharges were included in the price.

"Is it possible to get one keyed to a location other than the ones you already use?" I asked.

"Yes, but that is custom work and more expensive, especially if it is over a long distance," Elnos said. "It will also take longer because I need to send a qualified mage to the desired location for the initial charge. If you are looking to get something within a relatively short period of time, I recommend one of our pre-keyed options."

In the end, I decided to purchase two double-strength gulayas that were keyed to a beach just outside the city. Elnos promised to have them ready for me the following afternoon—they took twenty hours to charge.

As he rang up the sale, I noticed a flyer on the counter advertising the Chief Mage's upcoming wedding. It featured a picture of Lord Iannis and Sunaya, arm in arm, and I picked it up to study it further. The Chief Mage was a very good-looking man, tall with long hair and sternly handsome features, and Sunaya was a fierce beauty with a mane of black curls, piercing green shifter eyes, and a curvy figure that I couldn't help but envy.

"Mr. Ragga," I asked as I noticed the Chief Mage and his bride wore twin necklaces with a single small stone attached to the chain. "What are Lord Iannis and Miss Baine wearing here?"

"Ah." Elnos smiled. "Those are serapha charms. Like the gulayas, they had gone largely out of fashion in the past century, but they are coming back in vogue thanks to the happy couple."

"Yes, fashions do come and go. I don't think I've ever heard of them." I had a feeling that, as a mage, I ought to know what these were, but I'd missed out on a lot when I was forced into hiding.

"They are typically exchanged between two people who are going to marry or are already wed, and they bind a piece of one's soul to the other," Elnos explained. "The charms can be used to find one's beloved and check on their well-being. As I said, they are quite popular now—I've actually been making some to sell here in the shop, as more than one person has asked for them recently."

"Do you have any I can buy?" I asked eagerly. If Iannis and Sunaya had them, then I wanted a set for Fenris and me. In truth, I was starting to feel a little jealous of Sunaya. She was bold and beautiful and fierce, not to mention powerful. And she had known Fenris far longer than I did.

Don't be silly, I thought as Elnos went into the back to retrieve the charms. *Sunaya is clearly in love with her own man. And Fenris loves you, not her.*

Elnos brought out a case of necklaces with a variety of stones ranging from simple topazes to dazzling opals. I selected a pair with pretty blue stones that matched the illusion ring Fenris fashioned soon after we'd met. I no longer needed the illusion magic, but I still wore the ring on my right hand anyway, as it was the first thing Fenris had ever given me. Elnos handed me a card with instructions on how to activate the charms, then boxed up my necklaces.

"I can tell from your southern accent that you're not a native," Elnos said as he rang up my purchase. "What brings you out here to Solantha? The wedding, or the Convention?"

I hesitated, not sure what to tell him, then remembered Mirrine's story about why she was attending. And the Haralis paper I'd visited in my hometown had been sending someone too... "Both," I told him. "I'm a reporter from the *Deros Globe*, and I've been sent to cover the event—mostly the wedding, that is. I just arrived yesterday."

"An unusual occupation for a mage," he commented, "but then, so is being an inventor." He grinned.

"I think we mages ought to be a bit more adventurous in our occupations, don't you?" I asked as I took my package from him. After all, being a veterinarian was equally unusual for a mage. "We'd learn so much more about the world if we stuck our heads out of our ivory towers more often."

"I completely agree," Elnos said. "And you aren't the only reporter mage in town anyway. I've run into quite a few of your colleagues in the last week. If you're looking to find more of your kind, you should head over to the Solantha Press Club."

"Yes, I've heard of it, but haven't had time to go there yet," I lied. "Have you been there? I thought you were an inventor by trade."

"I was invited to a party there once—it's a posh place with a well-stocked bar. The staff help out-of-town press members with accommodation, schedules for planned events, credentials, and so on."

"Sounds like the perfect place for me, then."

I thanked Elnos and bid him a good day, promising to come back tomorrow to pick up my purchases. As I stepped out into the waning sunlight, I resolved to pay a visit to the press club at the earliest opportunity, if Fenris agreed to help me fake some realistic-looking credentials. It sounded like a useful source of information, and if they provided a full schedule of planned events, that might help us figure out which venue was most likely to be attacked.

SEVEN

FENRIS

With over two hours left until I was to meet Mina, and no cabs in sight, I decided to stroll through downtown. It was Solantha's seediest district and home to the Black Market, where various illegal goods, including those of a magical nature, were sold after dark. I had never been down here before, but as I walked through the streets, it was even less attractive than I thought it would be. Most of the local businesses seemed to be dives, grimy bars, betting parlors, and cheap brothels. If ex-Resistance members were congregating anywhere, it would be down here.

Of course, it was a long shot that I would spot anyone or anything useful—even though it was merely a fraction of the city, it was still a large district, and many walked the cracked streets that wound between buildings in various states of disrepair. There was reconstruction happening down here, too, but not as much as in the rest of the city. I got the distinct feeling that downtown was low on the list of priorities for the city planning department.

But as I walked along the sidewalk, keeping my head down and trying not to look conspicuous, I did notice something odd.

Two scruffy men gave each other a discreet hand signal while passing in the street—it was a quick touch of two fingers against their left hip, like a man reaching for his sword. At first I thought nothing of it, but five minutes later, I saw another pair of men do it. And then a hefty woman, while passing yet a different man.

Is this how the Resistance army recognizes one another? I wondered. Curious, I tried the gesture with the next man who approached, but he only glared at me, then shouldered past.

Perhaps I should find a dark alley and change into a different disguise, I told myself as the back of my neck prickled, not for the first time. I'd drawn strange looks more than once since I'd crossed into downtown—the clothing I wore was a little too new, too clean, making me stand out. I quickened my pace, heading for the nearest alleyway and hoping no one was skulking in it, waiting to try and mug me.

Not that he'd succeed. Most of the residents down here were human, and no match for me. But there was strength in numbers, and the last thing I needed was to draw the attention of some gang.

Before I could make my getaway, a huge man dressed in a dirty white shirt and leather pants stepped in front of me. "You lost?" he growled, sneering down at me and exposing yellowed teeth. Two of them were missing, and I wondered who in Recca would have dared to knock them out.

"I'm trying to find my way back to maintown," I said, taking a step back and holding up my hands. "Can you point me in the right direction?"

"I don't think he's lost at all," another man sneered, coming up beside the giant. This one had shoulder-length, greasy brown hair and a scar that slashed over his left eye. "Look at him in his fancy clothes. Only a mage would think he could blend in by wearing something like that. He's a spy!"

Other men were surrounding me now, and within seconds, they'd formed a circle. *Around ten of them,* I thought, doing a quick count, and my heart began to beat faster. These were not good odds. Taking my glasses off to show them my shifter eyes would not defuse the situation, I judged—humans in these parts had no love of shifters.

"I assure you, I'm just a tourist—" I began, but one of them lunged at me. I twisted out of the way and caught a punch to the chin from another man that knocked me back a step. Snarling, I grabbed the third man that came for me and flung him into the building behind me. His head made a sickening crack as it hit the brick, but I didn't have time to look at him—the other men were charging at me now, shouting battle cries, their eyes blazing with hatred and bloodlust.

I had no choice but to fight.

Yelling a battle cry of my own, I flung out my hands and blasted them with a blinding flash of light. The men screamed and threw up their arms, and I followed up by flinging balls of fire at them. Shrieks and the smell of dirty, roasting flesh filled the air as five of them were hit by the flames. With the others still stumbling about, blind, I turned on my heel and dashed through the alleyway, then vaulted the fence at the other end. I landed in the back of a small building and sprinted around it to the street beyond—

"And just where do you think *you're* going?" A man grabbed me by the arm, pulling me to an abrupt stop. Twisting around, I looked up into the face of a tiger shifter with close-cropped blond hair, dressed from head to toe in black leather. A bracelet with a familiar emblem sat on the wrist of the hand he was gripping me with, and my stomach dropped.

"Enforcers," I gasped—there were two of them; another man stood next to him on the pavement. "Thank Magorah you're here. I was nearly mugged by a group of men." There was no point in pretending I was human—the shifter would be able to smell that I was not.

"That tends to happen when you go walking about unawares in downtown," the second enforcer—a human—said flatly. "Like a pretty pigeon about to be plucked."

"I'm sorry," I said, lowering my head. "I wasn't thinking."

"Clearly not," the tiger shifter scoffed, releasing me. He narrowed his eyes, his nostrils flaring. "You stink of magic. Just what kind of trouble were you getting into down there?"

"I told you, I was mugged—"

"You're lying," the tiger shifter snarled, and he tried to grab me by the arm again. But I was faster, and I darted around him, then shot over another fence. The enforcers gave chase, but I sprinted through another alley, changed my scent and appearance to that of an old man, and quickly slipped into a dive, where I hid in the corner and grabbed a half mug of some truly foul-smelling ale somebody had left behind on the table.

The enforcers came through and asked if they'd seen a man matching my description, but my disguise held, and the tiger didn't suspect that I was the same man. I mentally thanked Sunaya for teaching me the importance of changing my scent in such situations. I waited a good ten minutes until after they were gone, then shuffled out, still as an old man, and headed back toward the port. I changed disguises into an old woman when I crossed into maintown and caught a cable car up to the port, then once more when I arrived.

To my relief, Mina was waiting by the car. She looked beautiful, with the sun setting behind her and the sea breeze ruffling her blonde hair, and if I hadn't been disguised as an old woman, I would have kissed her. I nearly laughed at the nonplussed look on her face when I pulled out the car keys and unlocked the door.

"*I ran into some opposition,*" I explained to her in mindspeak as I got in—there were plenty of people strolling about, and I couldn't risk changing back so soon after running away from enforcers. *"Let's get back to the hotel."*

"This isn't exactly how I expected to meet," Mina commented, sounding both amused and annoyed as she got into the car with me.

I started the car, and said nothing until we were crossing over the Firegate Bridge, leaving downtown and those too-keen enforcers far behind. "I decided to go for a stroll in Solantha's seedier neighborhoods and nearly got arrested," I said as I finally dropped my most recent illusion. I explained to her about the group of thugs who'd jumped me and the hand signals I'd seen them using right before they'd called me out as a spy.

Mina shook her head. "I never expected you, of all people, to be so foolish as to go into a bad neighborhood alone and unarmed," she said, frowning at me. "But I'm glad you're safe. Do you really think these people exchanging their hand signals are co-conspirators? They could just as easily be a gang of thieves."

I shrugged. "Perhaps, but it's worth investigating further. If it's a gang, it must be very big indeed, and would need to be eradicated also."

Mina reached for my hand. "Promise me that your next investigation will not involve rushing headlong into danger without telling anyone where you are," she said, her silver eyes bright. "The last thing I need is to find you in a jail cell, or worse, dead."

I lifted her hand to my lips and kissed it. "I promise," I told her, and prayed to the Creator that I would be able to keep it.

EIGHT

Upon our return to the hotel, Fenris took a long, hot shower to wash off the grime of the streets, and I lounged on the bed in a silk teddy, thinking about the day's events. Fenris had no bruises or lacerations for me to heal—whatever injuries he'd suffered had vanished during the ride back, thanks to his shifter abilities. Still, Fenris had been somewhat shaken as we'd driven back home—he had been very tense until we'd finally made it to the bridge, more so than I'd ever seen before.

I suppose I would be too, if I'd nearly been arrested. If Fenris landed in the Enforcers Guild jail, he would be in a world of trouble. There was a good chance that the Federal Director of Security, his greatest enemy, had asked the enforcers to report any sighting of Fenris. Polar, his original persona, was a wanted man already condemned to death in absentia.

Worried, I bit my lower lip as I pictured what easily could have happened. I would insist that he use a heavier disguise the next time he went out. Though Fenris had told me he'd spent most of his time in Solantha within the castle walls and in wolf form, someone in the Guild was bound to recognize him and perhaps report him to the Federal authorities in Dara. Solantha was a dangerous place for him to be.

"Don't look so troubled," Fenris said, gently taking my chin in his hand as he sat down next to me. He was wearing only a towel, draped low around his waist, and his bare, muscled chest gleamed in the lamplight. "I'm sorry I gave you such a scare, Mina, but everything turned out fine."

"I know," I said, skimming a hand along his broad shoulder. I loved the feel of his warm skin, and I let my hand trail further down, along his muscled back. "But I'm realizing just how great a risk it was for you to come here. I wish the gulayas I'd ordered today were ready—I would feel much better if you had one."

"Oh, so you did go back to that shop?" Fenris raised his eyebrows. "What did you think of it?"

"It was very interesting—the shop owner is an inventor mage called Elnos Ragga. Oh!" I jumped off the bed and rushed for my bag, which I'd left on the shoe bench. "I nearly forgot."

I retrieved the box and gave it to Fenris. "An engagement present," I said as he lifted the box.

"Mina..." Fenris's eyes shone as he gently lifted out one of the necklaces. The two were slightly different—the stones were identical, but Fenris's chain was made of thicker, heavier links, while mine was more elegant. "I didn't know you knew what serapha charms were."

"I saw Sunaya and Iannis wearing them in a picture and asked Mr. Ragga about them," I said. "I want to be able to reach for you and know that you're safe, even if you're not right next to me."

"And I wish the same." Fenris slipped his arms around my waist and kissed me softly. "This was a very thoughtful gift. I will have to thank Elnos in person for suggesting them, if I ever get to see him again."

I raised my eyebrows. "You know Mr. Ragga?"

Fenris's eyes dimmed. "Indeed I do. He was Noria Melcott's boyfriend. They worked together on various inventions, until she left to join the rebels. He, on the other hand, was a great help to us while we were fighting the Resistance."

I frowned. "How exactly does that work, if she was in the Resistance and he was fighting against it?" It sounded like a recipe for disaster and heartbreak to me. No wonder Ragga had talked about being forced to grow up so fast—he must have gone through quite a lot, though he seemed to be coping well enough, judging by his cheerful manner and successful business venture.

Fenris sighed. "The two of them met at the university where Noria studied, and she also worked in Comenius's shop part time. Sunaya was friends with Noria's older sister Annia, a fellow enforcer, and became close to Noria as well. But all that was before Noria decided to run off and join the Resistance."

"A stupid thing to do," I commented. "And very unfair to her boyfriend. But then again, he's a mage, and you said she was human, right? Perhaps it never would have lasted anyway."

Fenris shrugged. "I think it might have—they had so much in common, but unfortunately, not their politics. Anyway, Noria was sent up north to work on a deadly weapon that was meant to exclusively target shifters or mages. Elnos had to make a choice, and he chose to protect the thousands of innocent people who would have died had Noria and the Resistance succeeded."

"How horrible!" I gasped, truly shocked at the idea of a young girl committing genocide. "And you say that she was a close friend of both Comenius and Sunaya? How did nobody suspect?"

"Oh, everyone knew of her hatred for mages," Fenris said. "She never bothered to hide her feelings. But so many humans hate the regime; she was not unusual in that regard. And Noria did not realize the true extent of the weapon she was helping to create until it was too late. By the time she figured it out, she was already well within the Resistance's stronghold, and they refused to let her go or let her give up. In the end, we rescued her and eliminated the weapon and the compound."

"She sounds like an idealistic girl who chose the wrong side," I murmured.

"As so often happens in wartime." Fenris picked up the other necklace with a smile. "Enough talk about Noria, though. Let's put this gift to good use."

I scooped my hair back from my neck and allowed Fenris to clasp the chain of his necklace around my neck. He positioned the stone so that it sat directly over my heart, then placed my right hand over it and held it there.

"I'm not sure if Elnos explained, but serapha charms require that you imbue them with a small piece of your soul in order for them to work. You place the stone over your heart, then speak a short incantation that will transfer that piece into the charm. I'll do it first, and you can repeat after me."

"All right." I placed my chain around Fenris's neck. He pressed the stone to his heart, then closed his eyes and said the Words. His brow furrowed, as if in pain or discomfort, and the air around us sizzled faintly, as it always did when magic was being performed. White light flared between the cracks of his fingers, but it was gone nearly as quickly as it came, leaving me to blink away the spots floating in my vision.

"Wow," I said as Fenris lowered his hand. The stone was glowing bright blue now, the light from within blazing like a small star. "Is it always going to be like that?"

"No." Fenris smiled. "It will settle down after a few moments and return to look like a normal stone until I activate it again. Now let's do yours."

I took a deep breath and closed my eyes, then repeated the incantation Fenris had used. I felt a pinch deep inside me, in a place I wasn't aware existed, followed by a burning sensation, as if someone had jabbed a needle inside me. I gritted my teeth against the pain, but it disappeared before I knew it.

"Phew," I said as I opened my eyes and glanced down at the charm, which was glowing just like Fenris's. "I thought it was going to be worse than that." The stone felt hot against my bare skin, and I toyed with it briefly before lifting the necklace over my head.

We traded necklaces, and the stones' brilliance faded away, just as Fenris had predicted. Fenris taught me how to use them to check on each other's location, distance, and health, and then we ordered room service, too tired from the day's events to venture downstairs to the dining room.

"I could use a nap right now—" I said sleepily, and then the phone rang. This hotel catered to the ultra-wealthy and thus had phones in every suite, something that I had never seen before. It didn't seem like such a great luxury right this second, though—how could you enjoy peace and quiet like this?

Frowning, I snatched it off the cradle and answered. Was there a problem with our order?

"Apologies for disturbing you, Mrs. Shelton, but there is another visitor here for you," the receptionist said, sounding aggrieved. "A young lady with red hair."

I nearly dropped the phone. "*Barrla?*"

"Yes, that is her name," the receptionist said reluctantly. "I assume you want me to send her up?"

"Yes, please," I said, then hung up the phone. I quickly threw a robe over my flimsy attire, and Fenris dressed in the white cotton pajamas that the hotel provided. A few minutes later, a knock came at the door, and I opened it to see Barrla standing outside, dressed in traveling clothes and looking like she was out for blood.

"Where is that good-for-nothing Dalton?" she demanded,

storming inside. She scanned the room with narrowed blue eyes, as if Marris might be lurking in a corner somewhere. "Are you hiding him?"

"Of course not," I soothed, taking Barrla by the arm. "Why don't you sit and let me get you a cup of tea?"

"Don't try to calm me down," Barrla hissed, her eyes crackling with anger. "Marris up and left in the middle of the night so that I wouldn't be able to come out here with him. Who is he to tell me where I can and cannot go?"

"He was right to tell you that it was dangerous," Fenris said. "I myself was nearly killed in the streets today."

Barrla froze. "Killed? What do you mean, killed?"

"A group of thugs who might be former Resistance members jumped Fenris today," I said, guiding Barrla to a chair. "Solantha is a beautiful city, but if there truly is a plot to strike against the government, it definitely isn't safe right now."

"Hmph." Barrla crossed her legs as I boiled some hot water in the steampot and dug up a tea bag from the box of assorted teas provided by the hotel. "It may be dangerous, but that's even more of a reason for me to come out here. You are my friends, and you shouldn't have to deal with this alone. I'm not some shrinking violet."

Fenris and I exchanged a look. "This isn't like one of your adventure romances," he said to Barrla. "This may well lead to real bloodshed and death."

"That doesn't mean I can't be useful," Barrla insisted. "I used all my savings to come out here by air—you're not turning me away after I've only just arrived."

"Of course not," I said as I handed her the cup of steaming tea. "But don't be too angry with Marris, Barrla. He is infiltrating a group of terrorists, and since you are not a former Resistance member, you would only make things harder for him. He is relatively safe on his own since they know and trust him, but once they battle the mages, things could get very ugly. We are here to prevent that from happening."

"Yes, and I will help you," Barrla declared. When Fenris looked like he wanted to object, she said, "What is the point of making me a member of the League of Justice if I'm not allowed to participate?"

I sighed. "Fenris and I are...better equipped to deal with this than you."

Barrla glared daggers at me. "And how is that, exactly?"

I bit my lip and glanced at Fenris, who dipped his chin. *"You may as well tell her, since Marris knows,"* he said in mindspeak.

I turned back to Barrla. "Fenris and I can both use magic. I was born to a mage family, and Fenris has mage ancestors in his family tree too."

Barrla's jaw dropped. "You're pulling my leg. Mages? But isn't he a shifter?"

Fenris smiled wryly, then conjured a ball of light in his hand. "There is a reason I moved away from civilization," he said. "I'm not like Mina, but I have enough magic to make the mages uncomfortable if they knew about it. And shifters as well," he added ruefully.

"This is just like *The Mage's Secret*," Barrla said, shaking her head. "It's a romance between a mage and a shifter. Why didn't you tell me about this, Mina?" She sounded upset. "I know that everybody calls me a gossip, but I am capable of keeping secrets. You could have trusted me."

My insides squirmed with guilt at the hurt look on Barrla's face. "I'm sorry," I said, crouching down in front of her so I could look her in the eye. "I know now that I could have trusted you, but you have to understand that after hiding my true identity for over a decade, it had just become second nature. I didn't trust anyone with the truth, not even Fenris. He found out by accident. I came to Abbsville because I was running away from my abusive family, and I had to pretend I was a human so that they wouldn't find me."

Barrla stared. "Abusive? Like they hit you?" Her brows creased in confusion. "That happens in mage families, too?"

"Yes, unfortunately. We are not that different, really, and every evil you find among humans will also occur among mages here and there." I gave her a bitter smile. "That's all over now, though—Fenris and I went back to my hometown last month. We successfully claimed the inheritance my relatives had stolen from me, and I took my family name back. There isn't really any reason for me to hide anymore...but after pretending to be human for so long, I was nervous about your reaction," I admitted, looking down. "I'm truly sorry, Barrla."

There was a long silence while she mulled things over, and with each second that passed, I grew more nervous. Had I made a mistake?

But at last Barrla exhaled, and a tiny smile returned to her expressive face. "I can't exactly blame you for being afraid to confess to being a mage," she said, patting my shoulder. "Especially after what Roor and his mother tried to do to you. No wonder you were so terrified about that whole thing! I promise I won't tell anyone in Abbsville about this when we return. You *can* trust me, Mina."

I smiled at her. "I know," I said, and gave Barrla a hug. "You're a better friend than I deserve. I've felt guilty about deceiving you, and I won't do so again. But what people in Abbsville think or say about me doesn't really matter now. I probably won't be staying there for much longer."

As I said the words, I felt a little pang—I would miss my friends, the book club, the little surgery I'd only just begun to set up in Fenris's house. But I had a whole new life ahead of me, with endless possibilities. I couldn't turn away from that just because I was a little afraid.

"That makes sense, if you're rich now," Barrla said. "I don't intend to spend the rest of my life in the countryside either—I want to see the world and go on adventures, like you and Fenris are doing. And with any luck, I'll have a handsome man at my side...though if Marris doesn't apologize on bended knees, it will have to be someone else," she added with a militant gleam in her eyes. Clearly, her anger was still running hot. I wasn't truly worried for Marris—Barrla could never hold a grudge for long. If Marris played his cards right, I was sure she would ultimately forgive him.

We talked for a few more minutes until dinner arrived—we'd ordered another meal for Barrla, who was hungry after her long trip. While we ate, I arranged for Barrla to take the room I'd rented for Marris. After we'd finished dinner, she left us, and Fenris and I slipped into bed. The exhaustion I'd been holding at bay finally hit me, and I fell asleep almost immediately. We had a long day ahead of us tomorrow and needed all the rest we could get.

NINE

The next morning, the three of us met downstairs for breakfast and discussed our plans for the day. The weather was somewhat blustery and half overcast, but that didn't stifle our excitement. Barrla confidently ordered a substantial breakfast from the waiter, completely undaunted by the rich surroundings and snooty staff. She was agog at seeing Fenris without his shifter eyes and thrilled that she was finally participating in a real-life "operation." When I mentioned I was pretending to be a journalist, she suggested posing as my photographer, which would add credibility to my role. Together we would infiltrate the Solantha Press Club and see what we could uncover.

"I've taken photographs a time or two," Barrla said, "but never with a professional camera. I can say I'm new at this job if anyone notices me fumbling, but it would be best to look like a pro, if possible. Do you think we'll have time to practice?"

"We can snap a few photographs of city scenes if you want, before we get there," I said with a smile. I had no doubt that Barrla would take far more than a "few" pictures with the fancy new camera we were going to buy. It would be good for her to get a bit of practice with the equipment, especially since we were going to be spending some real money on it. If we stumbled upon anything that could constitute proof of a rebellion, photographic evidence might be a good thing to have.

We were just about to leave when Mirrine, the Forrane journalist I'd met the other night, came up to us. "Good morning," she said, looking as elegant as ever in another fitted suit, this one cream with black piping, and a pert little hat to match. "I hope I'm not interrupting, but I wondered if you were heading to Solantha this morning. I have an important appointment, and the car I ordered to pick me up broke down on the way here."

"Of course," Fenris said with a faint smile. "We would love to have your company, madame—there is plenty of space in our steamcar."

"You didn't tell me you already made a new friend, Mina," Barrla said, her blue eyes sparkling as she looked Mirrine up and down. I could tell that Barrla was impressed—Mirrine was the epitome of a worldly, confident woman, exactly the type Barrla aspired to be.

"Yes, we just met the other night," I said. "Mirrine, this is my good friend Barrla. She lives nearby and decided to come and see us while we were in this part of the Federation."

"Pleased to meet you." Mirrine raised her eyebrows, and I knew what she was thinking—Barrla was not a mage, but we were. But she didn't say anything about it, for which I was grateful. "Shall we get going, then?"

Fenris had the car brought around, and we sat in the front while Mirrine and Barrla settled themselves in the back. Having Mirrine around would put a crimp on what the three of us could discuss, but at least Fenris and I could still use mindspeak.

As we drove, Barrla began an artless conversation with our passenger. I winced at some of the more pointed questions, which were not entirely polite, but Mirrine handled them easily enough and didn't seem offended.

"Are you going into town to see a beau?" she asked Mirrine. "A woman like you must have many admirers."

"I do like men," Mirrine said with a cat-like smile. "But I find they are best enjoyed briefly and then discarded before they lose interest themselves."

"But what about marriage?" Barrla asked, sounding shocked, and even I had to admit I was surprised by Mirrine's cavalier attitude. "Don't mages consider that to be sacred?"

Mirrine laughed. "In theory, yes," she said, "but not all of us practice what we preach. Marriage can be a trap when you live as long as we do. You should be glad that you are human and will only have to live out a single century with whomever you choose to marry. Humans are even allowed to divorce in the Federation, aren't they? Most likely by the time the two of you have grown tired of each other, you will have lost your sexual appetites anyway. And you certainly will not have to involve yourself with selfish, calculating mages. As lovers or husbands, they are not worth troubling with."

"We are not all so selfish," Fenris said coolly, and I hid a smile—he was clearly offended by this wholesale condemnation.

"No," Mirrine said lightly, "perhaps not. But I find there are just as many bad apples as there are good in the barrel."

I took Fenris's hand before he could retort. "*She doesn't know you,*" I told him in mindspeak. "*You are a good man, and one of the most selfless people I know.*"

Fenris relaxed. "*Your new friend must be speaking from personal experience,*" he said. "*I wonder who left her so embittered.*"

"*Must have been her own husband—surely she had one at some point,*" I said, glancing at Mirrine in the rearview mirror. If two mages married for life did not love, and eventually came to hate each other, I could see how that could lead to searing anger and rampant infidelity. I could imagine all too easily how Mirrine might have been chained to an unfaithful spouse.

Fenris dropped Barrla and me off in maintown, then continued on to the Mages Quarter. He would take Mirrine to her destination, then sneak into the palace disguised as a servant to try and find out what Iannis and Sunaya were up to and how soon they were expected back.

In the meantime, Barrla and I went to a camera shop and selected a first-rate camera plus a whole bagful of accessories—mostly very expensive lenses and many different rolls of unexposed film. By the time we tallied everything up, I'd spent enough to buy a small steamcar.

"Oh, this is so lovely," Barrla said as we walked around with our new equipment. She took some pictures of pigeons feeding from a fountain, a family promenading with four children and a dog, and several townhouses she found interesting. "I can't wait to see how these turn out once they've been developed."

I laughed. "I suppose we'll have to add 'learn to develop film' to our list of things to do."

After half an hour, Barrla declared she felt comfortable enough to carry off her role, and we took a cab to the Solantha Press Club. It turned out to be only eight blocks away, but since I hadn't known which way to go it had seemed easier to let the cab driver take us.

The Solantha Press Club was an older, elegant, three-story corner building with a repeating pattern of a quill and a scroll carved along the edges of the windows and the roof—the press club emblem, which was also embossed in gold above the revolving door entrance. The lobby was done in dark wood and lush red carpet and had a distinctly masculine feel, right down to the air, which smelled faintly of aftershave.

Behind the large welcome desk were two pretty women

dressed in smart-looking wine-red suits with the club emblem stitched onto the lapels. They greeted us with a smile. "How may I help you?" the slim brunette on the left asked.

Barrla and I pulled our credentials—duly forged by Fenris—out of our handbags. We'd dressed in skirt suits similar in style to the one these women wore and three-inch heels that I'd spent a good portion of this morning practicing in so that I wouldn't wobble. My toes were already beginning to pinch, but I was proud that, so far, I hadn't tripped. After a cursory examination of the credentials, we were waved right into the lounge to the right of the lobby, a large rectangular room. It was all leather seats and low tables, mostly filled with middle-aged men whose cheeks were already ruddy from drinking. Quite a few of them had cigars, and I wrinkled my nose at the haze of bluish-gray smoke in the air.

"Where are all the female reporters?" Barrla asked in a low voice as interested male gazes turned our way.

"I imagine that they're out chasing stories, as these men should be doing instead of drinking like fish and smoking like chimneys," I answered in an equally low voice, though I kept a pleasant expression on my face. "I imagine that's where the young male reporters are too." These guys seemed to be the veterans, the ones who were past their prime and content to rest on their laurels rather than hunt down juicy leads.

As we had previously agreed, Barrla and I split up. She went to the back of the room to chat up a thin, silver-haired man who was drinking bourbon with a colleague, and in no time her bubbly laughter was filling the room. I spotted a man drinking alone in the corner who looked to be in his early fifties, with a compact build and thinning hair.

"Is this seat taken?" I asked, patting the arm of the leather chair across from him.

"Be my guest," he said, gesturing toward it. He looked up at me in surprise, clearly not expecting that I would take an interest in him, and I smiled as I took the chair. "I haven't seen you around before."

"I'm Mina Shelton, from the *Deros Globe*," I said, holding out a hand for him to shake. "I just got to town."

"Rubb Slade," the man said, shaking my hand. He frowned. "I thought the *Deros Globe* already sent a reporter."

"We're a large paper," I told him. "They decided to send me along to cover the wedding specifically, while my colleague concentrates on the Convention. My boss thinks that a woman is better suited to find out all the gossip around the Chief Mage's romance."

Rubb gave me a condescending smile. "Ah, of course. You'll write pages and pages about the gown and the flowers and the food, and how beautiful the bride is, I expect."

"I'm quite good at my job," I said simply, not rising to the bait. I lifted a hand to signal the server. "Why don't you let me buy you a drink?"

I ordered Rubb another glass of what he'd been drinking—an amazingly expensive brand of whiskey, it turned out, as the glass was delivered. Good thing I was rich now. He took a long drink from the glass, then let out a satisfied sigh.

"Good stuff," he said, lowering his glass. "Aren't you having some?"

"It's a bit early in the day for me," I demurred. "I was hoping you might be able to tell me more about the wedding venue."

Rubb scoffed. "Only that it's off-limits to non-mages, which you already know. They won't even tell us where the actual wedding is being held. Those of us who are covering it are only allowed to attend the receptions, so if you were hoping to sneak into the actual ceremony, you're out of luck. None of us here can help you."

"Do you think that's because they're worried the Resistance might try to attack during the ceremony?" I asked.

Rubb shook his head. "Mages have always been secretive about their little rituals," he sneered. "None of the press have ever been invited to a mage wedding in the history of the Federation, or anywhere in Recca as far as I know."

"That's true," I said—the various temples of Resinah were a closely guarded secret. Since mage weddings were always held at a temple among the closest friends and family, few humans would ever have attended one. "But what about the wedding reception? Is there any danger there?"

"Not likely," Rubb said. "The mages are paranoid, and security is everywhere. It would take a bloody miracle to get at the bastards."

I raised an eyebrow. "Sounds like you wouldn't be entirely sorry if that miracle *did* happen."

Rubb laughed. "*Sorry?* It would be the story of the century! And one I would relish telling, as would you. It's the kind of scoop every journalist dreams of."

"Oh yes, it would be very exciting to cover such a sensation," I agreed as I signaled the waiter. "But also pretty dangerous, so I think I'll pass. Anyway, since you say it is so unlikely, there's no point in thinking too much about it."

"Yes," Rubb said, a calculating gleam in his dark eyes. "Even so, I'd advise you not to get too close to the Chief Mage and his bride just in case something untoward *does* happen. They would be the prime targets, along with the Minister."

"I appreciate the advice," I said coolly as the waiter came by with the bill. I paid it, then stood up. "Thank you for the conversation, Mr. Slade. Enjoy your whiskey."

I turned on my heel and moved on to the next target, who proved to be far more pleasant, if a bit too long-winded. Barrla and I spent another hour there, and though we didn't learn anything conclusive, we did get a copy of the scheduled events, which listed not only the times and the venues, but also which big-wigs were expected to attend.

"This is quite detailed," I said as I scanned the list, which had been painstakingly copied by hand. "How did you get this?"

"By batting my lashes and asking nicely," Barrla said with a wink. "Men are so easy."

"They certainly are for you," I agreed with a laugh. "I'm glad you came along—this is more than I would have gotten on my own."

"I told you I would be useful," Barrla said, looping my arm in hers. "Now why don't we take a break and enjoy ourselves?"

Barrla tucked the schedule away in her purse, and we caught a cable car down to Witches End. She was absolutely delighted as we explored the magical shops, and purchased several charms and potions. Eventually I steered her toward Elnos Ragga's shop so I could pick up the gulayas I'd ordered the previous day.

"Welcome back, Mrs. Shelton," Elnos said with a smile as we entered the store. His eyes lit up as they settled on Barrla. "I see you've brought a friend. Your photographer?" He glanced at the large camera bag slung over Barrla's shoulder.

"Yes. I'm Barrla Kelling," Barrla said with a smile, offering her hand. "Mina didn't tell me that you were so handsome."

Elnos grinned. "You remind me of someone I used to know," he said, his eyes bright as his gaze lingered on her red curls. "Would you two like to join me at the café up the street for a bite? I was just about to head out to lunch."

"That sounds lovely," Barrla said. "I'm famished!"

Elnos handed over the gulayas, and the three of us walked a short way along the pier to a charming outdoor café that served sandwiches and salads under striped red-and-white canvas awnings. The waiter joked with Elnos and was very prompt in serving our selections. I guessed Elnos came here often and was a favored customer.

As the three of us drank cold tea and ate, Barrla and I told Elnos about the lazy reporters at the press club and how we were trying to ferret out information regarding a suspected Resistance attack. From what Fenris had told me, Elnos was trustworthy, and we needed all the help we could get.

"You cannot be serious," he said when we were finished, frowning deeply. "If there is such a plot, why would you—a journalist—know more about it than the mage authorities? Or are you working undercover for the Mages Guild?"

"We have connections," I said, "one of whom is plugged into Resistance circles. And I'm not working for the Mages Guild, though if we find any proof of what we suspect, we'll immediately involve the proper authorities. We've already sent them warnings and told them what we do know."

He stared at me, then at Barrla, who nodded in confirmation. "I guess after all this poor city has lived through in the recent past, it should not surprise me." He pushed his half-eaten sandwich away, and I felt a bit guilty for ruining his appetite. "Now that I think about it, though, this kind of thing is only to be expected."

"Solantha does seem to attract its fair share of trouble," I agreed.

"It sure seems so," Barrla said. "It's a very exciting city." I had to hide a smile at the tone in her voice—she clearly didn't think any less of Solantha for being dangerous.

"If there truly is a Resistance plan to attack this wedding, it must be stopped at all costs," Elnos said. "Iannis and Sunaya are my friends. I shall talk to my contacts in the Mages Guild myself, check if they are aware of the danger."

"Good." Hopefully that would make them take even more stringent precautions.

Elnos took another drink of his cold tea, then put down the empty cup with a decisive thud. "You know, after you left yesterday, I got to thinking about what kind of magitech device might be useful for a reporter looking for a good scoop."

"Magitech?" Barrla asked, looking confused.

"It's a term used to describe any device or tool that combines magic and technology," Elnos explained. "As an inventor and a mage, I delight in bringing new magitech devices to life. For the past couple of weeks, I've been working on a new variation of the ether pigeon, one who can spy. It was inspired by Miss Baine's ether parrot, the only one in existence. If you are working against the Resistance, you might be able to make good use of it."

"A spy ether pigeon?" I asked, leaning in a little. "How would that work?"

Grinning, Elnos pulled a small metal owl from his sleeve. "I've created a new spell which conjures an ether owl that can turn invisible," he told me, setting the owl in the middle of the table. It was roughly the size of my palm and absolutely adorable. "The ether owl will be able to transmit what it sees and hears through this twinned owl puppet, which can repeat the audio and play the video through the mirrors in its eyes."

Barrla gently picked up the bronze owl and turned it over in her palms. "Those are some very small mirrors," she said, examining the owl's eyes. "I imagine only one person will be able to look into them at a time."

"Yes, well, it's not meant as a presentation that can be broadcast to an audience," Elnos said. "It's a reconnaissance tool, and one I would like you to field-test for me."

I blinked in shock. "You're giving this to me?"

"Lending it," Elnos corrected. "It's the first working prototype. I don't plan on selling it, at least not yet, but I'd like you to make use of it in your investigation and then let me know just how useful you find it and if any improvements need to be made."

"I would be more than happy to," I said, taking the owl from Barrla. "Can you teach me the spell to summon the ether owl?"

Elnos told me the incantation, then wrote it down on a napkin for good measure. Holding the metal owl in the palm of my hand, I repeated the Words, and an identical glowing blue owl appeared on the table. It hooted softly as it looked up at me, cocking its head curiously, and Barrla squealed.

"Oh, it's so cute!" She reached for it, but her fingers passed through the owl's ghostly feathers. "Why can't I touch it?"

"It's called an ether owl for a reason," I said, amused at the pout on her face. "Go to the Solantha Press Club bar," I commanded the owl, then spoke the Word to send it on its way.

The owl disappeared, and its metal counterpart whirred to life, its mirrored eyes flashing. Within moments, the mirrors cleared, revealing the lounge Barrla and I had been sitting in before. The bird was hovering over one of the tables, where several of the journalists we'd talked to were gathered.

"I wish those girls would come back," one of them said. "After they left, I suddenly realized how boring you lot are."

Another one scoffed. "What, you think you'd be able to get a piece of that ass? Don't kid yourself, Waldorn. They're both way beyond your league."

"I bet I could get the blonde to open her legs for me," a third one leered. He was admittedly a bit younger and more attractive than the others, though that wasn't saying much. "She was pretty cozy with me when we were chatting earlier."

"How original," I said dryly, leaning back. "They're talking about how much better they would have liked to get to know us, Barrla."

Barrla frowned at that, and Elnos grimaced. "I'm glad I've chosen a different profession," he said, tossing a couple of coins onto the table. "I've got to get back to work, ladies, but it was great having lunch with you. Please come by the shop again soon."

Barrla and I said goodbye to Elnos, and I prepared to recall the ether owl since the journalists were saying nothing of importance. But before I could, I caught frantic motion in the owl's mirrored eyes, and I clutched it closer so I could see what was going on.

"Are you sure?" one of the journalists was saying eagerly. "The Minister is arriving today?"

"Of course I'm sure, you idiot!" another man said. "He'll be giving a press conference at his mansion in two hours. We have to get ready!"

"Two hours?" Barrla exclaimed when I told her what he'd said. She dug the schedule out of her bag. "That's not on the press schedule."

"No," I said, giving her a wide smile. "But we're going to be there anyway."

TEN

I t was a good thing we had a head start, as it took over an hour to get through the snarled traffic. On top of that, the extra guards outside the Mages Quarter checked our press credentials, and our steamcab's registration, before letting us in. I looked around curiously—this was the richest, most exclusive part of Solantha, although the houses differed in size. A few streets had brownstones with tiny front gardens alongside much larger mansions standing alone in the middle of well-kept gardens. Unlike every other part of the city, there was no construction here. The earthquake from last year must have completely bypassed this part of town. I wondered if that was due to magical intervention or if the Mages Quarter had simply been lucky.

"I see very few people on the streets here," Barrla said.

"Seems like it's mostly a residential area, no shops," I said. "So there wouldn't be much foot traffic." The few pedestrians we saw walking up and down the sidewalks either wore robes or the uniforms of maids or nannies.

"There are a few shops around here," the cabbie said, "clustered in two streets west of here, but they are too expensive for anyone but pampered mages. They have all the gold."

I tried not to feel too guilty at being one of those rich mages—after all, I'd lived without riches for over a decade, working as hard as any human. And besides, there were plenty of wealthy humans in the rest of the city, from what I had observed.

The cabbie turned a corner, and we found ourselves in front of a huge mansion decorated with the flags of the Federation. "So this is the residence the Minister rented," Barrla said in a hushed voice, sounding awed. "Who do you think lived here before? They must be very rich."

Everyone and their dog seemed to know that the Minister was in town. The entrance gates of the mansion were crowded with members of the press and at least a dozen mages trying to get in. The latter probably were federal officials summoned to report to their ultimate boss, Minister Graning. The cabbie dropped us off with a sarcastic "Good luck!" after I tipped him, and Barrla and I joined the queue lining up to go through security.

The gates were guarded by both humans and imposing mages wearing black robes. It was the mages who inspected us, checking our credentials and patting us down for weapons. Even Barrla's camera was closely scrutinized, as though they feared it might be a concealed bomb. The magitech owl they brushed off as a mere toy, to my amusement, and they didn't comment on my serapha charm either, even though it would have tipped them off that I was a mage. I guessed mage reporters weren't so uncommon after all.

Eventually we were permitted through the gates and into the courtyard, which was completely packed with press people and flunkies milling about. "Wow," I muttered to Barrla. "I had no idea so many members of the press had come to Solantha. With such little notice of the press conference, it's amazing that they all arrived here in time." It was as though they had some instinct telling them where and when to come here.

"I didn't know there were so many members of the press, period," Barrla said, sounding equally amazed. But she schooled her face into an expression of cool professionalism, and I did the same—we couldn't afford to look like a pair of small town girls who'd lost our way, not in front of this experienced and cynical lot.

Hoping to get a good look at the Minister, whom I'd never seen before, Barrla and I elbowed our way as close to the front steps as possible. There was already a podium set up, and several important-looking mages were standing next to it—probably members of the Minister's office. Barrla noticed that the photographers were all grouped in the front, so she went to join them with her camera in hand, while I stood further back with the other journalists.

"Hello there," a familiar voice said, and I turned to see that Rubb, the journalist I'd treated to that expensive whiskey, was standing next to me.

"Nice to see you again," I lied, hiding my instinctive dislike for the man. "Have you attended press conferences with the Minister before? Is it always like this?"

"In Dara he is not mobbed because people are more used to his presence," he said, as his eyes wandered over the scene. "It is ridiculous, but there you are. Power attracts weaker minds like shit attracts flies."

"Not very flattering, considering that we too are here to see him," I said dryly. Had he been trying to shock me? I'd seen my fair share of disgusting things as a country veterinarian—he would have to try much harder. "Is he likely to say anything of particular interest to my readers?"

Rubb shrugged. "I doubt it. These bigwigs consider anything they say to be important, no matter how stupid or trivial, just because they say it with a serious face. It's all a game, girl, not to be taken seriously."

"Of course," I said, as if I knew exactly what he was talking about.

"If it were Lord Iannis, now, I'd be more interested in what he has to say," Rubb continued, a gleam in his eye. "But it seems he is still out of town."

"I do hope he won't miss his own wedding," I commented. "That would make for a very different article than the one I planned to write."

"Maybe, but it would still make for an interesting story," Rubb pointed out. "'Derelict Chief Mage Disappoints Powerful Guests,' or something like that. It would put a swift end to his undeserved popularity." He smirked. "The articles would practically write themselves."

I didn't agree that Lord Iannis's popularity was undeserved, considering what Fenris had told me about his friend, but there was no doubt that it would be a social catastrophe if the bridegroom or bride were not back in time, after inviting the entire government to their wedding. I tried to edge away from Rubb, tired of his relentless negativity, but was blocked by all the bodies around me. With nowhere to go, I was forced to suffer his company.

It was a good fifteen minutes before the crowd finally hushed and the Minister took the stage. The mage to his left announced him as Lord Zavian Graning, Minister of the Northia Federation. I was not impressed at what I saw—while he looked both imperious and intelligent, he was not particularly tall or handsome, with ordinary brown hair and plain features.

"Thank you for coming here today," the Minister said, his strong voice carrying across the courtyard without the aid of a microphone—he was using magic to enhance it. "I'm going to share some highlights of the Convention agenda and answer a few questions from the press."

The Minister proceeded to drone on for several long minutes about some of the legislation and issues that the Convention was going to vote on, but when the Q&A period came, it was clear nobody cared about any of that. The questions were all about Iannis and Sunaya, and seemed to center around the Minister's personal thoughts about the upcoming wedding.

"How do you feel about the Chief Mage of such an important state marrying a shifter?" one of the reporters shouted, a question I found particularly interesting. "Is it not going to set an unfortunate precedent?"

"Lord Iannis is not just marrying a shifter," the Minister replied. "Miss Baine is also a powerful mage in her own right, and has repeatedly proven herself against the Resistance. As for setting a precedent, I see little danger of that since there are not two like her in the entire Federation." The briefest of frowns flitted across his face, and I gathered he was quite thankful that Sunaya didn't have a doppelganger. "I wish both of them well, and will be hosting a reception in their honor in just a few days."

That last bit was nothing new, since his planned reception, which was being held in a large Solantha concert hall, was featured prominently on the schedule we had studied. It was in the middle of the coming week, the night before the Convention opening and just days before the wedding. But would the Chief Mage and his bride be back in time? To not turn up at the Minister's reception for them would be an intolerable insult, and nearly as much of a fiasco as not showing up for the wedding itself. I imagined the event would have to be cancelled at the last minute, in that case.

"Do you know where Lord Iannis and his bride are, and

when they are expected back?" another reporter asked, obviously thinking the same thing I was. "Why has he left so suddenly, right before the Convention? As the host, should he not be here at your side at this moment?"

"Lord Iannis has left on an important mission for the Federation," the Minister answered. "He is expected back shortly."

"Minister," a female voice called, and I turned to see Mirrine standing just a few feet to my left. I'd completely forgotten that she would be here! Hopefully she would not blow my cover, but she was not even looking in my direction, her eyes fixed on the Minister. "Do you see any likelihood that such a disparate match will lead to a happy union? Miss Baine may be a powerful mage, but there are considerations of age, nationality, and power differentials. Surely they will find it difficult to reconcile all that."

I spun back around just in time to glimpse a look of shock on the Minister's face. It was gone so quickly that I could almost have imagined it, but no—I knew what I saw. But why would he find the question shocking? Surely he'd had similar thoughts many times himself, as did every mage who heard about the unusual couple. Since mage marriages were forever, both the bride and the groom were taking a great risk.

"Nobody can tell the future," the Minister responded blandly, "but I have every confidence in Chief Mage Iannis and his bride. That will be all."

The other reporters began shouting questions all at once, but the Minister turned on his heel and went back inside the house, two escorts trailing him.

"Typical," Rubb muttered. "These mages always like to act holier-than-thou, as if they never have affairs and their eternal marriages are always blissful. I doubt the Chief Mage and his shifter bride will have a happy marriage for long...*if* they ever get married at all."

I stared at him. "Is there something you're not telling me?" Once again, I got the distinct feeling that he despised the Minister and all mages...but there was an undercurrent to his words, almost as if he were making some kind of prediction.

Rubb shrugged. "There's less than two weeks until the wedding, and yet the 'happy' couple is missing in action. That's got to mean something, don't you think?"

And with that parting shot, he disappeared into the crowd.

My foray into Solantha Palace turned out to be a waste of time. First I had to wait twenty minutes so that some bored guard would allow me into the Mages Quarter at all—I was already disguised as a servant in Iannis's livery, but had to use sleight-of-hand to make them think I also had the special badge that everyone from inside the area was supposed to show.

It would have been easier to slip into the Palace without attracting notice, but doing so would mean that I could not openly ask what I wanted to know. Nor could I loiter anywhere for too long without being told to help out with the work. It was very different from my previous existence here, when I'd only answered to Iannis and had been his friend and adviser rather than a paid employee. I couldn't help feeling strange as I walked these well-known corridors and rooms after being so certain that I would never do so again. Everything looked much the same, and I had to subdue a foolish wish to visit the library and say hello to Janta. I had much more pressing business—I couldn't afford to immerse myself in old manuscripts as I had in the past.

Through careful probing and discreet questions, I managed

to find out from the servants that it was Sunaya who had left first, and very unexpectedly. They did not know where she had gone or why, but Iannis had followed, presumably to bring her back in time for the wedding. There was some speculation that they were on the Central Continent. It was lucky that Iannis had brought gulayas back into fashion, if they had in fact traveled so far away, or there would be little chance of either of them getting to the wedding on time.

The Palace staff were torn between confidence in Iannis's formidable power and fear that, for whatever reason, he and Sunaya would remain missing in the crucial period ahead. Everybody agreed that Iannis at least had left of his own will, and that whatever danger was keeping them from their post must be something quite extraordinary.

Frustrated, I concluded that nothing more was to be learned here. Hopefully they had joined up, wherever they were—Iannis and Sunaya made a formidable team. When they returned, I would make them tell me exactly what had happened, but right now, another trip downtown, with a better disguise, might be a better use of my time.

I took a cab across town, then ducked into an alley and changed my appearance to that of a large, scruffy man in his early thirties with beat-up clothing—exactly like the type of man who had accosted me the other day. I was determined to find out if those men were, in fact, part of some outfit being gathered against Iannis, and what they were planning.

You may not find out anything, I reminded myself as I trudged through the streets, keeping a vaguely threatening expression on my ugly face. The locals paid me no heed this time except to move faster when they saw me, confirming I looked just like every other thug around here. The criminals who had attacked me were unlikely to know much—they struck me more as hired muscle than criminal masterminds.

But still, I might yet get a lead to the brains behind this operation.

Over the next hour, I observed several more people exchanging the hand sign I'd seen before. I was almost certain they were all part of a group—if not the Resistance, then some very large criminal gang. Sometimes the parties would keep walking, and other times, they would join up and go off somewhere together. After the fourth time, I moved from my vigil beneath the awning of an abandoned building and followed a small group. They never interacted openly beyond the exchange of signals, but maybe I would overhear something once they were in private.

Keeping a respectable distance, I followed the trio of men around the corner, where they entered a building site. The place was crawling with workmen, but half of them were just standing around, apparently waiting for a foreman to come around and give them orders. It seemed wasteful, considering there were building materials and equipment lying around, but I couldn't stay to investigate or I would be caught.

The next man I shadowed turned out to be a better target— he went into a bar, where I could easily observe him. I followed him in and sat in a booth with a mug of beer and a magazine, hoping to hear something of interest. But the man sat at the bar alone, nursing a beer for a good hour and looking so bored that I wondered if he was just killing time.

I was nearly ready to give up and move on, but something niggled at me, telling me to stay. So I joined the fellow at the bar and ordered a beer.

"Morning," I said as I discreetly flashed the hand signal—it was only a few minutes before noon, with no one else in the bar as of yet.

"Morning's almost gone," the man grunted, returning the signal. "All this waiting is getting on my nerves. I'm this close to chucking the whole thing and going back to my grocery job in Osero. At least there I knew what to expect every day."

I nodded sympathetically, even though I didn't really know what he was talking about. "I feel the same way," I said as the barkeep set a fresh beer in front of me in a chipped glass mug that had obviously seen better days. "But I would kick myself if I missed the showdown. We both know it's going to happen eventually."

"Exactly," the man agreed, then took a long drink from his mug. "I'd just rather not die of old age before it does."

"I'm looking forward to the mages finally getting what they deserve," I said, trying to sound out the man for more information. "They need to pay for all these centuries of grinding us into the dust."

"Yeah, but it's not going to be easy," the man said darkly. "I heard all about the raid on our compound in Osero—the mages cut our people down like we were nothing, even though we outnumbered them, and obliterated the whole site with some terrible magic weapon. I heard only ashes and rubble remained. And there will be even more mages here. Even if we take out the leaders, the others might still rally against us."

So there *was* a plan to take out the leaders. "Maybe," I said, "but you can never tell with mages. The last time Solantha was hit by the Resistance, it nearly fell apart."

The man nodded, brightening a little. "That's true. The only reason it was saved was because the Chief Mage and his bitch came back at the worst possible time. If we can take out all of the leadership, things might fall into place. But even if they don't," he said, lifting his mug, "this is still a historic moment, and I damn well want to be part of it. And at least we get enough money for beer and food while we're waiting."

"Hear hear," I said, clinking my mug with his. "Do you think the plan is viable? I have to admit I have my doubts."

He shrugged. "Beats me. No point in speculating when we don't have much to go on. But give me any chance to strike at these arrogant mages, and I'm in."

I finished my beer and wandered off, annoyed that the details I managed to get from this beer-guzzling revolutionary were so vague. The man was probably just repeating propaganda he heard from the organizers—he had not struck me as particularly smart, and operational security would likely keep these grunts in the dark until the moment they were needed. The organizers of this plot clearly knew what they were doing.

I needed to try a different tack to find out who the officers and financiers of this operation were. That they remained shadowy figures reminded me of the Benefactor—right up until the end, the vast majority of the Resistance had no idea who she was, or even that she *was* a she. The Benefactor herself was dead now, but someone had taken it upon themselves to continue her work. Perhaps some of her lieutenants, seeking to avenge her? Not that Thorgana had been a woman to inspire loyalty and liking, the way I remembered her. But then I was biased against anyone who tried to exterminate mages like Mina, Sunaya, or Iannis. Regardless of how I felt about her, Thorgana's cause obviously lived on.

My wanderings led me up into maintown, and soon I found myself standing outside the Ur-God temple where Sunaya had once listened to Father Calmias preach about the virtues of genocide. The building was imposing and took up an entire block all by itself. I had passed it quite a few times during my years in Solantha without ever thinking about its possible importance. How like Sunaya to infiltrate where no other mage or shifter would ever dream of entering...she had a real knack for running into useful clues, and I could only hope to do half as well.

Doing my best to look like a human in search of spiritual

guidance, I entered the temple and sat in one of the pews, bowing my head as if in prayer. According to mage tradition, the Ur-God was simply a different name for the Creator of all things, but I could not bring myself to actually pray under these circumstances, wearing my thug-like disguise. Would Resinah approve of what I was doing? Since I hoped to prevent bloodshed, to save her descendants, I could only trust that she would.

The inside of the temple was decorated with loving care, with vaulted ceilings and garlands of roses carved into the stone. It had that hushed air of reverence that usually permeated sacred spaces. Several pews were occupied. From what I could tell, the faithful here were workers and businesspeople stopping by during their lunch hour for some divine guidance, their heads bowed and their hands clasped in prayer. My stomach grumbled at the reminder of the time of day—I would have to seek out sustenance soon.

After ten minutes or so, I rose and approached a robed elderly man who was busy rearranging the flowers on the altar—a caretaker, I assumed. "Excuse me, sir," I said in a low voice. "Is Father Calmias here today?"

"I'm afraid he's out right now," the caretaker said. "Is there something I can help you with?"

"I was just wondering how he's doing," I said casually. "I heard a rumor that his teachings have changed since the Uprising, and I wanted to ask him about it."

The man frowned, looking me over with a critical eye—did he take me for a diehard anti-mage fanatic who would take issue with the more peaceful gospel the preacher now espoused? My current disguise might not have been the best for this place...

"I wouldn't say that Father Calmias has changed his teachings completely," the caretaker said after a short pause, putting down the gold-plated vase he'd been polishing so he could give me his full attention. "But after a revelation from the Ur-God himself, he is now preaching tolerance and forgiveness toward all races. Rightly so, of course, as we are all the Ur-God's creations, even if we humans were the first and original sentients on Recca."

"I guess that could be confusing for some of the congregation, since he preached the opposite for so long," I said. I could see that he was just repeating by rote the gospel Father Calmias was now espousing—his scent told me he had mixed feelings on the matter.

The caretaker nodded, apparently relieved that I had reacted so calmly. "Regrettably, the change has created a schism in the congregation. Most listen to Father Calmias, but a vocal minority have rejected his new teachings and left for other temples, unable to let go of the anger in their hearts. I pray that they will eventually see the light."

I thanked the caretaker for his time and left a small donation before seeking out a nearby restaurant for a hearty meal. After my hunger was sated, I strolled around in maintown for a bit, curious to see if anyone around here was using the same hand signals. But the humans in this part of town were, by and large, well dressed and civil—they went about their business as normal, and if some stopped to chat in the street, there were certainly no gang signals exchanged between them or any groups of them skulking off into shadowy alleys or seedy bars.

With a couple of hours left until I was to meet Mina and Barrla for dinner, I had time for one last foray into downtown before calling it quits. It was late in the afternoon, and the streets were mostly empty except for a few loiterers who looked just as inclined to try and steal my purse as they did to beg for a few coppers. Dirty, downtrodden, hopeless, with nothing but a life of crime to look forward to.

I wondered if Sunaya knew how wretched this place was, and if she had plans to do anything about it. It wasn't easy to help the poor, since so many of them were resistant to good advice and suspicious of outsiders butting into their lives. But conditions like this would only breed more crime.

As I passed a narrow alley between a brothel and a gaming den, a trio of burly men rushed out. "You there," one of them said, and I was surprised to see he was an enforcer. The two flanking him were most certainly scum, and yet they weren't in chains. "Have you seen a scantily clad woman running about?"

"No," I said truthfully, bewildered. "I haven't seen much of anyone out here today."

The enforcer grunted, and the group shouldered past me, looking to be in a foul mood. I continued on, but this time with my eyes wide open, scanning the streets for the woman they described. About two blocks away, my ears picked up the sound of panicked breathing, and I caught the sharp, sour scents of fear and pain.

Curious, I followed the scent into an alleyway. It grew stronger, even beneath the stinking garbage, and sure enough, I found a slight young woman in a short, torn, see-through dress cowering behind a dumpster. She jumped at the sight of me, banging her shoulder into the brick wall, and gasped for air. I held my hands out, palms up.

"Shhh," I said soothingly, noting the terrible bruises on her arms and her left cheek. "I'm not here to hurt you. Is there anything I can do to help?"

The woman trembled, clutching her arms around her thin body. She seemed too frightened to give me an answer. From the wild look in her eyes, I could tell that she would try to attack if I came any closer. Sighing, I waved a hand and conjured the illusion of a T-shirt and jeans onto her body.

The woman gasped as she looked down at herself. "Wha—"

"The men are looking for a scantily-clad woman, so that should help," I said briskly, opening up my money pouch and taking out a few coins. "Here, take these and get yourself somewhere safe."

The woman nodded silently and snatched the money from my palm. She gave me a look of wary gratitude, then hopped up onto the dumpster and scrambled up over the roof of a garage.

"There she is!" a man shouted, and I winced. So much for the disguise.

I heard footsteps pounding on the asphalt as the men gave chase, and I ran back out, unwilling to let them hurt a defenseless woman. On catching sight of me, they turned as one, raising their cudgels.

Three humans against one shifter—I didn't need to use magic, I told myself as I grabbed the enforcer and threw him against the nearest wall. I had this.

One of the other two was unexpectedly fast, and it was harder than I had reckoned to outfight two thugs with cudgels when I was unarmed. I was not doing too badly, though, and was just pushing their hard heads together when I heard a noise from the roof of the squalid houses in the alley, like a heavy body climbing onto the tiles. Before I could drop the two criminals I was holding and investigate, something hard slammed into the back of my head, making stars explode across my vision.

I crumpled to the ground, my head splitting in agony, and heard the sound of a woman screaming as everything went black.

TWELVE

After all the excitement at the press conference, Barrla and I went to check out the locations of the main events. With our press passes, we were able to access most of the venues, and got through a third of the ones on the schedule. Barrla took lots of photos, which we planned to show Fenris and Comenius once they were developed.

The conference hall where the Convention was to be held was on the outskirts of town, in the middle of a park surrounded by a high fence. Barrla and I concluded that due to its isolation, it would be relatively easy to guard. Even now, before the Convention had begun, we spotted a dozen black-clad mage agents prowling the grounds as we approached, repeatedly checking our credentials and watching us with distrustful eyes the whole time.

"If anything does go down here," Barrla muttered as we left, "we will be prime suspects. It can't look good to them that we're snooping about and taking pictures, and they have our names, too."

I shrugged. "We'll have the Chief Mage and his bride to vouch for us," I said, though I was a little worried as well. They weren't back in town yet, and didn't know me, after all. But they were good friends with Fenris, and I was going to have to bank on that if things did go south. And even if we were suspected, we were innocent, and the authorities wouldn't have any proof saying otherwise.

After that, we visited two of the reception venues, which would be harder to guard, as they were inside big hotels in crowded city blocks. Each place was large enough to hold up to a thousand guests and had multiple entrances, if you included the fire escape doors. One hall was being prepared for a different function later in the evening, a banquet for a large company's staff and clients. There would be six hundred to sit down, a hotel trainee told us, but the area had been halved with sliding walls, while the other half would be used for a seminar the next morning and was being filled with chairs.

I tried to imagine where I would attack, if I were with the Resistance, and easily came up with half a dozen scenarios.

"So Fenris really knows the guests of honor in person and will introduce you to them?" Barrla asked as we left. "You are going to be moving in very exclusive circles, Mina. We'd better do some clothes shopping later on."

"I'll be in disguise, most likely, since Fenris prefers to keep a low profile among all these mages. Besides, a thousand people in one spot is hardly exclusive," I pointed out. How did Sunaya Baine feel about attending all these huge events night after night? I guessed she would be relieved to escape to the privacy of her honeymoon. I would be, in her place. Of course, nobody was giving receptions in Fenris's and my honor. I didn't envy her at all in that regard.

"These hotels are the most vulnerable spots we've identified," Barrla said, echoing what I had been thinking. "Only, which one are they going to target? There are five major receptions scheduled here in town, including the Minister's." That one, two days before the wedding, would be held in a large concert hall, which we had not yet inspected. It was closed to the public during the daytime, though from the outside, they seemed to have reasonable security.

"I feel like the heroine of *Shifter Undercover*," Barrla declared as we sat in a steamcab heading back towards the Mages Quarter. "You remember, that was the one where the lion shifter had to pass as human, wearing false glass lenses in her eyes, to catch the villains who had framed her clan."

"False lenses? That sounds most uncomfortable," I commented. Barrla loved to bring up outlandish scenes from her novels and compare them to real life, but I couldn't remember her mentioning that one before.

"Yes, but being a shifter, she could stand the pain and was continuously being healed."

I shook my head. I'd have to check with Fenris on whether something like that was even possible. I was glad that, as a mage, I would never have to use such painful methods.

We managed to enter the Mages Quarter with little trouble this time, but we were unable to get into the Palace grounds, where the main wedding celebration would be held. I wasn't too worried about that—Fenris had considered the Palace an unlikely target, as it was strongly warded. With any luck, Fenris and I would be able to be there, in disguise, and mingle with the other guests when the time came.

I looked forward to that, and wondered if I might take any inspiration for my own wedding. I wanted to be married sooner rather than later. If only we could make some headway with this investigation, Fenris and I could turn our attention to our own future. A small wedding would suit me just fine—neither of us had families to invite, so there was no need for a grand affair, even though I could afford it.

With the sun beginning to set, and our stomachs growling,

Barrla and I adjourned to the seafood restaurant where we were supposed to meet Fenris. It had been recommended by the concierge in the Marwale as one of the best in all of Solantha. Fenris had made reservations ahead of time, and the host immediately led us to our table, which had a prime location right by a window that overlooked Solantha Bay. With a smile, he handed us leather-bound menus and took our drink orders.

"I am surprised that Fenris isn't here yet," Barrla said after a few minutes as we slaked our thirst on sparkling water and white wine and munched on bread and butter while studying the list of appetizing dishes. "It doesn't seem like him to be late."

"No, it isn't," I said with a frown. "He's normally very punctual. Perhaps he ended up meeting with someone on short notice? It would be great if he was able to find some clue to who is behind all this." I tried to be optimistic, though I had an uneasy feeling in my stomach. "Why don't we just go ahead and order—I know what he likes, and he'll be grateful not to have to wait for the food when he finally gets here."

But as the minutes began to tick on, and our entrées arrived with no sign of Fenris, I grew increasingly worried. I couldn't even taste the plump shrimp I was eating or appreciate the chef's subtle seasoning. If Fenris knew he was going to be delayed, why not send an ether pigeon to let me know? Antsy, I looked down at the serapha charm hanging from my neck and gently pressed my finger to the stone to activate it. It began to glow, letting me know that Fenris was alive, but to my dismay, the glow was a little diminished.

"What is that?" Barrla asked, leaning forward.

"It's a serapha charm," I told her, then briefly explained what it did. "The diminished glow usually means that the other person is injured or ill," I said, my heart sinking into my toes. "Something must have happened to Fenris."

"Then we need to go and find him," Barrla said, putting

down her fork. "Didn't you say that thing can tell you where he is?"

Nodding, I closed my eyes and focused in on the little tug deep in my chest. "He's still in the city," I said. "Somewhere west of where we are now."

"Well that narrows it down," Barrla said dryly. "Is this like a game of hot and cold? The charm will tell us whether or not we're close?"

"I'm afraid so," I said, wishing that we had a better option. "It's too bad I haven't mastered the art of sending ether pigeons...but even if I could reliably produce them, it might be a bad idea if Fenris is not in a safe place to receive them." He was in human disguise, after all, and nothing shouted "mage spy" like having an insubstantial bird pop into existence next to you and relay some mysterious message.

"Better not, then," Barrla said, tossing her napkin onto the table and signaling to the hovering waiter to bring our bill. "At least we have some kind of lead on him. Let's go and find him before it's too late."

THIRTEEN

FENRIS

A throbbing pain in my head dragged me from the darkness, but it took me a while to gather my wits. My head was on fire, my tongue was parched, and I hurt all over—not a usual state for a shifter. What in Recca had happened to me?

Breathe, I ordered myself, taking in a deep draw of air through my nose. I focused on getting my heartbeat under control and relaxing my muscles. Eventually the pain faded a bit, and I risked opening my eyes to take stock of my surroundings. The small room looked very much like a prison cell, though I had never seen it from this particular perspective. I was lying on a hard cot, and I could hear breathing and motion coming from other cells down the hall.

I must be in the Enforcers Guild basement cells.

Groaning, I pushed upright into a sitting position and looked down at my torn, bloody clothes—the very clothes I had worn in the hotel that morning. My disguise had lapsed during my period of unconsciousness. Panic shot through me—had any of the enforcers recognized me? How recognizable would I have been unconscious, with my eyes closed? Was Director Toring even now being notified of my capture?

At least you're still alive, I tried to console myself, *and while there's life, there's hope.* Bracing myself, I shifted into wolf form to heal my injuries, then back again. Panting, I leaned against the wall—a wave of weakness washed over me. I had a feeling it had been many hours since I'd last eaten.

Dredging up what little strength I had left, I conjured another illusion, disguising myself as the human again. But this time I modified my appearance to look less like a ruffian, improving the quality of my clothing and making my skin look cleaner and my hair less shaggy. It was always possible that nobody had noticed my change in appearance, and if some enforcer came to check on me, I wanted to look more like a confused citizen than a scruffy thug. With any luck, someone in authority would come along soon, and I could get out of here without making a scene or betraying my identity. My coin purse, which had contained my forged ID and all my money, was gone too. All I had left was Mina's serapha charm, whose magic ensured that only I could take it off. Had they tried to do so? Would anyone searching my unconscious body have realized it was not just an eccentric necklace?

As an hour passed with nothing but my gloomy thoughts to keep me company, I began to worry that no one would come to interrogate me or let me out. Why was I here, anyway? Most likely due to that wretched enforcer who was chasing the ragged woman downtown with those pimps. Mina would have been worried when I didn't turn up at dinner. I must not contact her, or lead anyone to her, while I was in peril of being recognized.

After a time, I decided enough was enough—I had not mastered over a thousand spells so I could sit around in a cell, twiddling my thumbs and waiting for some gruesome fate to befall me. I tried to pick the lock with a general-purpose unlocking spell, but a ward flared to life the moment my magic touched it, no doubt put there by one of the Mages Guild apprentices.

"Dammit!" I cursed under my breath as an alarm blared— tampering with the lock had set it off. What a foolish beginner's mistake. I should have used my mage sight to check for wards, but somehow, in this human environment, had not expected any. Perhaps my wits were still addled from that blow to the head.

Heart pounding, I flung myself back onto my cot and closed my eyes, hoping that no one would notice. There were a few other prisoners in the cells, and it was possible that the guards might not be able to tell which lock had been tampered with.

The alarm subsided after a while, and as the minutes ticked past in silence, I began to relax a little. But the sound of heavy footsteps approaching had me tensing again, and I gritted my teeth as the door at the end of the hall swung open.

Four enforcers stopped outside my cell—two humans and two mages, I realized with dismay. One of the mages opened the cell with a key, and I was unceremoniously yanked from my cot and dragged upstairs.

"Where are you taking me?" I demanded, doing my best not to struggle. I was vastly outnumbered, and resisting would only make things worse. Besides, I was trying to portray a harmless human imprisoned by mistake.

"Captain wants to speak with you," the mage who'd opened the cell said shortly. None of them seemed particularly inclined to talk to me.

I frowned. The captain? Why was he taking an interest in me? I turned various scenarios over in my mind as the enforcers took me up to the fourth floor and marched me into a large office at the end of the hall.

"Captain Skonel," the mage enforcer said as he opened the door. "The prisoner you asked for."

Ahhh, yes, I thought as I looked at the man sitting behind the desk. I remembered now. Skonel had been acting captain the last time I'd seen him, and on probation, but his appointment would be permanent by now.

"I didn't realize we had a mage on our hands," the captain said, his gaze full of suspicion as he studied me. He was tall and wiry, whereas his predecessor had been rather broader and more imposing. "What's a mage skulking about downtown for? And why aren't you in robes?" His scent was redolent with animosity.

"I demand to know why I've been arrested," I said angrily, taking on an imperious tone—if the captain thought I was a mage, then I better act like one. "I was minding my own business when some thug hit me on the head. He should be in a cell right now, not me!"

"That 'thug' was the owner of Lance's Ladies," the captain said, and I remembered the name—it was on the sign of the brothel I had passed. "He claims that you refused to pay for their services and destroyed some property in a drunken rage. He even paid a bounty for you."

"So you're going to believe a brothel owner over a mage?" I scoffed. It seemed that Sunaya had not rooted all the corruption out of the Enforcers Guild, if pimps and enforcers were still working hand in hand.

"I'm inclined to, since I have no idea who you are and what you were up to in such a seedy area."

"My name is Uthrel Galorian," I said, using the name of the hero from an ancient Loranian saga. Iannis would instantly recognize the name, though it would mean nothing to these humans. "I am working directly for the Chief Mage and his bride, Sunaya Baine. They will both vouch for me. These ridiculous charges are bogus—I was never even *inside* that damn brothel and wouldn't dream of using their services. I was investigating human trafficking on behalf of the Mages Guild."

"And why is it," the captain said tightly, "that the Mages Guild is conducting criminal investigations *on my turf*, without informing me?" His voice rose dangerously. This must be a sore spot with him, but it was too late to change the story now. Besides, from what I'd observed, he was doing a poor job of policing the area.

"We suspect that some of your enforcers are involved," I said, "and we did not want to involve you without concrete proof, in case you have a mole in your office. The fact that your enforcers dumped me into a cell with a false story when I was the victim of assault is proof that our suspicions are justified. I demand to know the name of the enforcer who delivered me here. He or they must be in league with the gangs downtown!"

"You're in no position to make any demands of me, much less waltz into my office and accuse my men of corruption," the captain snapped, his face coloring with rage. "I'll look into this little story of yours when I have the time, which won't be anytime soon with all that we have going on in Solantha right now. Until I can confirm who you are and what you were really doing there, you'll remain in your prison cell."

"You have no authority to hold me!" I shouted with righteous indignation as the guards grabbed me. "The Chief Mage will be furious when he hears about this!"

"Good," the captain growled, and I had to give him reluctant credit for courage, if not for good sense. "Maybe then he'll realize how it feels when someone stomps all over *his* jurisdiction."

As the enforcers dragged me back to my cell, I considered fighting my way free. But the odds were against me, and I didn't need yet another bounty on my head.

"Just in case you think about trying to escape again," the mage enforcer sneered as I was shoved into my cell. Before I could ask what he meant, he slapped a pair of runed manacles on my wrists. I gasped, then immediately ducked my head as the illusion I maintained flickered away. Hurriedly, I retreated into the shadows before the enforcers noticed, but they had already turned away, talking and laughing amongst themselves as they left. The bastards.

Dammit. I should have fought them after all. I glowered at the manacles, and the runes on them glowed back, almost as if they were mocking me. As long as I had these cuffs on, I couldn't do any magic. I was well and truly stuck here, and if anyone recognized me as Fenris, I was doomed.

In hindsight, I might have been better off telling the captain who I really was—the claim that I was working for Iannis would have been much more believable then. It was possible my fortuitous "death" in the quake had forestalled Garrett Toring and his agents from putting me on any wanted lists, and I could have bluffed my way out of this predicament. But it was too late for me to change my story without looking even more shifty.

Of all the times for Iannis and Sunaya to be missing, this was surely the worst.

FOURTEEN

MINA

Abandoning the restaurant, Barrla and I followed the pull of the serapha charm, hoping it would lead us to Fenris. At first we got into a cab and gave the bewildered driver step by step directions, but soon we were snarled in traffic. We paid the driver for his time and continued our search on foot, doing our best to navigate the streets even though we didn't really know where we were going. It was dark by now, and despite the gas lamps, the city felt strangely menacing. I cursed the heels that slowed us down.

Finally, several hours and two sore pairs of feet later, we found ourselves standing outside a tall, dingy gray building. "The Enforcers Guild?" Barrla panted, using a handkerchief to mop the sweat from her brow as she moved the camera bag to her other shoulder. "This isn't good."

"No." I bit my lip as I stared at the faded lettering above the entrance. If Fenris was here, there was a good chance he was taken prisoner. "We have to get him out of here."

"A prison break? I've never tried one of those before," Barrla said, sounding far too eager.

"Let's start with some questions first."

We entered the building together. Despite the late hour, it was quite busy with foot traffic—I imagined there was a change of shift going on.

"Excuse me," Barrla purred as she sauntered up to the gangly young man sitting behind the reception desk—an enforcer trainee. "Is the captain in? My associate and I would love to interview him for the *Deros Globe*. We'd love to know how he's coping with all the upcoming festivities." She gave him a coy smile, and his cheeks turned pink.

"*Fenris?*" I called in mindspeak while Barrla flirted with the trainee, trying to convince him that his captain would love to be interviewed by out-of-town journalists. I could feel him—it almost seemed as if he was right beneath me. "*Are you here?*"

"*Mina?*" Fenris replied, and I nearly sagged with relief. He sounded alarmed but coherent—I didn't sense that he was in any pain. "*What are you doing here?*"

"*I've come to find you, of course,*" I said, a little crossly. "*How in Recca did you end up in a cell?*"

"*I was following up a lead downtown when a thug knocked me out,*" Fenris said, sounding chagrined. "*It seems that the enforcers and the pimps down there work hand in hand. They could have killed me, but instead they brought me here unconscious, claiming I'd refused to pay for a whore and destroyed some brothel's property while drunk.*"

"*A whore?*" I started to ask, and then shook my head. I didn't even want to know. The main thing was that he'd survived the greatest danger. "*Fenris, I thought we already agreed you weren't going to go back there alone.*"

"*I know, I know. I'm sorry,*" he said, and he sounded so upset with himself that I decided not to belabor the point. "*They've put runed handcuffs on me, Mina. I can't use my magic.*"

"*Doesn't that mean you're no longer disguised?*" I asked,

alarmed. The last thing Fenris needed was to have his identity revealed while he was already in a jail cell.

"Yes, but with any luck they won't be back to see me for some time. They say they are 'looking into' my story." Fenris briefly explained to me how he'd told the captain that he was in downtown on a mission for Iannis. *"You must go to Comenius at once and explain what happened, and have him check to see if Iannis and Sunaya are back yet."*

"I can't just leave you—"

"You can, and you will," Fenris said firmly. *"It will do me no good if you stay here, and it's best if you keep your distance anyway. Somebody needs to be around to stop the attack."*

Tears pricked at my eyes, but I nodded. "I'll go and tell Comenius, but I will *be back if he cannot help. I won't abandon you. Fenris."*

I could have sworn I felt Fenris sigh on the other end. *"I love you, Mina. Please be safe."*

"I love you too."

"Thursday at two o'clock sounds perfect," Barrla said as I tuned back into her conversation with the trainee, who was holding a telephone receiver now. "That will work for us, won't it, Mina?"

"Hmm? Oh, yes, of course," I said, blinking down at the young man. Thankfully he didn't seem to notice my lapse in concentration—he only had eyes for Barrla. "That would be fine."

Barrla finished setting up the appointment, and we left. "Did you manage to contact him?" she asked under her breath as we stepped outside.

I nodded. "He's in a cell below, being held under false charges, and they've blocked him from accessing his magic. He's asked us to go to Comenius for help, but I fear only the Chief Mage will be able to get him out."

Barrla scowled. "There's got to be something else we can do, isn't there? This seems so unfair!"

"I do have those double-strength gulayas," I remembered. "But I'll have to get close to Fenris in order to use them, and they'll probably search me first. If I could activate one as I grasped his arm, I might set him free...though there's always a chance it won't work with the bars between us." And even if it did work, we'd both be branded as fugitives.

"We could use the ether owl to spy on the captain," Barrla said as we hailed a cab. "That way we can at least find out what he plans to do with Fenris and then figure out how to thwart it."

"That's not a bad plan," I said as we got in. "But first, let's talk it over with Comenius. He might have a less risky alternative."

FIFTEEN

Barrla and I managed to make it to Witches End just shy of eleven at night. We rushed up the stairs, relieved to see the lights were still on, and the door was opened by a dark-haired woman I could only assume was Elania, his wife.

"My goodness," Elania said in a throaty accent as she ushered us in. "I knew Fenris would pick a beauty to settle down with, but you are a vision." She took me by the shoulders and looked me up and down. "What brings you here so late at night?"

"Thank you," I said, blushing at the compliment, especially considering who it came from. Elania was one of the most gorgeous women I'd ever seen, with long, shiny black hair piled onto the top of her head, exotic features, and a ridiculously curvy figure draped in a black dress that showed off her assets. She couldn't have been more different from Comenius's fair coloring and conservative nature, and yet somehow, they seemed a good fit. "Do you mind if we sit down? We're in a bit of a bind, and we need some help."

"Of course," Comenius said as Elania shut the door behind

us. "What seems to be the problem? Is it something to do with Fenris? Why is he not with you?"

Barrla and I sat down on the couch while Elania brought us tea. "He's being held at the Enforcers Guild on false charges," I said. "He was doing some investigating in downtown, and if I had to guess, someone didn't like what he saw or learned. A brothel owner is claiming he didn't pay for services rendered and damaged his property in a drunken fit."

Comenius stared. "Neither of those things sound like the Fenris I know," he said.

"What did Fenris say in his defense?" Elania asked. "Surely he was able to spin some story to explain what happened. He is an intelligent man. In any case, those are not very serious charges. He should have gotten off with a fine."

"He told them that he was on some mission for Lord Iannis, but the captain didn't believe him," I said. "He's holding him there until he can verify his story."

"Well that would work fine if Iannis was actually here," Comenius muttered. "I still haven't heard anything, and I've been checking every day."

"Do you think it might help to hire a lawyer?" Barrla asked. "If they find out who Fenris really is, he might need it."

Comenius shook his head. "The enforcers despise lawyers, and a real mage working on Iannis's behalf would not bother. We need to talk to someone who can get Fenris out of that cell."

"Kardanor may be able to help," Elania suggested. "Aren't you supposed to meet him for coffee in the morning?" she asked Comenius.

Before Comenius could answer, someone banged on the door. Alarmed, Comenius went to answer it and found Marris standing outside, dressed in paint-splattered overalls.

"Sorry I'm late," he said, panting a little as he came inside. "I ended up—"

He froze at the sight of Barrla, who was standing and glaring at him with her arms crossed over her chest.

"What in Recca are you doing here?" he gasped.

"I'm helping Mina prevent a catastrophe," Barrla snapped, her blue eyes crackling with ire. "Which is more than you can say right now."

"I've been infiltrating the Resistance!" Marris protested. "And *you're* supposed to be safe back home!"

"Stop!" I said sharply, holding up a hand. "You two can table this fight for later. Barrla is here to stay, and if you want to help, Marris, then give your report. Fenris is unavailable right now, so you'll have to tell us what you've found, and we'll relay it to him as soon as possible."

Marris scrubbed a hand over his face as Barrla grudgingly took her seat. "Fenris told me to meet him here, but he never actually introduced me to you," he said to Comenius and Elania. "How do I know I can trust you two?"

"They're old friends of Fenris," I said. "You can speak freely."

Marris sat down on the couch and snagged a cabbage roll from a plate Elania held out to him. "So far, I've determined that there are masses of former Resistance soldiers in town disguised as workers for various construction companies. I've joined their ranks, and we've been sleeping in pretty crowded conditions in half-finished apartments. Okay for a week or two, if you are used to roughing it, but there's some grumbling in the ranks. Oh, and it's humans only this time, none of our former shifter mates have been called in for this."

"That's not surprising," I said. "They would probably have refused anyway."

Marris nodded. "We've been given pocket money, and those of us who actually help out with the work get a bit extra. I've been painting walls, as you can see from my clothes." He gestured toward his paint-stained shirt. "All of us have been ordered to be ready until something happens that throws the city into chaos, and then we are to go to pre-assigned areas which we will hold and secure until all opposition is subdued."

"Damn," Comenius said. "Do you really think there are enough to hold the city?"

Marris nodded grimly. "New recruits are arriving daily, and there are so many of us that we are practically tripping over each other's feet now."

"It sounds like the Resistance is planning to take out all the top mages in one go," I said. "Do you think that's the case? That would certainly cause instant chaos."

"I don't know how they're going to do it, but that does seem to be the plan. If they are able to pull it off, they definitely have enough men to hold the city against a confused and blindsided population."

"Do you have any idea who the bosses are?" Barrla asked. "Have you talked to anyone who isn't a peon?"

Marris gave her a look. "No, but my employer is Moredo Constructions, and other workers are employed by different companies. I wouldn't be surprised if the company owners were the ones orchestrating things. At the very least, they're working for the person who is, and will know who they are."

"That is very useful information," Comenius said approvingly.

"Yes, the best lead we've had yet," I agreed. "We'll need to look into these companies further."

"Marris," Barrla said, softening her tone. "Now that you've found this out, come back to the hotel with us. There's no need to put yourself in further danger—if things come to a head, you might end up in a crossfire between your Resistance buddies and the mages. I don't want to lose you so soon."

"Someone is looking out for me," Marris declared, "or I

would not be alive now. Compared to some of my past exploits, this is pretty tame—at least so far."

"That can change from one moment to the next," Barrla warned.

Marris nodded, but from the gleam in his eyes, I could tell he was looking forward to whatever mayhem might be in store. "If it does, I'll fight my way through to you, sweetheart." He grinned at her. "Anyway, I feel totally out of place in that fancy hotel. I'm more useful with the Resistance—and I can earn money as a painter while keeping my ears open." He checked his watch. "I have to go back before the others become suspicious."

Barrla rose from her chair, and Marris took her in his arms and kissed her soundly. "I'll be back soon," he promised. "Take care of my girl for me, Mina."

He gave us a smile and a wink, and then he was gone.

Barrla sighed. "I really hope that idiot doesn't get himself killed," she said mournfully as she slumped back in her chair.

"Marris has survived this long," I reassured her. "And he cares for you, Barrla. He won't let all of this keep him away for too long."

"I'll talk to Kardanor tomorrow," Comenius said, drawing our attention back to the problem at hand. "He's the Secretary of Reconstruction and will know more about these companies than anyone else. I'll also ask him to talk to Director Chen about getting Fenris freed. She may be more of a stickler for the rules than Iannis, but she knows what Fenris has done for us. I'm not sure she knows about his true identity, though—I did not know myself for a long time. Perhaps we can just skirt that issue. In any case, I expect she is going to rip Captain Skonel a new one for keeping a mage in his prison and not promptly informing her."

"Thank you," I said with feeling. I wished I could go to this meeting myself, but I knew I wouldn't be of any use. If I really had to, I could use the ether owl to eavesdrop.

Comenius called the Palace to check in on Iannis again. Iannis still wasn't back, so Comenius left a message requesting an appointment with Kardanor for the next day.

"You should go back to the hotel and get some rest," Comenius advised. "You'll want to be at full strength for tomorrow."

"I don't know if I'll be able to sleep," I said, pacing back and forth. "Every time I think about Fenris, alone in that dark cell without his magic, I tense up." My stomach was still a mess of knots, and my food was still untouched on the table.

"Didn't you say something about gulayas?" Barrla asked. "That you wanted to have them in case we needed to break Fenris out as a last resort?"

"Right." But that would require access to him, impossible at this hour of the night. "I guess it will have to wait. There's nothing for us to do here."

We thanked Comenius and Elania for their hospitality, and they sent us on our way with a basket full of leftovers and a relaxation tonic. And as we drove back to the Marwale, I sincerely hoped that Barrla and I wouldn't have to prep for a prison break tomorrow.

SIXTEEN

When I finally felt Mina leave the building, I sagged in relief. The last thing I needed was for her to be caught up in this disaster. How could I have been so stupid as to let myself be caught like this? I should have escaped when I had the chance, damn the consequences. Yes, I might have been forced to leave the city before I could see Sunaya and Iannis again, but I had already ensured that they would be warned.

Anything was better than lying on this hard cot, surrounded by nothing but interminable silence.

Well, *silence* wasn't quite right. There were a few other people down here in the cells, and even though they weren't close enough to talk to, they made plenty of noise. Unable to sleep, I had nothing else to do but stretch out on the hard cot and listen to them. One drunk a few cells down was banging against the wall, shouting over and over that he demanded to see his mother. Another was snoring loudly.

"That's enough of that!" an enforcer commanded, storming back to the cells to confront the rowdy prisoner. I held my breath as he passed my cell, then relaxed—he hadn't bothered to glance my way.

"You can't hold me here—" the drunk began to yell, but his words were cut off by a yelp and a crackling sound. I wrinkled my nose at the scent of burned skin and hair—had the enforcer hit him with some kind of electricity? A thud to the floor confirmed that whatever it was had knocked the man out cold.

"Stupid bastard," the enforcer muttered, stalking out.

My stomach grumbled, and I was tempted to stop and ask him when we'd be fed. But the risk of being recognized was too great, so I stayed in the dark corner of my cell, my face averted, and did my best to ignore my hunger.

Now that the drunk wasn't making a scene anymore, I was able to hear other things. The enforcers were playing poker in an adjacent room in between rounds to check on their prisoners, and I tuned into the conversation.

"You sure it's not going to bring trouble, holding a mage down here?" one of them asked. He sounded a bit nervous. "The last time we locked up was Sunaya, and she ended up becoming the Chief Mage's bride. What if this guy's important?"

"Don't be ridiculous," the other enforcer scoffed. "Not every mage in this town has the Chief Mage's favor. Sunaya definitely didn't when we cuffed her—the fact that she's where she's at now is a combination of luck and knowing how to use what's between her legs."

"Man, I'd sure like a piece of that," another one said, and they all laughed. I shook my head in silence—if Sunaya were here to overhear that, she would have ripped them all to shreds. It was too bad that there were still those amongst her former coworkers who considered her little more than arm candy for Iannis.

If only they knew what she was truly capable of.

"That's all well and good, but I heard that he told the captain that he *was* working for the Chief Mage," the nervous guy said. "What if that's true?"

"The captain is within his rights to detain him," the second enforcer said. "As long as his story remains unverified, we can hold him as long as we want. Seeing as how we're so busy thanks to all the mages in town, we can't be blamed for taking our time to check out his story," he added smugly.

"And how do we know that this won't come back to bite us in the ass?" the first one demanded. "Everyone knows that the guys Meltin brings in from downtown are people the gangs want to get rid of, not real criminals."

"You sayin' you're gonna rat Meltin out?" the second enforcer said, his tone decidedly menacing. "Sounds like you're just jealous of the side money he's making. If you want in on the action, all you gotta do is say so. But nobody likes a tattletale."

I gritted my teeth and committed the name to memory. As soon as I was in a position to do so, I was going to seek retribution on Meltin. Unfortunately, I had no idea when that would be. As far as I could tell, these enforcers planned to keep me jailed indefinitely and had no intention of verifying the truth of my story. And with these stupid magic-blocking cuffs, I couldn't even send an ether pigeon to Iannis for help.

Mina knows you're in here, I reminded myself. *She'll get help.* Being forced to depend on her chafed my pride, but if we were to become a married couple, we'd better learn to rely on each other.

But would Mina be able to get me out before the Minister and his mages caught up with me? What if my identity was revealed before then? I should have asked Iannis what the exact status was, when I had the chance. My stomach turned at the thought of Mina standing by, helpless, as I was formally charged and executed. I'd never been this close to realizing that nightmare, not since those horrible days in Nebara Palace, when I'd waited under house arrest for Garrett Toring to arrive with the Minister's warrant to formally arrest me for treason.

These thoughts chased themselves around my mind for what felt like hours. Eventually, I fell into an uneasy doze, which was a welcome relief from the hunger pangs...

"Hey!" A loud voice woke me, and I bolted upright. "Rise and shine, sweetheart! The boss wants to see you."

"Now?" I tried to keep my voice even, but true panic swept through me as the cell door opened and two enforcers marched in to grab me. Surely this was some kind of mistake...it had to be long after midnight. Why would the captain trouble himself at this hour? Was the jig finally up? I ducked my head so that the enforcers wouldn't see my shifter eyes, but if they noticed that my appearance was different, they didn't make any comment about it.

"Here's the prisoner again, Captain," one of the enforcers said as they dragged me back into the captain's office, where he stood talking with another man. "Anything else you'll be needing?"

My stomach plummeted as the two men turned to me, their mouths dropping open in amazement. "Fenris!" they said in unison, and I wished right then and there I had the ability to will myself to disappear. Staring at me, my shock mirrored in his own eyes, was Garrett Toring, the Federal Director of Security.

My worst nightmare, given flesh and bone.

"Is it really you?" Garrett asked as the enforcers finally released my arms. At least he had said *Fenris* rather than *Polar*. Did that mean the jig wasn't up after all?

"Yes." I shrugged nonchalantly, deciding to pretend that it was no big deal. The less guilty I looked, the better.

Garrett stared at me intently for a long moment. "Uncuff

him, please," he ordered Captain Skonel. "It is clear that a mistake was made."

"Uncuff him?" Skonel gave me an uneasy look. "But why did he not say—and that alarm, it should not have rung for a shifter—"

"*Now*. And leave us. I need to speak to him privately." Garrett's voice brooked no argument. Being in charge of Federal Security had made him more imperious than ever.

The captain glowered, but he motioned to his enforcers to do as Garrett asked. I held in a sigh of relief as the cuffs came free and rubbed my smarting wrists as the captain and his enforcers took their leave of us. Skonel was furious at the insult of being kicked out of his own office, but he had little choice considering Garrett outranked him.

The door closed behind us, and a tense silence filled the room. I met Garrett's eyes steadily, betraying nothing. Long seconds passed as he continued to study me as though I were a particularly vexing puzzle.

"Why did you let Iannis and Sunaya think you were dead?" he finally asked, and I blinked in surprise. That was certainly not the first question I expected. "You caused both of them unnecessary heartache."

"I..." I stalled for a moment as I quickly scrambled together a plausible story. I could hardly say that I had left to save them and me from Garrett's own probing, after he had come dangerously close to the truth. "I was badly injured during the quake when I helped Sunaya and Rusalia escape that collapsed building. I don't really remember how I escaped, to be honest, but I'm pretty sure I was hit on the head because I was dazed when I woke up and couldn't remember anything for a little while. By the time I regained my memories, I decided it was simpler to stay away. It gets... tiring, being the third wheel in Iannis and Sunaya's relationship, if you catch my meaning." I tried to look wistful, as though I'd had to suppress my feelings for Sunaya and found it painful. "I thought it might be easier for all of us to let them move on without me."

Garrett nodded sympathetically. "I know all too well what that's like," he said, and then gave a little laugh. "You know, I actually suspected you of somehow being Polar ar'Tollis until Sunaya told me the truth."

"Oh?" I asked, keeping my expression carefully blank even as my heart raced. What "truth" had Sunaya told him? One false step now could sink all of us. I held my breath, willing him to give me a clue.

"Yes, she explained everything to me," Garrett said. Was that a small grin on his face? "I completely understand that you wouldn't want to advertise that you are Polar's bastard son, brought up like some guilty secret that had to be hidden away. It must be hard enough to be a shifter amongst mages without everyone knowing that you're a hybrid."

Stunned, but pleased, at the strange narrative that Sunaya had spun, I managed a laugh of my own. "I'm afraid I'm not half the mage my father was," I said. "My shifter blood has prevented me from inheriting his full magical strength."

"Your father *was*? Do you know if he's dead, then?" Garrett immediately asked, looking like a keen bloodhound all of a sudden.

"I do not know for sure," I said, hiding my annoyance at Garrett's eagerness to execute me, "but I have a feeling he is no longer alive, and Lord Iannis agrees. Life as a fugitive would not have suited him. My father was a proud man."

"That's very interesting," Garrett mused. "Though I can hardly take your word for it. We need proof before we can stop hunting him, but at this point I'd just as soon find him dead than alive."

"Of course." I hid a shiver. Sunaya might have fooled Garrett for now, but it was clear that he had not yet given up.

"So, how much of his magic did you inherit, as well as his taste for studying those old scrolls? Sunaya is also a hybrid and yet very strong, but of course we do not know how much power her unknown father had or has." Garrett sounded like he had considered the issue more than once. "I suppose inheritance varies from family to family. In any case, you must not continue to hide yourself like this. Your grandparents have been staying in Solantha for months, hoping that you will resurface."

"My grandparents?" I reeled back, not bothering to hide my shock.

"Yes. They're convinced that you must still be alive, since your body was never recovered. They'll be very happy that their intuition was on target."

"That can't be right," I said, trying and failing to wrap my mind around the idea that my parents had come all the way to Canalo looking for me. "My father always told me that they were too proud of their mage lineage to accept a shifter into their family." Certainly, if I *had* fathered a secret wolf shifter child, I would not have expected them to welcome it.

"Maybe they were once upon a time, but that is certainly not the case now," Garrett said. "Your grandfather was quite anxious and saddened when he heard you had perished in the quake. There is no reason for you not to seek them out, or to deny your heritage anymore. Sensible people do not blame children for their parents' sins."

I shook my head, stunned at Garrett's unexpected compassion. I was so used to seeing him as my enemy that I wasn't sure how to handle his earnest efforts to help me.

"Do you know where my grandparents are staying?" I finally asked, deciding to play along. I might as well track them down to see if they really *were* my parents. Was the old mage who went to see Boon Lakin my father? An unexpected cocktail of joy and anxiety filled my heart. I hadn't seen my parents in years...what would they think if they knew that Fenris and Polar were the same person? Did I dare tell them the truth?

"Yes, they're staying at a hotel right here in town. The Golden something-or-other," Garrett said, screwing up his face as he tried to remember.

"The Golden Wave?" I guessed. It was a small but elegant hotel on the outskirts of the Mages Quarter that I'd passed on more than one occasion.

"Yes, that sounds right. Why don't we get you something to eat, and then you can be on your way?"

FENRIS

"Tell the captain we're leaving," Garrett said to the captain's deputy, who was loitering just outside the office. Captain Skonel and the enforcers from earlier were nowhere to be found, which wasn't surprising—the captain wouldn't want to hang out in his own waiting room, for everyone to see he had been kicked out. "I don't expect to be back again today, but if he has need of me he knows how to reach me."

"Before we go," I said, slowing to a stop, "I want Enforcer Meltin investigated. It seems he has an illicit arrangement with the brothel owners and gang leaders downtown, which is how I ended up in this unfortunate situation in the first place."

The deputy's face hardened, and I could tell that he was just as reluctant to take criticism about his Guild as the captain was. "I'd also appreciate it if Meltin returned my coin purse to me," I said pointedly.

"Yes, see to it that it gets done," Garrett said briskly. "We can't have corruption in the ranks, especially at a time like this."

"Yes, sir," the deputy said with a sharp nod, though his scent told me he was seething inwardly. He turned to go back into his office, and I reluctantly followed Garrett to the elevator. Despite my hunger, I wasn't looking forward to sharing a meal with him, but it was the least I could do after he rescued me, and I saw no way to avoid it without rousing renewed suspicion.

"So this Enforcer Meltin is responsible for putting you in a jail cell?" Garrett asked as we walked out of the building. Not a single person stopped us, though at close to two in the morning there weren't many people around. "How exactly did that happen?"

"It's a long story," I said, reluctant to discuss it out in the open. "Perhaps best told over some food."

Garrett agreed, and he took me to a twenty-four-hour diner a few blocks away that the enforcers liked to frequent. There were one or two enforcers seated in booths, nursing coffee, but other than that the place was empty, and we easily found a table that ensured us a measure of privacy. The wooden tables were shiny from use, and nicked here and there. The electrical light was flickering strangely, but the scent of warm food from the kitchens was highly appetizing, and I placed a huge order.

It was very strange to be sitting with Garrett, but I forced myself to get over it. As I devoured multiple burgers and milkshakes I told him about the human trafficking ring I had stumbled over, and that Meltin had falsely charged me with stealing from a brothel in order to keep me from digging too deeply.

"So were you working for Iannis, as you had told the captain, or not?" Garrett asked, his brow furrowed. "I thought you said that you planned to stay away from him and Sunaya."

"I did," I said. "But a couple of weeks ago, I learned by chance that there is a plot against the Convention or the wedding...I've not yet found out which. I came back to warn Iannis, of course, only to find that he was mysteriously gone."

"Indeed, at the worst possible time." I could tell that Garrett was not very upset about it—he probably thought it would improve his own chances to be named the Minister's successor. "Why did you not come straight to me with what you learned, or at least to Director Chen?"

Why indeed? I shrugged. "There was not enough information to act on. I wanted to find out more first. That was why I have been haunting such a bad part of town. The human trafficking was just bad luck. I didn't tell Skonel what I was really after, since I suspect that there are moles in his organization. Too many enforcers hate mages, and your quarrel with the captain tonight will not have improved matters."

Garrett scowled. "The man failed to inform me that they had taken a mage prisoner—you, as it happens—and I only found out by chance. He exceeded his jurisdiction, but I'll be surprised if he does it again."

So that was what they had argued about. I had reservations about Garrett's increasing powers, but for once they were working to my advantage.

"I did have a friend send warnings to you and Director Chen," I said. "And I was going to contact you again when I had more information."

"We get dozens of those every day, mostly from crackpots." Garrett sighed. "I already had an uneasy feeling, and we have stepped up security as much as possible outside Dara. Not even a flea is going to get into the Convention without being thoroughly checked. But until now, I was not truly inclined to take an anonymous warning—or several—too seriously."

I told him about the Resistance veterans being assembled and the strange hand signs I had observed. Garrett stopped eating and listened intently. "So there are a whole lot of men from out of state waiting for something to happen, and they're given money to cover their living costs in the meantime?"

"Yes." I described the fellows who had been lurking on a building site. "That gives us some leverage," Garrett said at once. "The bosses have to know what these supernumerary workers are, and who placed them there. I'm actually not too surprised. You don't get far in the construction business by being ethical and honest."

"I know." I vividly remembered the corruption we had so recently dealt with, before the earthquake.

"But we don't know exactly how they intend to strike. With only days before the Convention starts, I won't pussyfoot around—I'll round up anyone who might be in the know and make them talk." From the determination in his face, I had no doubt Garrett would act on that intention immediately.

"I wish you didn't have to resort to such desperate measures," I said. "I had hoped I would be able to find out who is behind this on my own."

"Without our resources and authority to arrest people, you had little chance," Garrett pointed out. "Thorgana's missing husband is a prime suspect, of course, but we have been unable to locate him, despite our best efforts. I put my best men on it, but he seems to have completely vanished from the face of Recca. For all we know, he's dead."

"Well, there was a large network to finance and direct the Resistance. Do you have a list of her main deputies?" I asked.

"Yes, and I've been tracking them down. I've managed to find a few, but these bastards are tricky—more often than not, they poison themselves before I can get anything useful out of them."

"Fanatics." I shuddered at the thought of being so blindly committed to a cause that I was willing to kill myself without hesitation. "That's not very helpful."

"Do you suppose they have another anti-magic device?" Garrett asked. "We destroyed the one we found out about, but it's possible Thorgana had another up her sleeve. If she somehow got that into the Convention venue, or anywhere close to the government, we'd all be sunk." He glowered, and I could tell that the notion was highly unsettling to him.

"I have a feeling it is something more violent," I said. "I wish Iannis and Sunaya were here. Sunaya has a knack for finding out dangerous secrets just in time to prevent the worst."

Garrett nodded. "That she does. Their absence has made my job significantly harder, and the Convention is starting in a few days. It's going to take place regardless of whether Iannis arrives on time, but if he's going to miss his own wedding, he will be a laughingstock. It would also be humiliating for Sunaya." He drank from his beer and put the glass down on the wooden tabletop. "Speaking of Sunaya, if she does make it back in time, she'll appreciate it if you attend the wedding. No need to let her see how you feel about her."

"Yes, I want to be there," I admitted, and my smile was genuine. "And I have moved on, so it won't even be painful."

Gratitude welled up inside me, and I made a mental note to thank Sunaya heartily when I saw her again. Thanks to her skillful manipulation of the truth, I could attend the wedding and walk about openly as Fenris without fear. Perhaps I might even be able to move back to Solantha and live close to my friends. A giddy rush of joy filled me, and I sat back in my chair, suddenly overwhelmed with the magnitude of it all.

"Are you all right?" Garrett asked, looking concerned.

"I'm fine." I waved him off, then sat up so I could take another bite of my burger. We talked for a bit longer, until Garrett finally said, with a huge yawn, that he was going to take himself off to bed. I had no choice but to let him pay the bill since I was copperless, and he brushed aside my offer to reimburse him. I promised to inform Garrett of any new discoveries, and he seemed satisfied with that. He even offered to let me be there when he finally caught the responsible parties, but I took that to be an empty promise. In the clear light of day, he'd revert to the ice-cold official I had known for years.

As I watched Garrett from the booth window as he walked up the street, the tension that had been digging into my shoulders finally left my body. I had never seen Garrett behave so affably before, except once with Sunaya. He had a crush on her, which was why he had been so sympathetic when I'd insinuated I'd felt the same and had kept away for that reason. But I couldn't let myself forget that he was still an enemy—if he ever discovered the truth, he would not hesitate to arrest me and have me executed. Sunaya must have been awfully convincing when she told Garrett I was my own son.

The absurdity of it all had me chuckling in the booth, and the waitress gave me a strange look as she passed. Of all the solutions to this maddening problem, that was the last thing I would have thought of. Only Sunaya would have come up with such a far-fetched tale and have Garrett believing it!

Shaking my head, I left the diner. The full moon beckoned overhead, a song in my veins, and even more insistent was the tug on my serapha charm that told me Mina was safe in our hotel room, waiting for me.

It would take a long time to get back to the Marwale without a steamcar, but it was too late to rent one, and I had no intention of staying away from Mina any longer than I had to. Giving in to the lure of the full moon, I shifted into wolf form, then loped down the deserted street, my veins singing with anticipation.

I couldn't wait to see her again.

EIGHTEEN

Warm hands slid over me, stirring me from a deep slumber. For a minute, I thought I had to be dreaming, and I rolled over, burying my face into the pillow as I attempted to burrow deeper into the dream. The hands were strong and calloused, and Fenris's masculine scent teased me, making me miss him fiercely. If dream Fenris was all I had right now, I would gladly take him.

But then those hands pulled me back against a hard, bare chest, and my eyes popped open. This wasn't a dream. I was here in my hotel room, hints of dawn streaming through the blinds and gilding everything in a golden-pink light. And Fenris...

"By the Lady," I gasped, turning in his arms. "How did you get back?"

"Shh." Fenris slipped his hands into my hair, stroking a thumb across my right cheekbone. "I missed you," he growled right before he kissed me. His tongue teased the seam of my mouth, making me forget my questions as hunger stirred within me. Opening to him, I kissed him back, stroking his tongue with mine as I ran my hand down his broad back. His muscles flexed beneath my touch, and he grabbed my butt, his strong fingers digging in lightly as he pulled me flush against him.

A bolt of desire struck me as I felt his length press against my belly—he was fully hard, and fully naked. Abandoning his back, I reached between us, and he groaned against my mouth as I wrapped my fingers around his cock and gently began to massage him.

"Yes," he panted, placing his big hand atop mine and moving it faster. "Like that."

I stroked him for a few minutes, taking pleasure in the way the planes of his face grew taut, his yellow eyes blazing with need for me. Eventually, he batted my hand aside with a growl, then flipped me onto my back and pushed my nightgown up around my hips. I cried out as he entered me in one smooth motion, pleasure rippling through me as he filled me to the brim.

"Yes," I moaned, digging my fingers into his shoulder blades as he began to pound into me. "More."

I held on for dear life as his thrusts grew faster and more desperate, arching my hips as I did my best to meet his ferocious pace. He crushed his mouth against mine, and I bit his bottom lip as a surge of possessiveness hit me. I knew what he was feeling—I felt the exact same thing, that deep relief, chasing the tail of the sharp-edged fear that had gripped me when I thought I might not see him again.

"You're mine," I told him, grasping his face between my hands and holding him still so I could look into his eyes. "You're mine, and *nothing* will take you from me again."

"Yes," he agreed, thrusting deep inside me again. And I finally let myself fly.

AFTER OUR FRANTIC LOVEMAKING, Fenris and I slept for a few much-needed hours. It had taken me forever to fall asleep after such a stressful day, and from the way Fenris had instantly collapsed on the bed, I gathered that he hadn't slept much, if at all, last night.

But some time later, the sensation of him nuzzling my neck stirred me from my slumber. "Mmm," he growled, nipping at the sensitive skin. "You smell good. I don't know why, but your scent is becoming more addictive by the day."

"And *you* smell like you've been running all night," I teased, turning in his arms and lightly shoving his chest. My mood turned serious as I searched his face, the realization that I'd come far too close to losing him sinking in. "What in Recca happened last night, Fenris? How is it that you're here now?"

"I can hardly believe it myself," he said, shaking his head. "Garrett Toring, the Federal Director of Security, rescued me from that jail."

"Rescued you?" I gasped. "Isn't he the one who wants to execute you in the first place?"

"Indeed he is," Fenris said, a bemused look on his face. "And he very well might have, if not for Sunaya. Apparently she spun some tall tale about Fenris being the illegitimate son of Polar and a wolf shifter. It's an utterly ridiculous notion, of course—I never would have dreamed of doing something as crazy and irresponsible as engaging in a secret affair with a shifter."

He wrinkled his nose, and that was the last straw—I burst into laughter. "You think that's funny, do you?" Fenris asked, arching a brow as my shoulders shook.

"It's very funny," I said, my tone still full of mirth. "The idea of you being your own son, and that we've been skulking about unnecessarily..." I cupped his cheek. "Now you can show this handsome face in public!"

Fenris grinned a little. "I knew you would say something

like that," he said, leaning in to kiss my nose. "I'll have to commit Sunaya's story to memory, though, and check with her for details once she returns. I can't afford to slip up, or we'll all be in the suds."

"Yes, and I'll have to thank her for saving you, even if she did so indirectly." After this, I was really looking forward to finally meeting Sunaya. "Thanks to her, you and I will be able to live openly together," I said softly.

A swell of emotion hit me then, and it seemed Fenris too, for he crushed me against him tightly. "I'm so grateful to have you in my life," he murmured into my hair as I stroked my hands up and down his broad back.

We held each other for a long moment, simply soaking in each other's company. "I have some news to tell you too," I finally said, pulling back a little so I could look at his face. "Marris came by Comenius's shop when I went down there to ask for help."

"Oh? What did he say?"

"Basically, that masses of ex-Resistance soldiers are being imported and disguised as construction workers. They're to remain ready at all times for some big attack, and they've been assigned certain 'sectors' that they are supposed to hold once the fighting starts. In the meantime, they are given enough money to feed themselves, and the ones who actually participate in the construction are given extra."

"Ahh, so they're not all standing around doing nothing," Fenris said. When my brow furrowed, he added, "I figured out much the same thing when I was in downtown today. I followed a group of men to a building site. They were wearing construction gear, but most of them are just pretending to belong there. Some of the actual workers were pretty annoyed at them."

"I would be, too, in their place."

"Later, I had a drink with another man who was obviously

with the Resistance, and he mentioned being given coin for food and beer, but the waiting chafed on him. If his attitude was typical, they cannot afford to wait much longer without having morale problems. Did Marris tell you which sectors are being targeted?"

"No—I think the foot soldiers only know which ones they're being assigned to. I guess nobody has the full plan except the higher-ups, whom we haven't yet identified. But Marris says that he thinks we should question the construction company owners, because they are employing the Resistance soldiers. They must know something."

"I suspect that is being done even as we speak," Fenris said, his eyes narrowed thoughtfully. "Garrett immediately thought of that, and he is not one to let grass grow under his feet with the Convention about to start. I could also have a word with Kardanor Makis, who knows all about the reconstruction."

"Actually, Comenius said he was going to speak to him about it today." My eyes widened as I realized Com would still be trying to save Fenris from the enforcers. "I ought to tell him that you've returned before they send Chen marching down to the station to find you."

Fenris laughed. "I'll send him an ether pigeon," he said. He quickly conjured one and told it to relay to Comenius that he had been freed and would be going to the Palace later to meet with Chen. "I may as well," he said to me after he'd released the pigeon. "Now that I no longer have to worry about hiding my identity."

"Sounds like we've got a busy day ahead of us," I said as I slipped from the bed, intending to grab a shower.

"Indeed. And I need to find time to visit my parents, too."

I froze, halfway to the bathroom. "Your *parents*?"

"Yes. Garrett told me that they arrived in Solantha shortly after my 'death' and have been living here ever since, waiting for me to resurface. They refused to believe I was dead, since my body was never recovered."

My mouth dropped open. "They've been here this entire time? Pining after their long-lost grandson?" I felt a pang of sympathy for them—it must have been horrible, holding on to a mere thread of hope all these months.

"They have," Fenris said grimly, looking far too unhappy for a man who was about to be reunited with his parents. "I'm honestly not sure how to approach them. They have never been particularly fond of shifters, and while they were loving and dutiful parents, they are tremendous snobs and regard almost everyone as beneath us. I don't know how they'll react once they see me, even if they already 'know' I'm a half shifter. And I'm not sure how well I'll be able to carry off the lie, either."

Fenris looked so troubled at the notion that I sat down on the edge of the bed and took his hand in mine. "I understand your apprehension," I said. "But there is no way to judge how they will react to the truth until we meet them in person. Losing their only son may have led to a change of heart. I say that we go and see them, and then we can gauge whether or not it's safe to tell them about your true identity."

Fenris smiled. "They will love *you*, at any rate," he said, rubbing his thumb across the back of my hand and sending tingles up my arm. "You are a beautiful, wealthy heiress, and a full mage, besides. Just the kind of woman they had always urged me to marry."

"Yes," I said, leaning in to nuzzle his nose, "and it's a good thing you're just the kind of man *I* want to marry. Now let's get ready for the day, or we'll never leave this hotel room."

Fenris growled in response, then rolled me onto my back and pinned me to the bed for another long, scorching kiss that told me we weren't going anywhere. At least not for a while.

NINETEEN

FENRIS

By the time Mina and I finally got dressed and ready for the day, it was far past the usual time for lunch. We found Barrla hanging around the hotel lounge with one of her shifter romances, and she nearly fell out of her chair when she caught sight of me.

"By the Ur-God!" she cried, shooting to her feet. "I thought you were still in prison!"

Barrla wrapped me up in a fierce hug before I could stop her, then immediately went and did the same to Mina. Several guests and staff members stared at us with blatant curiosity. I did my best to appear nonchalant. Thankfully I had taken time to shave and dress in freshly pressed clothes, so I didn't *look* like a man who had recently been jailed.

"At least now I know why you were so late this morning," she said saucily to Mina. "Had a happy reunion last night, did we?"

Mina's cheeks colored, and I coughed. "Why don't we discuss our discoveries over lunch?" I suggested, taking Mina's arm. "Unless you've eaten already?"

Barrla laughed. "You two are such sticks in the mud," she

said, but she followed us to the restaurant. Over a hearty meal, Mina and I filled her in on everything that had happened. Barrla was happy that I no longer had to hide my identity and had managed to escape prison without breaking any laws.

"Does this mean we'll be able to visit the palace together?" she asked eagerly, her eyes sparkling with delight. "I've been wanting to see the inside ever since we saw the towers from the Firegate Bridge! They wouldn't let us in when we went to visit, even with our journalist credentials."

"We will do that," I said, "but not today. It's best I make this first trip on my own, since I'll have to talk to the Director of the Mages Guild about catching the plotters."

"That's no fun," Barrla pouted.

"We're going to have some fun of our own, Barrla," Mina declared with a smile. "While Fenris meets with Director Chen, you and I are going to stake out the Minister's house again, along with the rest of the venues that we didn't have time to hit yesterday. We may yet catch the plotters in the act."

"That doesn't *sound* like very much fun," Barrla grumbled. "But I don't suppose detective work is all fun and games."

"Unfortunately not," I said, doing my best not to laugh. There was something endearing about Barrla—she was so expressive, in a way that reminded me of Sunaya, though without the snark and cynicism.

With our plans decided, we drove back to Solantha, and I dropped the girls off at the entrance to the Mages Quarter before continuing on to the palace. The valet was shocked when I pulled up, but he quickly hid his surprise and told me that he was very pleased to see I was back.

I gave him the key to the rented steamcar, then headed for the palace entrance. It seemed so surreal, walking through the palace gardens again, brilliant blossoms of every shade and color rioting around me and filling the air with a multitude of fragrances. Glittering butterflies flitted through the air alongside bees the color of burnished gold, and I looked past them, up and up, to where Solantha Palace towered above me in all its glory.

This place had been my home for three years. And now that I was back...it didn't quite feel like a homecoming, I admitted to myself. This could never be my home again, not if I intended to settle down with Mina. But the sight of it nevertheless healed a crack in my heart, and I strolled up the front steps with a smile on my face.

"Good afternoon," I greeted Canter, the surly old mage who manned the front desk. He nearly keeled over at the sight of me and was sputtering as I strode past—the old coot had never liked me. Humming a cheery tune, I strode down the hall toward the south wing, passing many startled mages on my way.

"Hello, Dira," I said as I walked into the Mages Guild lobby. "Is Director Chen in?"

Dira jerked her head up from the pile of paperwork she'd been reading, her eyes widening. "Fenris!" she exclaimed. "Yes, of course, let me tell her that you're here—"

"No need." Director Chen's cool voice flowed into the room, and I turned to see her enter the lobby. She looked exactly as I'd seen her last, dressed in one of her many silk Garaian robes, her fine black hair secured at the back of her head with a pair of ornamental chopsticks. Her beautiful face softened into a smile, one that I returned easily. "A guard told me that he saw you hand your car over to the valet, but I hardly believed it myself. Lord Iannis and Miss Baine will be overjoyed when they hear of your return."

"Yes, and I will be very glad to see them," I said. "I've been waiting impatiently for them to arrive."

Director Chen's smile faded. "As have we all." She hesitated for a second, then said, "Shall we go find someplace to sit?"

We adjourned to Director Chen's office, and I was very

pleased to see that she'd switched out her wooden visitors' chairs with the uncomfortable dragon carvings for something easier to sit on. Was she mellowing under Kardanor's influence? Over cups of fragrant green tea, I gave her a full report of my investigation into the Resistance plot and told her about my encounter with Garrett.

It turned out that Garrett had already talked to her earlier, when I'd still been in bed with Mina, and their minions had arrested two dozen suspects, who were even now being processed and interrogated. All the heads and managers of the main construction companies had been caught in their net and were screaming bloody murder—or for their lawyers, at any rate. The existence of the plot had already been confirmed by several witnesses, and they were hopeful of learning the particulars before the end of the day.

"So you really are the son of the former Chief Mage Polar ar'Tollis?" she asked when I'd expressed my hope that one or more of them would break soon. "I must say, you kept that secret very close to your chest. We've known each other for nearly two years and I had not the slightest idea! I only learned the truth from Director Toring just now."

I shrugged. "Given that Polar is condemned to death for treason, can you blame me for keeping that relationship private? And it's not like he permitted me to openly use his family name," I said, a little uneasy at having to lie to her. "It was even harder to hide the fact that I have some magic."

She shook her head in amazement. "I really should have guessed that part, in hindsight, considering how much time you spent on those magical tomes."

"I did try to be discreet, but not enough, as it turned out."

"I'm very glad that Director Toring isn't holding a grudge against you, considering how much he hates your father," she said. "Too often we hold children responsible for the actions of their parents, and you most certainly don't deserve that after everything you've done for the Federation."

"Thank you," I said, a bit startled by the praise. Chen and I had never disliked each other, but neither had we worked together much, so I hadn't expected her to act so warmly toward me.

"I am waiting to be informed of the result of Garrett's and the Guild's investigations before I tackle the main suspect myself," she continued. "Moredo is the largest of the construction companies currently working on city renovations. The owner bought up the two disgraced companies that were bankrupted after the quake. Surely he must be neck-deep in this nefarious plot, and Kardanor tells me he never trusted the fellow. I've ordered Maltar Moredo, the main shareholder, to be brought here. But first I'm leaving him to cool his heels for a couple of hours. Hopefully he is getting very nervous."

"Ah, and that gives you time to check on what the other suspects have said, to confront him with the evidence."

"Exactly. Will you help me interrogate him, as you used to do for Lord Iannis? He always praised your shifter senses and said they were far superior to a truth wand." With a wry smile, she added, "Of course, lately it was Miss Baine who helped out with that sort of thing."

I smiled. "In Sunaya's absence, I would be more than happy to offer my services."

Chen returned the smile briefly, but it faded, and she pressed a finger to her left temple. "I must admit I am worried about Miss Baine," she said. "She vanished right in the middle of the palace gardens, and Iannis suspected that she was abducted by someone with a grudge against him. He traveled to Manuc to find her...but that was two weeks ago. I hoped he would be back long before now."

My stomach sank at the fear in Chen's voice, but I did my

best not to give in to my own worries. "I'm sure Iannis would have sent word if the circumstances were truly dire," I told Chen. "Both he and Sunaya are powerful, resourceful mages. We must put our trust in their ingenuity."

Director Chen nodded, her face clearing a bit. "You're right, of course," she said briskly. "And there is far too much work to be done for me to be dwelling on this. I'm sure you'll want to get settled in—your room is waiting for you, and all your things have been left untouched."

I blinked—I hadn't even given a thought to my room. "I won't be staying at the Palace," I said, "but I would like to take a few things I left behind, and I expect it will take some time to go through everything. I'll go do that now, and you can send for me there when you are ready to interrogate your suspect."

Chen seemed a little surprised that I wasn't moving back in, but she didn't question me further—the large stacks of paperwork crowding her desk, many files marked with red "Urgent" stamps, were more important than where I was going to lay my head for the evening. I did not envy her job at all, especially with Iannis gone and all these additional complications. I was glad I no longer was a Chief Mage myself...I had enough problems to deal with as it was.

TWENTY

FENRIS

Leaving Director Chen reading the transcript of the morning's interrogations, I headed for my old room in the west wing. As Chen had said, it had not been touched at all since my "death," and it brought back a lot of memories.

Compared to all the other bedrooms in the palace, my room wasn't very large. When I'd first arrived in Solantha almost four years ago, I'd deliberately chosen a modest room so as not to rouse suspicion or envy among the resident mages. Over time it had become even smaller, as I'd accumulated a surprising number of possessions. I only had a small wardrobe hanging in the closet, but there was a locked chest filled with odds and ends, including potions and amulets, and various other supplies.

The true value in what I had left behind was my book collection—two out of my four walls were covered in shelves filled with texts, most of them magical, some of them gifts from Iannis on special occasions. I had sent off the most important items to a storage company in Osero during that time, when Garrett had been sniffing at my heels, and I had recovered them thanks to Marris, but there were plenty left. As soon as I walked in, I immediately began to sort through them to see which I wanted to take along, and which I might be able to force myself to part with.

Why part with any of them? I asked myself sometime later as I was leafing through a book on magical history. Now that I was a free man who could openly practice magic due to the supposed relationship with my absent "father," there was no need for me to haul all these books back to Abbsville, where I would only be forced to hide them away. Mina and I would settle down somewhere else, somewhere we could live openly as man and wife. But while we searched for that perfect place to call home, I might as well leave my possessions here for safe-keeping. Iannis had let them stay this long—surely a few more months wouldn't matter.

Satisfied with that decision, I turned my attention to the rest of my things. My coin purse still hadn't been returned, so I fished an old leather purse out of a chest, one that had already been pre-filled with wooden chips. I reached my hand in and murmured a transmogrification spell, and a few seconds later, I pulled out a fistful of gold.

Highly illegal, but there was no one around to see me, and Iannis wouldn't mind.

I riffled through my closet to see if any of the tunics hanging there were worth bringing, and stuffed two of them, and a pair of my favorite boots, into my magical sleeve. I also took some of the rarer potion ingredients I'd left behind, and two magical texts that had some great beginner-level spells for Mina to prac-tice with.

*Speaking of Mina...*I reached for the serapha charm to check on her. It immediately glowed to life, reassuring me that she was alive and well, and the tug in my chest told me that she was still in the Mages Quarter. I wondered how her scouting mission with Barrla was going—surely they would have finished up at the Minister's by now. I hoped they hadn't run into any trouble. The Minister's bodyguards could be rough with paparazzi.

They're fine, I told myself. The serapha charm didn't convey much about emotional state, but I could see that Mina was in excellent health. She had a good head on her shoulders, and Barrla could be very disarming. They would be all right.

By the Lady. I shook my head, smiling a little as I realized I was acting like a mother hen. I could only imagine how Iannis must feel—Sunaya put herself in danger on a far more regular basis than Mina ever would. I had worried for Sunaya at times, but it was nothing like the fear I felt for Mina when I imagined her falling prey to the many dangers that could still befall her in post-war Solantha.

Footsteps outside the door distracted me from my musings, and I opened it just as a guard was preparing to knock. "Excuse me, sir," he said, looking slightly flustered. "Director Chen asked me to fetch you. She is about to start the interrogation."

Already? I glanced at my watch to see that ninety minutes had passed. I had lost track of time, which usually happened when I was busy with my book collection. I followed the guard back down to the Mages Guild, and he escorted me to one of two interview rooms Iannis had set aside to interrogate persons of interest. Director Chen was standing outside, along with a mage guard, and she nodded when she saw me.

"Good, you're here," she said. "Let's see what Mr. Moredo can tell us."

She opened the door, and I followed in behind her. The room was bare of all furniture and ornamentation, save a single table and four hard metal chairs. The light hanging above the ceiling illuminated a swarthy middle-aged human with a thick black mustache and a shiny bald head. He had the build of a man who had once been in very good shape but was going soft since he'd passed his prime. I judged him to be somewhere in his mid-forties.

"What is the meaning of this?" he demanded, raising his shackled hands. "How dare you bring me here in chains like I'm some criminal! Don't you know who I am?" He was a good actor, but I could scent his worry underneath the bravado.

"Maltar Moredo," Director Chen said coolly, tossing a file onto the table as she took her seat. "Owner of Moredo Construction, and a rather generous contributor to several charities. We appreciate all of the recent efforts you have made to help rebuild the city."

"Well it damn sure doesn't feel like it," Moredo snarled. I sat down next to Chen, and his dark eyes narrowed in distaste as he noticed me. "What is this shifter doing here?"

"While it is obvious that you are a charitable man," Director Chen went on, ignoring Moredo's question, "we have found some of your contributions to be rather objectionable. For example, you have been making regular payments to the Hope Fund."

"So what?" Moredo shrugged his broad shoulders, but his anger began to turn sour with the beginnings of fear. "I'm allowed to spend my money as I see fit. The Hope Fund helps orphaned children."

"Yes," Director Chen said, "but the Federation has recently connected the Hope Fund to the Mills Foundation, owned by the late Thorgana Mills. That Foundation has since been seized due to its criminal activity."

Moredo scowled, the fear around him growing thicker. "I don't know anything about no Mills Foundation," he snapped. "My secretary likes to volunteer at orphanages. She's the one who had me add the Hope Fund to the list of charities we donate to every month."

"He's lying," I said to Chen, and the man stiffened.

Chen gave Moredo a cat-like smile. "Even if I did believe you—which I don't, considering the large sum you give the Hope Fund every month—your company seems to be embroiled in other suspicious activities. It would seem that many of the workers you have been bringing into Solantha simply hang around the job sites and do nothing, day after day, even though you are in charge of several important, time-sensitive projects. Are you normally in the habit of paying people to do nothing, Mr. Moreno? Or could it be that you are paying them to do something else?"

Mr. Moreno crossed his bulky arms over his chest, but I could hear his heart pounding furiously. "I'm not saying one more word," he growled. "I want my lawyer."

"Normally, I would accommodate you," Chen said. "But we know that you are preparing some attack on the government, and time is of the essence."

"That's ridiculous!"

"He is lying," I said again. "Let me try something, if you would?" I had not been able to use some of the more experimental magical techniques I had studied while pretending to be an ordinary shifter, but now that I was supposed to be Polar's son and a hybrid, I might as well show what I was capable of.

"Be my guest," Chen said, gesturing at the suspect. "Whatever does the job."

Moreno laughed harshly. "Do your worst," he said, sitting back in his chair and raking Chen with a sneer. "You can't scare me."

I stared into Moredo's eyes, and as the seconds passed, his sneer began to give way to terror. He seemed even more afraid of shifters than mages. "W-what are you staring at me like that for?"

Ignoring him, I uttered the words of an ancient truth spell. Magic sizzled in the air around us, and Moredo shivered, no doubt feeling the effects. Pearls of sweat beaded on his brow, and he stank with fear.

"There. He should now be compelled to answer the next three questions truthfully," I said to Chen.

Her brows rose. "Useful," she said, before turning to Moredo. "I wonder what question I should ask first."

"I'm not telling you anything," Moredo spat.

"Question number one," Chen said, as though she had not heard him. "What is the true reason you have brought in all these extra workers from out of town? I already know it's not for construction—many of them stand around doing nothing at the building sites you have set up."

Moredo's face went purple as he fought against the compulsion. "I brought them in as part of the Resistance attack force," he finally ground out.

"I see," Director Chen said. "Question number two. What are the details of the attack you are planning on using these soldiers for?"

Moredo's forehead was shiny now, and I could see dampness seeping through the underarms of his shirt. "We've got a container of machine guns that just shipped in from Garai, and some fireworks," he grunted. "We're supposed to be distributing the guns to the men tomorrow and assigning them their stations. The fireworks are the signal—once they go off, the men will attack the Convention, kill all the Chief Mages, and seize control of the city."

I blinked, surprised to hear that this was the plan. The Convention venue would be carefully guarded by mages under Garrett's command, so it seemed foolhardy to attack it. Had Marris and his friends been drawn here as mere cannon fodder?

"I see." Director Chen stared intently at Moredo. "Where are the guns?"

"On the *Taixing Shan*," Moredo said smugly. "You'd better

hurry if you want to pick them up...my men are already on their way to get them."

WITH NOTHING more to be gained from Moredo—once his three questions were up, he refused to tell us anything more—Chen threw him into a prison cell, then ordered a warrant and assembled a task force to search the ship. We left in all haste for the port, where we were met by Garrett Toring and his own bevy of agents. Between all of us, there were fourteen people.

"This reminds me far too much of our mission to Garai," Garrett growled under his breath to Chen, who nodded in agreement. Sunaya and Iannis had told me all about how they'd blown up an entire warehouse full of guns located near the docks. I sincerely hoped we would not have to go through anything as exciting today.

Director Chen strode up the boardwalk, waving the warrant the legal department had drawn up in record time and shouting in Garaian. I assumed she was letting the men onboard know about our intent to search the ship. The few I spotted beyond the railing scrambled hastily, and to my amusement, tried to pull up the gangplank before we could ascend. Garrett quickly blasted them away from the railing with a spell, and they went flying into the sails before slumping onto the deck.

"Fools," he muttered as we boarded the ship. A few other sailors rushed out from below deck, but their faces paled at the sight of so many robed mages, and they hastily put their hands up. The majority of the crew must have been ashore—there certainly weren't enough here to man a vessel this large.

"Their captain is currently at Varod's Vixens, a brothel in downtown," Chen said in a clipped voice to one of her agents after she'd spoken with one of the sailors. "Go and arrest him, and any of his sailors you find with him."

"Yes, ma'am." The agent quickly bowed, then strode off with one of his colleagues to do the job.

"Put the rest of them in cuffs," Garrett ordered his men, "and let's search the ship."

I caught a motion out of the corner of my eye and spun around just in time to see one of the sailors pull a handgun from the waistband of his pants. Cursing, I blasted the weapon out of his grip before he could fire off a shot, then tackled the man. He went down with an angry cry, thrashing and screaming, and I silenced him with a well-placed punch to the jaw.

"Hell," Garrett swore as he and the other mages immediately activated their shields. A few more shots went off, but the bullets dissipated when they hit the shields, and within moments, the agents had subdued the rest of the men.

"Fenris, are you all right?" Chen asked in concern as I stood up, dusting off my tunic. "He didn't shoot you, did he?"

I shook my head. "No, and as a shifter, I can survive most wounds without much trouble. Don't worry about me."

"Thank you for that," Garrett said, clapping me on the shoulder. "You might very well have saved my life."

"It was nothing," I said, even though that was the furthest thing from the truth. I was not sure how I felt about saving my enemy's life—but on the other hand, I needed him around to ensure the safety of the city, and besides, he wasn't *really* my nemesis anymore. So long as he believed I was Fenris, and not Polar, he was harmless to me.

Putting the thought out of my mind, I followed Chen and Garrett below deck. Fanning out, we searched the cargo hold, and in no time found the crates of guns, ammunition, and fireworks.

"By the Lady," I said as I examined a shiny black gun with a barrel longer than my entire arm. "The idea of a bunch of Resistance soldiers running around with these is terrifying."

"Yes," Director Chen agreed.

After consulting her about a suitable guarded warehouse, Garrett ordered his agents to carefully pack up the entire illegal cargo. "Now let's get these out of here," he suggested, "before someone accidentally blows up this ship and gives the resistance soldiers the signal they are waiting for."

MINA

After Fenris dropped us off, Barrla and I spent the next hour walking slowly around the Mages Quarter. Barrla marveled over the grand architecture and the magical gardens—many houses boasted plants of unusual color and size that were the product of magical tampering. One house had a row of statues lining the path to the front door that would sing a cheerful hymn whenever someone set foot on the property, and another displayed clusters of large yellow blossoms that smelled like freshly baked pastries and made us hungry even though we'd only eaten two hours ago. We also admired the bell tree chiming softly in the afternoon breeze.

"One would never guess that mages are so stuffy and high-brow, judging by some of these gardens," Barrla said as we finally made our way to the Minister's manor. "The things that they can do with their magic seem so wonderful!"

I smiled. "Magic *is* wonderful," I said to Barrla, recalling the countless times I'd used it to ease pain and save lives. "Just like your pastries and cookies are wonderful. But that doesn't mean that all bakers who make pastries are wonderful, are they?"

"No, I guess not," Barrla admitted. "But still, you would

think that having access to so much power would put them in a better mood."

I bit back a smile at Barrla's naivety as the mansion came into view. I'd once heard someone say that the more powerful you were, the greater the responsibility you were forced to bear, and that was just as true of magical power as it was political power. More so if you had both, like the Minister.

Unlike the day before, the gates to the Minister's rented mansion were shut tight, and the courtyard where the press had gathered was empty save for a gardener trimming the hedges. Barrla and I observed the guards from a discreet distance, but even so, we were easily spotted, and two guards watched us with suspicion from across the street, discouraging us from getting closer.

"I have a feeling our press passes won't help us today," Barrla murmured as we casually walked on, knowing that if we stood still too long the guards would come over to challenge us.

"It's a good thing we don't really need to get inside," I agreed. "There are guards everywhere—I don't see how anyone hostile could get in." Squinting, I focused my magical sight—a trick Fenris had taught me that would allow me to see magical residue in the air. The gates immediately began to glow purple, and runes flared to life around the perimeter, now visible thanks to my enhanced sight.

"In addition to the guards, there are wards everywhere," I said to Barrla. "They seem similar to the wards set up around the Mages Quarter that keep out all humans except at the manned checkpoints. It will be very difficult for a non-mage to sneak in."

With nothing interesting to observe at the front gates, Barrla and I retired to a small, deserted park around the corner. We sat down on a bench beneath an oak tree, and Barrla pulled the ether owl that Elnos had leant us out of her camera bag.

"Good idea," I said as she handed it to me. The mage guards would not be looking for an ether owl—the owl was invisible unless one used magical sight, and they were not trained to look for it since it was a new invention. It would also avoid the wards, since it was approaching from above. I conjured the ether owl using the spell Elnos had taught me, then powered up the metal owl and looked into its mirrored eyes as its magical counterpart soared above the mansion. Barrla and I passed it back and forth, and for the next hour, all we saw were harried mage officials coming and going. There were no suspicious characters hanging around the neighborhood who might be spying for the Resistance. The only loiterer we observed turned out to be a neighbor out for a quick smoke.

"It's hot out here," Barrla said as she watched a man with an ice cream cart amble up the path. "I think we ought to take a break."

"Wait!" I hissed, holding up a hand as Barrla started to rise. A black steamcar had pulled up in front of the gate, and Mirrine, the Forrane reporter I'd met at the Marwale, was getting out. "That's Mirrine. I want to know why she's coming to see the Minister."

Barrla shrugged. "It will all be about boring politics, I guess. Do you want a cone too?"

"Chocolate, please," I said absently.

I watched Mirrine approach the gates as Barrla set off to procure our ice cream. As usual, Mirrine looked elegant, dressed in a sharp-looking peacock blue outfit today. She flashed her press pass to the guards and said something, and after a minute, they opened the gate and let her through.

Did she have an appointment? I hadn't seen any other members of the press come by—what made Mirrine so special? Curious, I had the owl circle around the building until he found the Minister's office on the third floor. I directed him to fly inside, and he perched on the windowsill to the Minister's left. Graning was sitting at his desk and looking very tense. There was a secretary in the room, gathering up papers, as if they'd been interrupted in the middle of a meeting.

"Are you sure this press interview can't wait until later?" the man was asking, looking somewhat annoyed that he was being kicked out. "We really do need to go over these reports from Director Toring, he said they were urgent—"

"Later, Tarley," the Minister said tersely, his eyes trained on the door. "I'll call for you when I am finished here."

Tarley nodded, then swept from the room with an armful of notebooks and files. Mirrine walked into the room a moment later, a faintly amused look on her face.

"Still the same curmudgeon after all these years, Zavian," she said, seating herself in one of the visitor's chairs without waiting for an invitation. "You would think that being the most powerful man in the Northia Federation would wipe that sour look off your face, but it seems that some men can never be satisfied."

"Just tell me what you want, Mirrine," the Minister said flatly. "Money is no object, of course—"

"I have no interest in your coffers," Mirrine said with a flick of her slender hand. "I have plenty of coin, but you already knew that. It is your policies that I am interested in."

"I thought we both made it quite clear that we would not seek each other out again once we separated," the Minister said tightly, and I frowned. Separated? As in…?

Mirrine laughed. "*You* made that quite clear when you flounced back to the Federation with no regard for our marriage vows. Of course, you were not faithful even before that, and at the time I was glad enough to see the last of you."

"That magical union that the vows are supposed to effect never took, in our case," he argued, though without true conviction in his voice. "I contend that the ceremony was not valid. Perhaps that Forrane priest did something wrong. I should have known better than to get married in a foreign country."

She snorted. "What a self-serving excuse. It worked fine at first, until you indulged in those affairs. And I never agreed to avoid you forever, but you never cared a whit about what I wanted, did you? I was a fool for marrying you as quickly as I did. If I had waited a bit longer, I would have discovered you for the cold, selfish man that you are, and you would not be in the unfortunate predicament that you are now."

What? I blinked in confusion. Everyone knew that the Minister's wife had passed away five years ago, and that wife was certainly *not* Mirrine. Mages married for life, and they were only permitted one partner at a time. They could remarry if their spouse died, but considering that Mirrine was alive and well...if they had ever married, then she must *still* be his legal wife. His only legal wife.

"What predicament?" Graning shrugged with what I suspected was feigned indifference. "You can make trouble, I suppose, but I fail to see what has changed."

"Perhaps you should have thought about your position before your country decided to sabotage and block Forrane's eastern trade agreements," she said coldly. "We rely quite heavily on our trade with the Bilamese, as you well know."

"That is not my problem," the minister retorted. "The Bilamese have disregarded our offer of a trade alliance. It is only natural that we would prevent them from allying with you instead, or other nations would think they can refuse us with impunity."

"I don't care about your reasons for sabotaging my country's economy," Mirrine said, cutting him off. "Right now, you have a choice. You can either remove the sanctions against Forrane and Bilam, or I can go to any one of the numerous reporters in town and tell them the juicy story of how Zavian Graning is a faithless bigamist." She gave him a sly smile. "I think we both know which you would prefer."

The Minister stared at her. "You cannot go to the press with this," he said. "You would be ruined too."

"*I* am not the one who remarried," Mirrine said. "You are. I have absolutely nothing to fear from telling the truth, being merely a victim of your cruel abandonment, whereas you..." She trailed off, her smile widening, and waved a hand about the room. "Well, you have a great deal to lose. You should be very glad I am asking for so little."

"I'll need some time to think about this," the Minister started, but Mirrine shook her head.

"If I leave this room without an agreement from you, I will march straight to the Solantha Press Club," she warned. "And before you think to have me killed or detained, I have written proof of your perfidy that will be published should anything happen to me."

The Minister clenched his hands so hard around the arms of his chair that his knuckles turned white. "I will agree to your demands," he said after a long, fraught moment, "if you promise to go home. I was a damn fool for marrying you, but I am not going to risk everything I have worked for just because of some silly trade dispute."

Mirrine laughed, then rose from her chair. "I'm glad to see you are still somewhat reasonable. And I will leave whenever I please," she said silkily. "I can't say I'm surprised by your reaction; you're still the same man who puts ambition over everything else, including your loved ones." Her smile faded, and she stared at him for a long moment. "You really were the worst sort of husband imaginable," she said softly. "I often pitied your second wife."

The Minister clenched his jaw. "Mirrine—" he began, rising from his chair as she started to turn away.

"Just remember," she said airily as she walked away, "if anything happens to me, this all goes public."

The Minister sat back down in his chair, his face red with anger. I watched for a few moments, waiting to see if he would pick up the phone. But he simply sat there, fuming silently.

"Here's your cone." Barrla's cheerful voice tore me from the scene. "Sorry it took so long. There were some children who could not make up their minds." She held out the ice cream cone with her left hand, holding her own with her right and licking delicately. "What did you learn?"

I sighed. "They argued about trade agreements," I said as I took the cone. I tasted it, taking care not to spill any drops on my clothes.

Barrla frowned. "You looked like you were listening to some juicy gossip."

"Yes, there was a bit of that too, something about the Minister's past... but if I am right about what I heard, it might be a very dangerous secret to know. I want to discuss it with Fenris first—please don't be angry if I don't tell you everything now." I trusted Barrla, but I didn't want Marris, who hated the mages so much, to learn about such a damaging scandal before I had discussed the possible consequences with Fenris. I would not put it past the Minister to have Mirrine killed after all, if his secret leaked out before she left the country.

"Well, at least promise to tell me as soon as you can," Barrla said, pouting. "You do realize that if this were a novel, you'd be setting yourself up as a victim? Keeping dangerous secrets to yourself is not a good idea."

"Nobody but you knows I even have it, and I trust you not to blab. I'll discuss it with Fenris as soon as I see him."

We sat out there for another hour, listening through the owl and hoping to come across anything suspicious. But all we overheard was government business, and there was no sign of any spies that we could tail back to their lair.

"Oh, this is just torture," Barrla finally said as we watched a secretary bring in white wine and takeout from what looked to be a five-star restaurant. "The Minister is enjoying fine dining and cool air while we are sweltering in this heat!"

"Oh, all right," I said with a laugh as she put the owl away. "Let's go have some dinner ourselves."

We packed up, then caught a cab to the port, where we would grab some food and much-needed drink before reconvening with Comenius. With any luck, he might finally have some good news for us.

TWENTY-TWO

After the excitement of catching the conspirators and rounding up the prisoners, I returned to the Palace to pick up the things I'd selected. There was just enough time before the meeting with Mina, Barrla, and Marris at Comenius's place. I was looking forward to announcing that the plot had been foiled, and that mages, shifters, and humans in Solantha could safely go about their business once more. They would all be happy and relieved at the day's events.

Even better, Mina and I could finally get on with our own lives now that we had taken care of the Resistance's plans for revenge. It was amazing how quickly things had moved, once everyone—Director Chen, Garrett and his agents, Captain Skonel and his enforcers—had worked together. Teamwork truly was the key—these Resistance conspirators didn't stand a chance against our combined skills.

I was adding a tome on defensive magic to my magic sleeve to share with Mina when there was a sudden commotion in the corridor. "They've finally returned!" I heard an excited servant whispering as footsteps rushed up and down, and my heart jumped. Could it be...?

"Iannis?" I asked tentatively in mindspeak, reaching for them. *"Sunaya?"*

"Fenris???" they both answered at the same time, shock and delight reverberating through the connection.

A burst of elation filled me at the sound of their voices, and I jumped off the bed and rushed into the hallway just as they turned the corner. They both wore rumpled clothing and looked weary from their travels, but Sunaya squealed at the sight of me, and the next thing I knew she'd shot down the hall and had wrapped me in a fierce hug.

"Dammit, Fenris!" She squeezed tight enough that I could do nothing but wrap my arms around her and return the hug. She smelled just as I'd last remembered her—a combination of something sweet, like honey blossoms, mixed with magic and the faintest hint of charcoal from her steambike. Her thick mass of dark, curly hair nearly choked me, but it was worth it to finally see her and Iannis again.

"I missed you so fucking much," she mumbled into my shirt, finally loosening her grip enough that I could breathe. She lifted her head, and guilt hit me at the sheen of tears over her brilliant green eyes. But in the next second, they disappeared, and her fangs flashed in that familiar impudent grin of hers. "Figures you would take advantage of the quake to ditch us and go find a mate. I can smell her all over you."

The tips of my ears reddened, and I cleared my throat. "We're not actually married yet," I said, taking a step back. "Though I hope to be, soon."

"You must invite us to the wedding," Iannis said, sweeping in for a quick, hard hug of his own. "I'm so glad you will be here for ours."

"I wouldn't miss it for the world," I said, smiling. I looked between the two of them, then said, "You both look exhausted. I'll let you rest, and we can talk more in the morning."

"Oh, hell no," Sunaya said, grabbing my arm. "You just got back—I'm not letting you out of my sight so soon."

"Technically *you* are the ones who just got back," I said as she dragged me down the hall and into the room she shared with Iannis. Sunaya and Iannis actually had separate bedrooms, but it was just for show—they slept together almost every night since the day they'd become engaged. "I've been here in Solantha for several days."

"You have?" Sunaya exclaimed as we sat down on the couches. Servants came in on our heels, delivering drinks and a platter of snacks. "What have you been doing here this whole time?"

"I came here to warn you," I said as I helped myself to a glass of wine and a small plate of cheese and crackers. "There was a plot afoot—some of Thorgana's former associates were gathering ex-Resistance members together here in Solantha and planned to seize the city after attacking the Convention in force. They hoped to kill the country's strongest mages in one go and improve their chances of seizing power. Luckily they were discovered just today—their leaders were imprisoned and their weapons have been seized. It was an impressive collaboration of the Mages Guild under Director Chen, the enforcers, and Director Toring's office."

"And you, too?" Sunaya guessed. "There is a tinge of gunpowder in your scent."

"I was there," I admitted. "Now that I have been outed as Lord Polar's illegitimate son, Garrett Toring has been surprisingly pleasant," I added wryly.

Sunaya chuckled. "So you know about that, huh? I hope you're not too offended—I kind of came up with it on the spur of the moment, and since I thought you were dead at the time, I didn't think there would be any ramifications to you."

I smiled. "It was inspired, but you'll need to tell me every detail of your invention so I don't accidentally give myself away."

"Never mind all that now. I want to know more about this plot," Iannis said, his violet eyes narrowing. "I knew there was a chance something like this could happen when the Minister announced he'd hold the Convention here. We took precautions, but we hadn't gotten wind of anything like this before I left."

The door opened before I could reply, and Director Chen strode in. "Thank Resinah you are back," she said fervently in a rare show of emotion, making a beeline for Iannis. "I was beginning to reach my wits' end. Are you both unharmed?"

"Yes, thank you." Iannis smiled. "I apologize for leaving you hanging, Director Chen, but I trust you've had things in hand. I gather that on top of everything else, you had to deal with this Resistance plot Fenris was telling us about?"

Director Chen nodded, taking a seat in one of the empty chairs. "Fenris sent an anonymous warning on his way here, but it was not taken seriously. We acted quickly, however, after he connected with Director Toring. Fenris helped me get the crucial information out of the main suspect, Moredo, another of those construction tycoons...Was that only six hours ago? It seems longer." She passed a hand over her brow in a weary gesture. "Then he also helped take care of the plotters, just in time for your return."

"You all did very well," Iannis said. "I am glad everything is in hand."

"Who else was involved?" Sunaya asked, leaning forward. "Did you find out any details of the planned attack?"

Director Chen and I fully briefed Sunaya and Iannis on what we had discovered. We were still going over the details when Chen was called away on an urgent appointment, leaving me alone with my friends once more.

"I'm glad you are able to go around Solantha in your own face once again," Sunaya said. "Sorry we weren't here when you first arrived. Your run-in with Garrett must have been scary as hell since you didn't know what I'd told him."

"How exactly did you run into him?" Iannis asked. "What did you say?"

I told them about my brief incarceration and what had led to it, and how Garrett, all sympathy, had turned me loose and told me to go visit my parents. "I still have to go and see them," I said ruefully. "I have to admit that I'm not entirely looking forward to that visit, since they believe me to be my own son."

"They came here first, and I was sorry I could not help them," Iannis said. "They will eventually find out that you have resurfaced. Better that you go and see them in person than having them find out from a third party."

"I'm so glad that Garrett bought the story," Sunaya said, looking relieved. "He seemed convinced when I spun it, but that was months ago and I wasn't sure how he'd react if he ever saw you again. I tried to make you sound like a poor victim of your parents' indiscretion, brought up by your old great-uncle in that remote country house of his and hidden away behind the library sofas whenever he had a visitor. I told him you grew up in that library, which explained your love of books and scholarship and also why you were so different from other shifters."

For a moment, I wondered how she would know about my great-uncle's country house, but then I remembered she had all my memories. Sunaya's making such use of them was an unexpected development, and yet it was just the kind of thing she would do.

"It's a bit insulting how readily he and my parents believed your story," I said. "I would never have treated any child of mine like that, shifter or no." Of course, Garrett had never known me that well, but my own parents...I consoled myself with the reflection that Polar's name was already ruined in my fellow mages' eyes, so this added scandal could hardly make matters worse. I was Fenris now, and should just let it go.

"But never mind all that," I said to Sunaya with a smile. "I am very happy you did this. Now that I am engaged to Mina, it means that the two of us should be able to live openly together. And my interest in ancient magical lore and my knowledge of Loranian no longer need to be hidden. I can even practice magic to some extent."

"And wear robes, if you want to," Iannis said. "That old great-uncle could have apprenticed you."

"I wish that you'd brought your Mina with you," Sunaya lamented. "I *really* want to meet her. She smells nice, Fenris—like lavender and sunshine. I bet she's one of those sweet and gentle types."

I grinned. "She is, but she does have a fiery side if provoked. She is very excited about meeting the both of you, although she is a bit nervous."

"She won't have any need to be," Iannis assured me. "We'll make her feel right at home. I don't know that we'll have much time for social affairs before our wedding, what with everything going on, but we'll have to get together before you two leave."

"*Leave?*" Sunaya demanded. "You're not going back to whatever cave you've been hiding in, are you, Fenris?"

"Not permanently," I admitted, "but Mina and I do need to settle our affairs in Watawis—that's where I ended up. We are thinking of moving back out to Canalo, but it will likely be nearby, and not within Solantha itself. Mina is very fond of the beach," I added with a smile, thinking of how carefree and beautiful she looked frolicking in the waves. If moving to a beachside town meant seeing her in a bikini more often, who was I to complain? She'd also want a houseful of pets, I expected, and a veterinary surgery to keep practicing her skills.

"Speaking of traveling," I said, "where in Recca did you two disappear off to? I heard that you might have gone to Manuc, but nobody knew for sure. What was so important that you had to leave at a crucial time like this?"

"It's a long story," Iannis said as Sunaya grimaced in distaste, as if the very memory pained her. "I'll have to tell you the details when I have more time, but in short, we had trouble with some of my Tua relatives. They were not pleased with my choice of a bride and would not be ignored on the matter."

Sunaya snorted. "That's the understatement of the year," she said, rolling her eyes. "Thankfully we managed to escape, and just in time, too. There's still so much to be done." She sighed, flopping back down onto the couch.

"I should go and find Mina," I said, noting that Sunaya's exhaustion was finally beginning to catch up with her. Even Iannis, who always seemed full of energy, was sagging a bit in his chair. I touched the serapha charm, and the tug in my chest told me that Mina was not too far away, in the direction of the port. Good, so they were with Comenius by now. After inadvertently standing Mina up the other night, I'd better not keep her waiting any longer.

"All right," Sunaya said sleepily. "You said you were staying at the Marwale, right?"

"Yes."

"That's much too far away," Iannis protested. "You and your friends must come stay here in the Palace tonight. It's getting late for such a long drive."

"I agree," Sunaya said before I could protest. "I'll have a suite readied for you and will tell the staff to expect you. Tell Com I said hi, and that I'll come see him when I'm alive again."

I promised to do so, and left Solantha Palace with a bounce in my step. I couldn't wait to tell everyone that the danger was past, and that Sunaya and Iannis were finally back.

TWENTY-THREE

MINA

Barrla and I arrived at Comenius's place to find that it was quite crowded. The shop had already closed for the day, and when the door to Comenius's upstairs apartment opened, we saw that Marris was lounging on the couch, waiting to give his report. A pretty blonde girl, who must be Comenius's daughter Rusalia, was sitting at the table doing homework.

"Come on in," Comenius said with a smile, waving us through. I took a deep breath in and inhaled the delicious scent of beef stew. "Elania was just finishing up dinner."

"That smells amazing," I told Elania as Barrla rushed over to embrace Marris.

"Thank you," Elania said with a smile that morphed into a frown as she turned toward me. "You look like you've been baking away in the sun!" she exclaimed, snatching a large white pitcher and two glasses off the countertop. Before I could say anything, she'd pressed a glass of what looked like lemonade into my hand. "Drink this," she ordered, handing one to Barrla as well. "It's my special restorative recipe for hot days."

"It works like a charm," Marris confirmed, holding up his

own glass, which was empty. "I was beat when I got here after painting all day in this heat, and that stuff perked me right up."

I took a sip from the glass and was pleasantly surprised when a rush of cooling energy filled my limbs. Invigorated, I drained the glass. "Wow. That was amazing." I made a mental note to get the recipe from her.

"I told you it would be." Smiling, Elania took the glass from me, then pulled me aside and said in a low voice, "You really should be more careful not to get dehydrated, especially in your condition."

I blinked. "My condition?" *Could she know…?*

Elania smiled slyly. "Yes," she confirmed, still speaking softly—Comenius was at the table helping Rusalia with a math problem, and Barrla and Marris were talking on the couch. "You are pregnant. Trust me—with my talent I am able to tell at once. I'm also a bit more sensitive to such things just now," she added, "as I too am in the early stages of pregnancy."

"Really?" I asked, excitement overtaking me. I'd suspected for the past two or three days that I might be pregnant, but I hadn't been sure—aside from a slight tenderness in my breasts, I didn't feel any different. "Does Comenius know?"

"Of course he does," Elania said with a chuckle. "And you should tell your man, too, if you haven't already. You must also urge him to visit his parents—they came around here asking for him. They believe that Fenris is their grandson, and they told Comenius to let Fenris know that they are staying at the Golden Wave Hotel."

"I will definitely make sure Fenris visits them," I said—we'd already discussed it. I knew that he was nervous about this reunion, but I found it touching that his parents wanted to meet him so badly, even knowing that he was a shifter.

We were in the middle of an animated conversation when a knock came at the door, and Comenius opened it to reveal

Fenris standing on the doorstep. "I have excellent news," he said, beaming as he came inside. "The Resistance plot has been foiled, and even better, Iannis and Sunaya have returned!"

"Really?" Comenius and Elania said together in excitement.

"How did they look?" Comenius asked. "Were they injured?"

"How has the plot been foiled so quickly?" Marris asked, looking confused. "I didn't hear anything about that."

"Without our help?" Barrla asked, looking disappointed and relieved at the same time.

Fenris shook his head as he pulled me into his arms for a hug. "Sunaya and Iannis were exhausted but in good health," he said, then turned to kiss my forehead. "And they are especially excited to meet you, Mina. They invited us to move to the Palace, since the hotel is so far away."

Fenris then proceeded to describe the day's events to us. Even Rusalia stopped her homework and listened in fascination when he described how the Resistance's plans were uncovered and their weapons confiscated.

Seeing there was a shifter and a strapping young man joining them for dinner, as well as Barrla and myself, Elania called for takeout to supplement the stew she was cooking. We settled down around the truly impressive spread of food and took turns briefing one another about our day.

"It seems strange that none of us have heard about these arrests yet," Marris commented around a mouthful of stew. "The foremen were issuing cudgels, whips, and axes to the men this morning, and we were assigned stations throughout the city. They didn't say anything about guns, though. They told us that in the next week we needed to have our weapons ready at all times."

"I assume tomorrow they will countermand those orders and tell everybody to disperse," Comenius said optimistically.

"Once they learn the leaders have been arrested, they will see that there is no point in staying."

"We've been stocking up on healing tonics and poultices, just in case," Elania told us. "I'm happy to hear that they won't be needed now."

"Now that the danger is over, at least you won't need to continue posing as a Resistance soldier," Barrla said to Marris. "Surely you can pull out now, rather than wait for them to send you home tomorrow. The last thing I want is for you to end up arrested by the mages once they spread their net wider."

"I've had more than enough of paint fumes and brushes," Marris admitted. "I may as well rejoin you, though I'm still not keen on staying in that hotel."

Barrla rolled her eyes. "You can handle it for another couple of days. I'm going to meet the Chief Mage and see the Palace, now that the danger is over."

"Fenris," I said as Barrla and Marris began to bicker about when they would return home. "Can we talk privately?"

"Of course." Fenris took my hand, and we excused ourselves from the table. We went outside for a walk along the pier, enjoying the briny sea air and watching the last vestiges of sunset merge into twilight along the horizon. Aside from distant seagulls cawing, and the waves lapping at the shore, it was almost completely silent, and a wave of peacefulness washed over me.

"This is one of the two gulayas that I ordered from Elnos," I said, pulling it out of my purse and handing it to Fenris. "They're programmed to transport us to a beach outside Solantha. I'm glad you got through the day's events without needing them, but since we are living so dangerously lately, I'd feel better if you carried this."

"Thank you." He kissed me. "That would have come in handy in jail and will work just fine as extra insurance." Fenris's eyes gleamed as he took the palm-sized charm, which was cast into the shape of a rose. "Sunaya's life was saved by one of these not long ago. I'm looking forward to tinkering with them when all of this is behind us," he said, tucking it into his magical sleeve.

"There's something else," I said. "Something that I found out when Barrla and I were spying on the Minister."

"Oh?" Fenris frowned. "Is everything all right?"

I took a deep breath, then glanced around to make sure nobody was listening. It didn't seem like anyone was nearby, but even so...I muttered the privacy bubble spell that Fenris had taught me, and waited until the air shimmered around us before speaking again.

"Wow." Fenris raised his eyebrows. "This must be serious indeed."

"When Barrla and I were spying on the Minister's mansion," I said, "Mirrine, the journalist from Forrane we met at the Marwale, came to visit him. I thought that she was simply there for an interview, but it turns out she was there to blackmail him. I suspect she is no more a journalist than I am."

"Blackmail Minister Graning?" Fenris's eyes widened. "With what?"

"It turns out that she and the Minister were married long ago, in her home country."

"Married!" Fenris exclaimed. "But that's not possible. The Minister had a Northian wife, whom he married for her wealth and connections. She died only a few years ago...ah." His eyes lit with understanding. "So our esteemed Minister Graning is a bigamist, then."

"Yes, and Mirrine is using that against him—she wants him to stop sabotaging a trade agreement between Forrane and Bilam," I said. "She said that if anything bad were to happen to her, the truth would be published, so I imagine she has letters that are waiting to be sent out if she dies, or is imprisoned, or disappears."

Fenris's mouth quirked up into a smile. "A clever woman, that Mirrine," he said. "Threatening Zavian Graning would take some very steady nerves. He is a dangerous man. Does Barrla know about this?"

I shook my head. "I said I had to discuss it with you first, since it might be a dangerous secret. For now, only you, I, and Mirrine are aware of it."

"Good." Fenris squeezed my hand. "Barrla and Marris would be in over their heads if they decided to use this knowledge and might very well end up dead. I will tell Iannis about this, though—he of all people would know how to use this information without repercussions."

As we walked a little further along the pier, I wondered if I should tell Fenris that I was pregnant. He would be overjoyed—my stomach still jumped in excitement whenever I thought about it. But I decided to wait a bit longer. As a veterinarian, I knew that during the early days, the viability of a pregnancy was not a sure thing. It would be cruel to get his hopes up and then immediately dash them.

Besides, knowing Fenris, the moment I told him that I was carrying his child, he would whisk me back to the Marwale and refuse to let me anywhere near the city, which wasn't something I could abide. I wanted to be his full partner, not someone who had to be wrapped up in cotton wool and coddled. Like Barrla had said, I had come too far in this venture—I wanted to see it through until the end.

"It would be nice to get married here, in the same temple as your friends," I said instead, leaning my head against his shoulder.

Fenris kissed the top of my head. "I think that is an excellent idea," he said. "Our engagement is scandalously short by mage standards, but since we are nobody of importance around here, there is no way for anyone to know we have only been engaged for a few weeks. Solantha Temple is lovely, and Sunaya and Iannis can be our witnesses. Unless...did you want a bigger wedding?" he asked, sounding uncertain.

I smiled. "No, a small wedding is fine," I said. "Since I don't have any family left, it's not like we need a big wedding. But," I said, poking him in the chest, "we must invite your parents."

Fenris winced. "Right. I guess we'll have to give them an invitation when we see them tomorrow, won't we?"

I grinned. "So you've already made an appointment to go meet them?"

"No, but I knew you were about to suggest it," he teased, leaning in for a kiss. "And as always, I am loath to disappoint my lady."

TWENTY-FOUR

"Where is everyone?" I asked as we stepped back into Comenius's apartment. We'd stayed out on the pier for a bit longer, watching the stars in the night sky, but we hadn't expected to only find Elania and Comenius when we returned.

"Rusalia went to bed," Comenius said from the kitchen as he helped Elania with the dishes. "She had a sleepover planned, but even with this latest news that the plot is foiled, I'll be keeping her much closer to home until the Convention and wedding are over."

"I don't blame you," I said as Fenris closed the door behind us. "I wouldn't want my children to leave my side if there was the slightest danger of big men running through the streets with cudgels and axes, looking to maim or kill anyone with magic. And though the leaders have been arrested, most of the simple soldiers are still around, and armed, from what Marris told us earlier."

Fenris winced as Comenius's face paled, and I immediately felt guilty for bringing it up. "You are quite right to be extra careful with your daughter," Fenris said as he led me to the couch. "Where are Marris and Barrla?"

Elania smiled. "Your friends have gone out dancing at a nearby club. They said they would come back this way when they were finished, and if you were gone by then they would find a way back to the hotel you're staying at."

"Good," I said, smiling. I was happy that Barrla and Marris weren't squandering their time together. Neither of them had any intention of leaving Solantha just yet, and there was no point in them wasting time squabbling with each other about it. In fact, both of them seemed to thrive in the lively atmosphere of this city and would probably look back fondly on this first adventure together for the rest of their lives.

"Knowing those two, it's very likely they will be out until the small hours of the morning," Fenris said. "We might want to head to the Palace and let them find their own way back to the hotel."

I frowned. "How are they going to get a ride this late at night, though? They can't afford a cab and would probably be swindled as out-of-towners anyway. I don't want Marris taking Barrla back to wherever he's been sleeping—she shouldn't be around all those Resistance soldiers."

"I'll stay up for them," Elania said as she came over with a tea tray. "I have some work I meant to catch up on anyway. If they come back very late, they're welcome to sleep on the couch."

I thanked Elania for her hospitality and let Fenris drag me off to the Palace. It was close to midnight by now, and if Elania was correct about my being pregnant, I needed to get enough sleep.

By the time Fenris and I arrived at Solantha Palace, Iannis and Sunaya were asleep. Thankfully, the staff had been told to expect us, and we were able to get inside without incident. Though they tried to show us to a suite, Fenris firmly moved toward his old room, and I went along, curious to see it for myself. There were lots of books and several large chests that took up most of the space, and the bed was small. But even so, it felt more cozy than cramped. Exhausted from our long day, we fell into it, snuggled together, and slept deeply.

I was just having a pleasant dream about our wedding day when a discreet knock at the door woke me up. I squinted—there was a note that some servant had pushed under the door. Disentangling my limbs from Fenris's, I climbed out of bed and retrieved it. "Wake up," I said to his broad back. "Sunaya and Iannis are inviting us to share breakfast in their suite!"

"Hell," Fenris swore, rubbing at his eyes. He sat up, and the sheet slipped down to reveal his naked chest. Desire stirred low in my belly, and I nearly reached out to run my fingers down his abs before I remembered that we had just been summoned. "I could have done with a few more hours' sleep, but then again, I *am* hungry."

"So they want us to have breakfast with them?" I bit my lip. "I didn't even bring a change of clothes with me."

"Don't worry about that," Fenris said soothingly as he rose from the bed and quickly treated my pile of wrinkled clothing to a cleaning spell. "They won't care. They already love you and they haven't even met you yet."

Sure enough, when we went down the hall to Iannis's suite and knocked on the door, Sunaya was delighted to see me. "So *you* are the infamous Mina," she said, smiling broadly at me after she'd embraced Fenris. "I'm so glad to finally meet you!"

"Fenris has told me so much about you," I said, smiling

shyly. I offered a hand, but Sunaya bypassed it, embracing me instead. Now that she and Iannis were standing before me, they seemed larger than life—Sunaya in her leather with her weapons strapped to her legs, and Iannis standing tall at her side, impossibly handsome with his long red hair and aristocratic features, his violet eyes glowing with health. Power seemed to subtly charge the air around them, and I knew instantly that they were a formidable couple.

"All bad things, probably," Sunaya said with a laugh, looking toward Fenris fondly. "I've given Fenris more than his fair share of headaches with all the trouble I get into."

"You are a trouble magnet, no doubt about it," Iannis said teasingly. He shook my hand. "I am very glad that you made it here to see us," he said to me. "When Fenris called me asking for an antidote for that poison, I must admit I worried if I'd ever get to meet you. Croialis has killed too many mages. I assume there was no lasting damage?"

"Not at all—and thank you for saving me." I blushed a little beneath Iannis's intense regard, but he and Sunaya seemed friendly enough, and the knot of tension in my chest loosened.

"It's the least I could do for the woman who has captured my best friend's heart." Iannis winked. "I am very happy for both of you."

"Thank you." Fenris slipped an arm around my waist, and I smiled. "We're planning on getting married before we leave and were hoping you two will be our witnesses."

"Damn right we will," Sunaya said, beaming. Then she frowned. "Though we are leaving for a honeymoon after our own wedding next week. Can you wait until we're back?"

I exchanged a look with Fenris. "*Up to you,*" he said in mindspeak.

"I'd rather not wait," I decided. "We don't need any great

fuss, and we don't have many people to invite. I know it's irrational, but I have a feeling that the longer we postpone our wedding, the greater the danger that something might prevent it."

"I wouldn't say it's irrational at all," Sunaya said dryly, "considering that's exactly what happened to us. Fucking tyrants," she muttered under her breath.

"We would be honored to be your witnesses," Iannis added, giving Sunaya a look as if to say *behave*. I hid a smile when she stuck out her tongue—despite being two of the most powerful people in Solantha, they clearly had an easy dynamic between them.

"We know that you aren't going to want a huge shindig or anything," Sunaya said, "but since everyone else can't go to the temple we should have some kind of celebration that includes them. Fenris did make quite a few friends while he lived here."

"You're absolutely right," I said to her with a smile. "My human friends Marris and Barrla will want to be included, and I would love for Comenius and Elania to be a part. And perhaps that nice Mr. Ragga, too. I think he could become a friend, if we stay around here."

"I'm glad to see the two of you so full of energy again," Fenris said, beaming at his friends. "You were both exhausted when I left you last night."

Iannis shrugged. "Nothing a good night's sleep and a restorative tonic couldn't handle," he said. "It feels good to be home. There were moments when I wasn't sure we would make it back in time for the wedding. Had we known of this new Resistance plot we would have been even more desperate to return."

"It sounds like you had your hands full," I commented, curious what kind of adventure could imperil this formidable mage. The magazines claimed he might be the strongest in the entire Federation, and I had a feeling they might be right for once.

"Indeed we did," Iannis agreed. "I should feel guilty about all the extra work it made for Chen, but I don't regret missing weeks of preparations for the Convention. I never wanted it to be in Solantha and would rather have concentrated on rebuilding after the quake without these complications. There are not enough hotels for everyone, although the ones that are open make out like bandits from the scarcity of rooms."

"Speaking of which, you did bring your luggage along?" Sunaya asked. "I've had a guest suite readied for the two of you."

"I'm fine with staying in Fenris's old room," I said. We'd slept comfortably enough last night, and I could tell Fenris liked being surrounded by his own things.

"The bed is much too narrow," Sunaya said with a wink. "And all those bookcases take up too much space."

Iannis must have noticed that I felt a little flustered, for he mercifully changed the subject. "I must thank you for your efforts to neutralize the plot, Mina, and you even did it without getting thrown in prison," he said, with a grin in Fenris's direction. "Do you agree that all danger is over now?"

I thought about it for a moment before replying. "Since I was not present when the plot was defeated, I can only go by hearsay. It worries me that, according to our friend Marris, the workers were still being armed and told to be ready any day now."

"It always takes a little time for the troops to hear what is going on with their generals," Fenris said. "By this morning, hopefully they'll have got the word and will be dispersing. Though Marris seemed to think some might start to riot in their disappointment."

"I'll warn the enforcers to be prepared, if they try anything," Sunaya said.

"By the way," I said, remembering my discovery of the previous afternoon, "while it has nothing to do with the Resistance plot, I did find out something significant with the help of Mr. Ragga's ether owl. He said he was inspired by the bird you created," I recalled.

"Trouble?" Sunaya asked, and a large ghostly parrot materialized on her shoulder, cawing at me. His caw sounded a lot like a laugh.

"Yes!" I laughed, leaning forward to get a better look at the parrot, delighted. He flapped his wings, then jumped to my wrist when I held out an arm. The touch of his feet on my arm sent tingles racing across my skin even though I felt no weight—it was an odd sensation.

"Elnos is a good man," Iannis said. "His inventions are brilliant, and he has worked for me on more than one occasion."

"About your discovery..." Fenris reminded me as I reached out to touch the parrot's ghostly feathers. My fingers passed right through. The glowing parrot cocked his head at me, then disappeared in a flash of light.

"Right." I cleared my throat. "My friend Barrla and I were spying on the Minister yesterday afternoon."

"Spying on the Minister?" Iannis's eyebrows rose. "What for?"

"Barrla had a notion that the plotters might target him, and that we could catch a trace of them if we kept the area under surveillance," I explained, not mentioning that she had gotten the idea from one of her beloved shifter romances. "We did not identify any Resistance spies, but it was a good chance to field-test the ether owl." I pulled the tiny metal owl out of my bag to show them. "This device links up with the ether owl and allows a person to see and hear what it observes while it remains invisible to the target. I understand it's a magitech construct."

"That sounds just like something Elnos would invent," Sunaya said admiringly as she took it from me to examine. "It could be very useful to investigate suspects. Is he selling these yet?"

I shook my head. "He says it's just a prototype, and that he may never bring them to market."

"I hope he doesn't," Fenris said, scowling at the bird. "It brings up bad memories for me. Gelisia also used a bird to spy on me, but it was pure magic, not magitech like this."

"It's intriguing," Iannis said as he took the owl from Sunaya, looking it over with a critical eye. "I'll have to ask Elnos to let me borrow this when you are done with it, so I can study it further. Let's hope the Resistance isn't working on something like this too. A device like this would be devastating to our security measures."

"Anyway," Sunaya said, "what is it that you found? The Minister is such a stick in the mud, I figure if he had any vices they would have already been discovered by the paparazzi."

"A woman named Mirrine that Fenris and I met earlier came to visit the Minister," I said. "She told us that she was a reporter, but I think she works for the Forrane government, because she was blackmailing the Minister into lifting some sanctions that were hampering trade between Forrane and Bilam."

"Blackmail?" Iannis asked. "What sort of blackmail?"

"She's the Minister's wife. Yes, I know the Minister already had a wife," I said before Sunaya and Iannis could interrupt, "but apparently these two were married before that, in Forrane. It didn't work out, and the Minister decided to leave her and go back to Northia. From the way she talks about husbands in general, she didn't seem too sad to be rid of him. She said she pitied the second wife."

"Damn," Sunaya said, her eyes gleaming as she leaned back in her chair. "That's quite a juicy secret."

"It's also a dangerous secret," I said. "I didn't tell my friend Barrla, for her own safety, and because her boyfriend still has Resistance sympathies. Only Mirrine knows the truth, and now the people in this room. She seemed to fear that the Minister would kill her, and has taken precautions."

"This would ruin the Minister if the truth ever came out," Iannis said, a grave expression on his face. "Everyone knows that Zavian Graning and his late wife had an unhappy marriage to begin with—she was a sickly woman, and he was rarely by her bedside, too busy climbing the political ladder. He was not even there when she died five years ago, and her powerful family is still angry about it. If her relatives found out that, on top of this, he was a bigamist, they would be furious. They would drag his name through the mud, and he would have to resign his office in disgrace."

"We'd better not tell Marris that," I said wryly, "or he would immediately notify all the papers. He hates the Minister."

"Your friends Barrla and Marris sound like quite a couple," Sunaya said. "Where are they now?"

"I think they spent the night on Com's sofa," I said. "They're probably looking for a hotel room now, since they cannot stay with Comenius forever."

"I would like to talk to Marris myself and find out exactly what these recruits were being told, and how their morale was," Iannis said.

"Let's call Com and offer them some of our empty guest rooms," Sunaya suggested. "From what I've heard, they probably won't get a room anywhere else in town, since the Convention is about to start. I'll be too busy to be much of a hostess, but at least you won't feel lonely with your friends around you. Besides, maybe your friend Marris will learn that mages aren't so bad after all, just like I did when I first came here," she added with a smile.

IT TURNED out that Marris and Barrla were still at Comenius's place. Though Marris seemed hesitant when I talked to them on the phone, Barrla assured me they would be right over in the first steamcab they could find. They arrived quickly enough, looking flushed and bright-eyed and much more relaxed than when I'd last seen them. A servant brought them to the sitting room of the suite that Sunaya had moved us to.

"You two look like you've sorted out your issues," I said as they joined us in the sitting area.

"Nothing like a night of dancing to melt the stress away," Barrla declared. She looked over at Sunaya and Iannis, who had come over to greet them despite having a thousand other things to worry over. She nearly fell over, her eyes going wide. "By the Ur-God!" she squeaked, immediately folding into a curtsy. "My Lord and Lady...thank you for inviting us."

"No need for all that," Sunaya said with a smile. "I'm not exactly a lady, anyway."

"Yet," Iannis added, kissing her brow.

"These are my good friends, Barrla Kelling and her beau, Marris Dolan," Fenris said. "As I said earlier, Marris has been posing as one of the workers for the Resistance and updating us on new developments."

"Is that so?" Sunaya cocked her head at Marris. "And you haven't felt any urge to rejoin your comrades and take up their cause against mages?"

Marris stiffened, and I swallowed as the atmosphere in the

room grew tense. "I'd be lying if I said I hadn't thought about it," he said, meeting Sunaya's gaze squarely. "But in the end, Fenris convinced me that it's not in anyone's best interests to engage in terror attacks. I still think the mage regime needs to change, but not at the expense of innocent lives."

Sunaya nodded. "I agree with you," she said, and I let out a silent breath of relief. Clearly Marris was speaking what he considered the truth, or she would have called him out. "I used to hate the mage regime myself, until I found myself tangled up with it. This guy here has taught me that there are still a few good guys at the top"—she twined her fingers with Iannis's—"and that it's not all black and white."

"I think your union provides hope to humans and shifters," Barrla said. "Seeing a shifter and a mage wed proves that it's possible for the different races to live as equals. There's a whole series of interracial romance novels that are really popular, so I think a lot of people secretly want the barriers between us all to dissolve."

"We are certainly heading in the right direction for that to happen," Iannis said, "but not if the Resistance is allowed to prevail. They think they are helping their cause, but their violent acts and vitriolic speeches only widen the divide. Those who consider humans the superior race are no better than the most bigoted mages."

Marris looked unconvinced, and I wouldn't have minded discussing this further, but a messenger came rushing in with some urgent message for Iannis and Sunaya. They took their leave of us, promising to come back and visit again when they had a free moment.

"Wow, I never expected to actually stay in the Palace," Barrla said, looking around the room. "After they would not even let us take a peek inside with the press credentials we flashed! Do you suppose they will mind if I take pictures of the place?"

"I'm sure Sunaya and Iannis won't mind," Fenris said, and that was all the encouragement Barrla needed. Taking me by the hand, she tugged me from the chair.

"You better come with us," she told Fenris. "Someone needs to make sure we don't get lost!'

TWENTY-FIVE

FENRIS

Since we had nothing better to do for the moment, I went along with the girls and gave them a tour of Solantha Palace while Barrla took dozens of photographs. Marris had begged off in favor of getting some more sleep, and while I could certainly use more shut-eye myself, I knew Mina would be disappointed if I didn't come along.

Besides, it was a delight to watch Mina's eyes go wide and her face light up with pleasure as I showed her the various wings and introduced her to the staff. She was particularly excited when I took her to the Palace's vast library. Both Mina and Barrla spent a good twenty minutes discussing literature with Janta Urama, the head librarian.

"I am glad that you've returned," Janta said to me, her voice quiet but pleased as we stood near a row of shelves. I could scent her sincerity. "I've missed your presence here in the library, Fenris."

"I hope to visit often," I assured her, "though not every day like I used to. Mina and I plan on moving back to Canalo after we settle our affairs, but we will be living outside the city. Mina is not fully trained yet, and access to the library will be helpful for that."

"Well make sure you bring her with you the next time you come," she said, smiling at Mina. "I've already got a few books in mind that I think both of you ladies will enjoy—I'll have them set aside for you when you come back."

Mina and Barrla beamed. "I would like that very much," Mina said.

We took our leave of the library, promising Janta that we would return and inviting her to the small wedding that Sunaya and Iannis were putting together for us, whenever it would be scheduled. Famished, we grabbed a quick bite to eat at the Palace cafeteria, then finally parted ways with Barrla and headed out for the appointment I had been half dreading, half looking forward to.

Meeting my parents.

"You'll be fine," Mina said, patting my arm reassuringly as I drove the short distance through the tree-shaded streets of the Mages Quarter. "I swear, I've never seen you this nervous about anything, Fenris. Your parents have been searching for you— they aren't going to spit on you when we turn up outside their hotel room."

"I know that," I said, and really, I did. It was absurd to think that they would reject me. "It's just...I never expected to see them again. After Iannis changed me into a shifter, and I woke up, I resigned myself to letting them believe I was dead. In fact, they *still* think I'm dead," I said, and I couldn't help sounding a little bitter about it.

"We might be able to change that," Mina said cautiously, "depending on how this visit goes."

I shook my head. "They'll be angry with me regardless of whether or not I tell them the truth," I said. "If I confess that I am Polar, they will be upset that I didn't trust them enough to let them know I was still alive. And if I don't, they are still bound to be angry with me for not telling them about my supposed affair with a shifter, and their 'grandson.' No doubt they will bring it up."

"That doesn't mean they will hold it against you," Mina said gently. "They have clearly decided to accept you as a member of their family, even if you are a half shifter."

"That is because they have no choice," I said. "My only sister died years ago, and my parents are too old to have children now. I am their only descendant."

Mina said nothing, simply wrapping her fingers in mine, for which I was grateful. There wasn't really anything she could say to alleviate my dread, and in truth, I knew I was being silly for letting myself get worked up about this. Of course my parents would be looking forward to seeing me, regardless of whatever misgivings they had about a shifter in the family. But still...this subterfuge, it felt *wrong*.

And yet the charade had to continue. Not just for my own safety, but for Iannis's. I didn't know how my parents would react to the truth, even though I loved them and knew they loved me. My father had always been a stickler for the rules. If he saw how low I'd sunk, that I'd voluntarily changed myself into a shifter...he might very well refuse to have anything to do with me.

The Golden Wave was a small boutique hotel at the edge of the Mages Quarter, right along the beach. I pulled up in front of the sparkling gold and white building and handed the car keys to the valet before going inside.

"Excuse me," I said to the receptionist sitting behind the glossy white counter. "I'm looking for Mr. and Mrs. ar'Tollis. Could you tell them that Fenris is here to see them? They've been expecting me."

"Of course," she said smoothly, picking up the phone. My

stomach tightened as she dialed, and I moved away a little, intentionally tuning her out so that I wouldn't have to hear my parents on the line.

"Mr...ah...Fenris?" the receptionist said a moment later, and I turned back. "They'll be down shortly."

"Thank you."

Mina and I sat down at a small group of sofas in the back of the lobby, and I kept my eyes trained on the elevator on the other side of the room. A few minutes later, its door opened, and my breath whooshed out of me at the sight of my parents for the first time in four years. They did not look different since they had been maintaining their looks by magic for some centuries now, but there was a heaviness to their eyes, a look of mingled sadness and hope at seeing us, that gave me a jolt of guilt and regret.

"Fa—*grandfather*," I said as I rose from my chair, catching myself just in time.

My father's eyes narrowed a little as he took me in. "You are Fenris?" he asked.

"Of course he is," my mother said, gliding over to me without hesitation and taking my face in her pale hands. "Look at how much he resembles our son. He has Polar's strong chin and the shape of his eyes." Her own blue eyes were brimming with unshed tears.

I smiled. "I'm glad you think so," I said, indulging her—I looked nothing like my former self, but if my mother wanted to see similarities, so much the better. "I've been told I bear little resemblance to my father, but I do share some of his interests."

"And who is this pretty young lady with you?" my father asked, looking at Mina. "You don't look like a shifter," he said to her, and I detected something like relief in his tone.

"This is Tamina Marton, my fiancée," I said. "Mina, meet my grandparents, Rotho and Balina ar'Tollis."

"I'm very happy to finally meet you." Mina smiled as she extended a hand to my father. "Fenris has been very anxious about this meeting, but I knew that you must be fine people if you are his grandparents."

"Well that's very nice of you to say," my father said, sounding a little flustered. "You are a full-blooded mage, if I am not mistaken?"

"Rotho," my mother scolded, making a shooing motion with her hands. "Forgive my husband for his impertinence," she said, taking both of Mina's hands into her own. "Of course you're a full blooded mage—I saw it right away. I am overjoyed my grandson has found and won such a fine young lady. You two make a very handsome couple."

"Thank you," Mina said, "but I take no offense. I come from an old family of mages in Haralis, though I'm the last of my line," she told them. "Fenris and I happened to meet up north while we were both traveling, and we hit it off right away. We are getting married here at Solantha Temple, and you are invited to the wedding, of course. We hope to start a family soon."

"Oh, that sounds lovely!" my mother exclaimed as I hid a wince. I hadn't been sure about inviting them to the wedding, since I needed to be careful what to divulge to them, but now that Mina had done so, there was no going back.

My father had blinked at the mention of children, no doubt wondering what kind of offspring a half shifter and a mage might produce, but to my relief, he didn't say anything about it.

The four of us finally sat down, and my mother ordered a tea tray and some cookies to be brought. Over refreshments, Mina and I told them a little bit more about our relationship and our plans for the future.

"I must say I am relieved that you managed to escape that horrible quake," my father said. "When we heard that you had died…well, despite never having met you, we were quite upset. Why did you take so long to return?"

"I'm not sure if this was ever explained to you," I said warily, "but the Director of Federal Security, Garrett Toring, thought that I was my father in disguise. Catching Polar had become something of an obsession for him, since it led to a temporary setback in his career. I was worried that he might try to convict me for my father's crimes, so I decided to disappear for a while. I did not know that Sunaya had convinced him of the truth until after I returned."

My father shook his head. "Even after all these years, it still boggles my mind that Polar was involved in such a scandal," he said. "He was always such a sensible boy—much like you seem to be. Your grandmother and I always believed that if he had not been so wrapped up in dusty old scrolls and books, he might have settled down with a nice mage girl, like you," he said to Mina. "But clearly he had time enough for women, if he ended up having a shifter child out of wedlock."

My father's tone turned bitter, and I had to bite down on my tongue to keep back a sharp retort. It was clear he still looked down on shifters in general. Mina put her hand on mine in silent support.

"Perhaps my father had reasons for not wanting to settle down with a mage woman," I said instead. "As I hear it, it was one of his own subordinates, a female he was courting, who betrayed him."

"She was doing her duty—" my father began.

"She was a catty slut," my mother said firmly, cutting him off. "I never did like Gelisia Dorax, and no matter what anyone believes about your father, he was trying to do the right thing," she told me. "I only wish that he'd been smarter about it so that he didn't have to give his life for it."

My stomach sank into my toes at the sadness and disappointment on my mother's face. "I don't know what my father would say to that, if he were here," I said, and it was true enough. This situation was so strange I had trouble wrapping my head around it. "But I'm sure he did not intentionally mean to cause either of you pain."

"Yes, well, enough of this sappy talk," my father said brusquely. "Polar may have made some mistakes, but at least he has given us you, and we are grateful for that much. Now tell us, what are your plans for the wedding?"

We chatted with my parents for a while longer, and to my relief, the tensions between us eased as we turned our attention toward happier topics. I learned that my father had come out of retirement and gone to work as an informal adviser to the current Finance Secretary in Nebara. At one point, over a century ago, he had held that very position himself, but as the father of a disgraced traitor, he probably could not assume any public office again. Gelisia had indeed been committing financial irregularities, they had discovered, but the new Chief Mage was very level-headed and easy to work with, and he had eradicated any lingering trace of corruption.

My mother, in the meantime, had taken up volunteering at the local human orphanage, much to her bridge group's surprise —she said she had been inspired by Polar's sacrifice to save a human girl's life and decided to take an active interest in those less fortunate than herself.

Two hours flew by before we finally took our leave, promising to send them a message when we had a date for the wedding and to come back and visit as soon as we could.

"*There*," Mina said in mindspeak as we walked away. "*That wasn't so bad, was it?*"

"No," I told her as we approached the valet. "*Once we got over that initial unpleasantness, it was actually quite a nice visit. But it is clear that my parents are still angry with me for lying to them and not entirely comfortable with me as a shifter. Having you around, and knowing that I was settling down with a girl from a respectable mage family, helped more than I would like to admit."*

"It does seem that it might be better to let them think that you are their grandson," Mina conceded. *"I am sorry that things did not go better, but your parents were happy to see you, at least. I think that in time they will grow used to having a half shifter grandson."*

The valet brought the car around, and I gave him a hefty tip before getting in with Mina. "It's just...it is difficult to swallow their anger with me," I said aloud to Mina as we drove away. "I am a little angry at my father, too, and unlike him, I have no way to vent my frustrations to his face. I sought advice from him on what to do about my dilemma before I resorted to illegal means, and he was completely unsympathetic. He couldn't even understand why I was so conflicted about condemning a child to death and told me that I just needed a vacation."

Mina pursed her lips. "There is no denying that your father is not a particularly compassionate man," she said. "But it does seem that he is willing to try, at least for your sake. Isn't that the best we can ask for?"

"I suppose," I admitted. I looked sideways at Mina, and the turmoil in my gut eased a little as I noticed the way her golden hair caught the sunlight. She was so beautiful...

Mina cocked her head, noticing the look on my face. "What?"

"Has anyone ever told you that you are wise beyond your years?" I asked, reaching for her hand even as I turned my attention to the road. "I am over five times your age, and yet you are the one who is keeping me grounded."

Mina laughed. "I recall that our situations were quite reversed when it was my family we were dealing with," she said, pressing a kiss against my knuckles. "It is hard to separate logic and emotion when it comes to your relatives. That is why we have each other—to shore up our weaknesses. As a unit, we are unbreakable."

"Unbreakable," I murmured, smiling. "I like that quite a lot."

"Me too," Mina said. "Now let's turn our combined energy toward our wedding and the future we'll build together."

TWENTY-SIX

After our visit with Mr. and Mrs. ar'Tollis, Fenris and I returned to Solantha Palace with the intention of offering Iannis and Sunaya our help with the myriad event preparations that still needed to be done. I knew Sunaya had to be running behind with everything since she'd been gone for so long. Although Fenris wasn't especially thrilled by the notion, I was looking forward to helping her pull the wedding of the century together.

We walked into the Mages Guild lobby, hoping Sunaya might be down here in her office. Sure enough, she was standing at the reception desk talking to Dira, Iannis's secretary. Another young woman dressed in business casual attire was standing by her side—a human, I gathered with a little surprise.

"Sunaya," Fenris began, and she spun around so fast that I jumped a little.

"There you guys are!" she exclaimed. "We've been waiting forever for you two to come back. There's so much to be done!"

"Er, so you know that we've come to help with your wedding, then?" Fenris asked as Sunaya and her companion began herding us back down the hall.

"Oh, don't worry about my wedding," Sunaya said with a wave of her hand. "My assistant here, Nelia, has everything right on schedule. We're going to focus on *your* wedding now."

"*My* wedding?" I squeaked as we were ushered upstairs, toward the west wing. "I thought you were just handling the reception?" Fenris and I had plans to go to the temple and arrange a wedding date with the priest, but that wasn't until later this week.

"Don't worry, ma'am," Nelia said, smiling shyly. "I'm very used to planning events. Everything will be perfect. I've already booked the temple for the day after tomorrow, an hour before sunset. Just let me know who you want to attend, and I'll get invitations sent out to them by special messenger."

Fenris tried to protest, but Sunaya wouldn't hear it, and I had to hide a grin at her no-nonsense approach. She had Nelia drag him off to our suite, where the Chief Mage's personal tailor was waiting to fit him, while she brought me into her sitting room.

"Good afternoon," a plump woman in a deep purple dress said cheerfully, rising from the couch. An array of measuring tapes, bobby pins, and other sewing-type implements were spread out atop the coffee table, along with a huge stack of fashion plates. "My name is Gardina Lawry. Are you the blushing bride-to-be?"

"I guess I am," I said, a grin overtaking my face now that some of the shock was wearing off. "Are you here to fit me for a wedding dress?"

"I am." She gestured to the stack of magazines on the table. "Why don't you flip through these and see if there's something you like?"

"I took *forever* picking out a dress," Sunaya said as we sat down to peruse the magazines. "My sense of style isn't exactly traditional, so I ended up cobbling together a couple different styles. I know you don't want a big wedding, but there's no reason at all why you shouldn't have the perfect dress, so I told Mrs. Lawry to bring a variety of fashion plates for you to check out."

"I appreciate that very much," I said, opening the first magazine. A dazzling array of dresses in all sorts of colors and fabrics awaited me between the pages, and I quickly found myself entranced.

I spent the next hour paging through the fashion plates and discussing different options with Sunaya and Mrs. Lawry. At some point, Nelia came back in, and I imagined that Fenris was probably already finished with his fitting and had sought refuge in the library.

Finally, I settled on an ivory gown with off-the-shoulder sleeves and lace appliques covering the bodice and skirt. Nelia suggested white silk flowers for my hair, which I approved.

"You are going to look lovely," the seamstress gushed as she took my measurements. "I already have a dress almost exactly like the one you want in my shop—a few alterations and it'll be ready for your special day."

The seamstress finished up, and as she took her leave, Nelia pulled out her notepad. "Let's get a list of who you want to invite while you're still here," she said. "I'll have the invitations rushed out so they all arrive by tomorrow."

"Fenris's, ah, grandparents should definitely come," I said, changing "parents" to "grandparents" at the last moment. This was tricky. Only a few hours ago, I'd told them that we would let them know as soon as we had a wedding date. I guessed it was going to be sooner than any of us thought! "I'd love it if Elania and Comenius could attend, even though they're not strictly mages. And if he has time, Mr. Ragga, from the gulaya shop."

Sunaya smiled. "I'm glad you hit it off with them so well," she said. "Comenius and I are old friends."

"Are you?" I hadn't realized—Fenris hadn't said much about their friendship.

"Yeah, that's how Fenris knows him in the first place," she said. "Comenius was one of my first magic user friends, and he's been here with me through all the ups and downs, long before I learned to use my own magic." She smiled fondly, and I wondered how close they had actually been. "I'm glad that he and Elania finally tied the knot, despite some speedbumps on the way. Having to take in Rusalia out of the blue was not easy for either of them."

"I can imagine." I opened my mouth to mention Elania's pregnancy, then closed it. It wasn't my place to share that kind of news. Changing the subject, I asked, "What about Barrla and Marris? I know they're human, but Barrla is my best friend. I can't imagine getting married without her by my side."

Nelia bit her lip, but Sunaya gave me an understanding smile. "Iannis and I can get them in," she promised. "The First Mage is not going to mind if a few non-mages attend. I wish I could have my best friend at my side for my wedding day," she added with a sigh.

"Do you mean Annia?" Fenris had told me about her, and the trip he, Annia, and Sunaya had undertaken to recover Iannis after his crash. She sounded like an interesting woman. "I gather she is still off looking for her sister Noria?"

Sunaya nodded. "Annia was supposed to come back for the wedding, but something came up." Her expression clouded over briefly, but then she seemed to shake it off. "No worries, though —I know she's with me in spirit, and she'll be back when she can. As for your wedding, I'll definitely make sure Barrla and Marris get in. It's been a little while since I had the chance to break some rules," she added with a wink.

After I finished talking over some of the wedding details with Sunaya and Nelia, I sought out Barrla and Marris in their room in the east wing. A quick knock on the door confirmed that they weren't there, but when I wandered a little farther down the hall I found them in one of the parlor rooms eating scones while Barrla was deep in her current novel and Marris leafed through some men's magazine.

"Mina!" Marris exclaimed, noticing me first. He put the magazine down and straightened in his chair. "We came looking for you earlier but you were gone."

"Sorry about that," I said, taking a seat next to Barrla. "Fenris and I went to visit his grandparents, and then Sunaya corralled me to do some wedding preparations. The time must have slipped away."

"It would have been nice if you'd told me you were leaving," Barrla said, pinching my arm lightly. "But never mind that. How did the visit with Fenris's grandparents go? Are his parents still alive, too?"

"No parents, but the grandparents were overjoyed to see him, even if they are mages," I lied, not wanting to get too much into the details as Barrla and Marris didn't know the full truth behind Fenris's heritage. "They had been told he died in the quake, but his grandmother refused to believe he was dead since a body was never recovered. They are originally from Nebara, and I'm glad that they stayed, or Fenris would have never known to look for them."

"I'm sure they're going to be thrilled when they find out you two are getting married," Barrla said. "Are you sending the invitations out today?"

I blinked. "How do you know about that?"

Barrla grinned. "Sunaya told me all about it when she came around looking for you this morning. You *did* tell her that you were smuggling me into the wedding, right?"

I laughed. "Of course. I wouldn't dream of having it without you."

"A mage wedding," Marris murmured, looking a little awed. "I never thought I'd be attending one, especially not with you as the bride, Mina."

"You don't have to come if you don't want to," I said quickly. "I know how uncomfortable you are around mages."

Marris smiled. "I wouldn't let Barrla go without me," he said, "and besides, I'm starting to get used to it. I thought staying in the palace would be just as uncomfortable as that fancy hotel, but I'm realizing not all mages are bad. I really like Sunaya—she seems more human than the others, which is ironic since she's not human at all."

"She's a total badass," Barrla said admiringly. "I can see why it would take a man like Lord Iannis to keep up with her."

"You know, I do feel a bit guilty that my buddies have gone through all this for nothing," Marris said. "Not that it's a good thing that they were looking forward to killing the mages...but they're going to be pretty disappointed."

"Maybe, but at least they'll still be alive," I reminded him. "Many of them would have died if the plot had gone through, and those who didn't would be rounded up and executed afterward. You did them a favor in preventing that, even if they wouldn't see it that way."

"Doesn't it seem strange to you that they decided to target the building that had the strongest security?" Barrla asked. "I would have chosen a different venue if I had been planning the attack, one that offered better chances of success. But then again, I guess sane, logical people would not get involved in such schemes in the first place."

"I wish that the guy who'd confessed, Moredo, was still alive so we could ask him how they made that decision," Marris said. "Nasty business, suicide."

"He committed suicide?" I had been so wrapped up in

family and wedding thoughts that this jolted me. "When did that happen?"

"Last night, in one of the cells of the Enforcers Guild, I gather," Marris said. "Everyone in the Palace is discussing it. You really hadn't heard?"

"But what if it wasn't suicide?" Barrla's eyes lit up. "What if he was assassinated in order to keep him from talking, because he hadn't told the entire truth? I remember reading a novel once where a prisoner was murdered by the warden to keep him from talking, and it was passed off as a suicide."

"If it was murder," I said slowly, turning the idea over in my mind, "it would mean that one or more enforcers were in on the plot." Judging by the way they had treated Fenris, I did not have much trouble imagining that some enforcers in Solantha sympathized with the Resistance. After all, the majority of them were human, and they seemed to resent the mages' higher authority.

"Could be one of his associates somehow managed to slip into the prison and commit the murder," Barrla suggested. "The Resistance has many sympathizers."

Marris shrugged. "Yes, *if* it was a murder. But speaking as a Resistance sympathizer, not all of us are up for underhanded killing. It's not the same as fighting openly, face to face."

"That's a good point," I said.

"I should probably say goodbye to my buddies today," Marris said, pushing out of the chair he'd been lounging in. "Since the plot has been foiled, they'll be leaving soon. Some of them will be pretty angry, so I'll have to be careful not to be seen with any of you until they've left town."

"Watch yourself," Barrla said as she stood up to kiss him. As they embraced, I decided to seek out Fenris and see what he thought about this unexpected death. If Barrla's instincts were right, perhaps we'd been premature in thinking all danger had passed...

TWENTY-SEVEN

FENRIS

"I hope Mina's suspicion is wrong," Iannis said as he hung up the phone. He sat back in his office chair and pressed the tips of his fingers together, his expression pensive. "With your wedding and the Minister's reception tomorrow, and the Convention for the entire coming week, we don't have time to hunt down the culprit if this suicide was faked."

"It's just a hunch," I said, though I was not so certain that was the truth. Mina had come to me with her and Barrla's suspicions, and after consulting with Iannis, we'd asked Sunaya to look into it. She had intimate knowledge of the enforcers and their cells, and had immediately set out to interview all witnesses. So far, she had not discovered anything suspicious about the man's suicide—he'd hanged himself from his belt, without witnesses. The only tangible result of her foray was the return of my purse and the news that Enforcer Meltin was currently residing in a cell, pending the result of an investigation into his activities. It seemed Captain Skonel had bestirred himself after all.

Iannis looked like he was about to say something else, but

the phone rang. "The Minister is here for his courtesy visit," Dira said. "Shall I send him in?"

"Yes, please, in one minute. If he has brought any staff with him, ask them to wait outside." Iannis hung up the phone. "I suggest you shift now, Fenris, and get under the desk before the Minister comes in."

Frowning, I did as he asked, reaching for the beast that always lay dormant, just waiting for the chance to come to the surface. My wolfish side sprang forth eagerly, and a pale glow engulfed me as my body stretched and reformed. It took only seconds for the change to complete, and just in time—the door opened right as I darted beneath Iannis's huge desk. This felt strangely like old times, but I did not entirely like it. My days of skulking and hiding were over after this, I decided as I rested my lupine head on my paws.

"Lord Iannis," the Minister said by way of greeting. I tried to peek beneath the sliver of space between the desk and the floor, but all I could see was the hem of the Minister's robes and his shoes. "I am glad to see that you've returned safely, though you cut it pretty close."

"Thank you, Minister," Iannis said politely. "The journey was unexpected and we returned as soon as we could, believe me. I am grateful that you kept an eye on things in our absence. Sunaya and I look forward to your reception tomorrow night. I do hope that the aborted plot did not cause any issues with the preparations?"

"Everything is well in hand," the Minister said. "I leave the details to my underlings."

Iannis poured a drink for both of them, and they spent the next few minutes discussing various state matters, particularly the legislation that was being voted on this week by the Convention.

"I don't want to keep you too much longer," Iannis said, "but before you go, I have a request, and I am hoping that you will grant it as a wedding present."

"Oh?" The Minister sounded curious. "What did you have in mind?"

"As you know, my friend Fenris is the son of the late Polar ar'Tollis. He may be illegitimate, but he is Polar's only heir, and he is about to be married to a respectable young lady mage. It would be a generous gesture if Polar could be pardoned posthumously, so that Fenris and his bride need not begin their marriage under the shadow of having an outlaw ancestor."

"Pardon Polar? You cannot be serious," the Minister protested indignantly. "Even if I wanted to, I could not wipe his slate clean—he committed a grievous offense against the Great Accord and must be punished to the full extent of the law. I truly don't see any need for this—Fenris and his bride will not be persecuted for his father's crimes. Perhaps if we had confirmation that Polar was dead I might consider it, but there is always a chance that he survived. If he were to resurface after the pardon, it would make a mockery of all we stand for!"

"I am very sorry you feel that way," Iannis said coolly as my heart thundered in my chest. What in Recca was Iannis thinking, bringing up something like this now? "I had hoped you might have a more flexible outlook on the matter, as I have recently learned that you yourself have not always followed the tenets of the Great Accord. Is it not true that mage marriages are permanent, and can never be broken?"

A deathly silence filled the room, and I held my breath, silently admiring and cursing Iannis at the same time. It was just like him to leverage the Minister's dirty secret on *my* behalf rather than using it for his own political gain. But what if the Minister did not bite? This was a very dangerous game Iannis was playing—if the Minister did not play along, he would almost certainly come after both of us.

"In case you were wondering," Iannis said in a friendly tone, "I did not learn of this from Mirrine. Your wife is a lovely, intelligent woman, and knows that it is safer for her if she is the only one who knows your secret. She does not know that I am aware of the truth."

"Is the pardon really all you want?" the Minister asked stiffly. I could scent his fury, but it was overshadowed by the acrid smell of panic. "I had been planning on naming you my successor, but in light of this...this *blackmail*, I am far less inclined to do so now."

"I have never been interested in your position, as you well know," Iannis said blandly. "I far prefer the temperate clime of Canalo to Dara's snowy winters. I am perfectly content with you naming Garrett as your successor, once you sign and seal these documents."

Iannis pulled a file from one of the drawers and passed it to the Minister over the table. The Minister said nothing, and I gathered by the sound of shuffling papers that he was reading the documents Iannis had prepared in advance. Jittery excitement filled my nerves, and I had to force myself to remain very still lest the Minister become aware of my presence.

"You're asking me to give an unconditional pardon to not only Polar, but also to anyone who may have helped him in any way, for any action involving him after he fled Nebara," the Minister said flatly. "That sounds an awful lot like *you* are the one who helped him escape."

"Whether or not I had anything to do with Polar's disappearance is irrelevant at this point." Iannis sounded utterly unconcerned. "There is no evidence to support that claim, whereas I can produce proof of your bigamy at any time. I've already taken precautions to ensure said proof is published, should anything happen to me following this conversation."

"Besides," he went on as the Minister sputtered, "this

doesn't really have anything to do with Polar. I strongly suspect he is dead, and even if he somehow survived he would be a fool to show his face in the Federation. This is for the benefit of Fenris and his bride, who have done nothing wrong."

"Very well," the Minister said grudgingly. Relief swept through me as I heard the scratch of pen on paper, and all the tension bled from my muscles. "Signed and sealed, as you 'requested.' I must say I am not looking forward to tomorrow's reception as much as I was before I came in here," he added tartly.

"I'm sure you will manage," Iannis said lightly as he tucked the documents back into his desk drawer. "Good day, Minister, and thank you for visiting. I shall see you tomorrow at the Formal Opening of the Convention."

There was a beat of strained silence, and I had to choke back a laugh as I imagined the look on the Minister's face as Iannis summarily dismissed him. But the moment passed, and the Minister rose from his chair and left without another word.

I stayed where I was for another minute, listening as the Minister's footsteps faded outside the hall. Only when I was certain that he wasn't coming back did I nudge Iannis's legs out of the way so I could get out from under the desk.

"You are absolutely insane," I told him after shifting back into human form. "What if this entire thing had backfired and the Minister ended up throwing us all into prison?"

Iannis laughed. "Come now, Fenris," he said, pouring another drink for both of us. "We both know the Minister values his position far more than I do mine. Yes, there was a chance he would have refused me, but he knows that he cannot afford to have his relationship with Mirrine publicized. From his perspective, this was the only logical solution."

"True enough," I admitted as I swirled my glass of scotch around. I took a small sip, and the liquid burned down my throat, filling my stomach with warmth and banishing my lingering nerves. "You don't think that I should start going by Polar now, do you?"

"No," Iannis said. "You may have the legal right to do so, but assuming your true identity would cause more trouble than it is worth. Besides, you are not truly Polar anymore. Your years as a shifter have turned you into a new man."

"Yes," I agreed, smiling. "I am quite content to let Polar ar'Tollis remain missing or dead. Those who matter to me are the only ones who need to know the truth."

"I do wish I had known about this secret earlier," Iannis said ruefully. "We might have been able to avoid the transformation spell entirely. It is too bad that the change is irreversible."

I shrugged. "I quite like being Fenris, actually," I assured Iannis. "I don't think I would want to change back even if it were possible. I have long made peace with who I am now—I may not have all of my magical strength, but the shifter abilities I've gained were worth the tradeoff. Besides, it seems like my powers are slowly regenerating."

"Is that so?" Iannis asked, his violet eyes lighting up. "You should document that, test the rate of improvement at regular intervals. Perhaps in a few years we can unearth some of the more experimental spells in my archive and try them together."

I laughed. "Let's focus on getting through our weddings first," I suggested, lifting my glass to him. There would be time enough to think about magical experiments after all this excitement was behind us.

"About that wedding," Iannis said, his expression serious. "Are you sure Sunaya is not rushing you and your bride? I know that Mina said she wants it to be soon, but two days is perhaps sooner than she thought—and what about you? There is a reason mage engagements are supposed to last for at least a year.

Minister Graning is a case in point. If you say the word, we can always wait a few more weeks."

I stared at him. "By the Lady, Iannis. You know me better than to think that I would rush into marriage just because Sunaya arranged to get us married now. Mina may be young, but we are both absolutely certain of our feelings. We're already living as man and wife anyway—it would be insulting for me to turn around and tell her to wait, when it's so obvious she wants this as much as I do. If anyone has a problem with that, they can go straight to hell."

Iannis grinned. "That was all I needed to hear," he said. "Now, are you sure you've got your wedding vows memorized?"

TWENTY-EIGHT

MINA

"Oh," Barrla sighed as the mage temple shimmered into view. "It's more beautiful than I could have imagined."

"Yeah, that was my reaction too when Iannis first brought me here," Sunaya said, and I silently agreed. The three of us stood outside the temple at the top of Hawk Hill, preparing to enter. Fenris, his parents, and the rest of our friends were waiting inside, and my stomach was a bundle of nerves. I wish I'd had more time to prepare—Fenris and I barely had time to choose our wedding vows and practice them.

"Stop fretting," Barrla said, squeezing my hand. "You look gorgeous, and you're going to do great. As long as you actually get to the 'I do' part, everything will be fine."

Sunaya laughed. "I don't think she'll forget that part," she said, her green eyes sparkling in the setting sun. She and Barrla had agreed to be my bridesmaids, and both of them wore matching blue silk dresses. They looked radiant, and I could already imagine how magnificent Sunaya would look on her own wedding day in just another week. She had shown me the dress yesterday—it was a work of art, though not entirely conventional.

The door to the temple opened, and Marris came rushing out. I smiled at the sight of him in a three-piece navy suit with a red tie—it was probably the fanciest thing he'd ever worn in his life.

"There you are," he said, grinning. "You look perfect. Are you ready?"

He offered me his arm, and I stared down at it, a lump forming in my throat. I wished my father had been alive to see this day—he would have been the one to give me away. But Marris had kindly offered to do so in his stead, so I smiled and laid my hand atop his forearm.

"I'm ready," I said.

Slowly, we entered the sparkling dome, the doors opening of their own accord to admit us. Normally there would be other worshippers here, kneeling on the floor and praying to the statue of Resinah that stood proud and tall in the center of the temple.

Instead, the temple had been cleared of all worshippers and was filled with our friends. Fenris's parents, Comenius and his family, Director Chen, Janta the librarian with two little girls at her side, Elnos, and a few others were seated in white chairs that had been brought out. Somewhere off to the side, a string quartet played a soft, melodious song that was often used at weddings.

I registered all of these things peripherally—my gaze went straight to Fenris, who stood before Resinah's statue with Iannis on one side and the priest on the other. He looked positively regal in his gold and ivory robes, and his yellow eyes were shining with pure adoration that was echoed in my own chest as I approached. I'd never before seen him in robes, but he carried them with pride.

I reached the end of the short aisle, and Marris gently placed my hand into Fenris's waiting palm. He inclined his head to both of us, then took a seat near Director Chen and Kardanor as Barrla and Sunaya took up their positions next to me.

"Family and friends of the bride and groom," the priest said, his sonorous voice echoing through the dome. "Welcome to Solantha Temple, where we have gathered today to witness the joining of these two souls in holy matrimony. In this sacred place, before the Creator and the First Mage, we take ourselves out of the usual routine of our day to be here for this unique moment in the lives of Fenris and Mina, where the two finally become one."

Fenris and I turned to face the priest as he addressed us next. "Though you may not have known each other your entire lives," he said in a solemn voice, "you have nevertheless been gravitating toward this day since you were born, and your union will last as long as you both shall live. As is our ancient custom, you pledge yourselves to each other and move forward into the future as one. Before you declare your vows, I want to hear you confirm that it is indeed your intention to marry today."

"Mina, do you come here today, freely and of your own will, to give yourself to Fenris in marriage?"

"I do," I managed to say around the lump in my throat, pleased that my voice remained steady.

"Very good. And Fenris, do you too come here today, freely and of your own will, to give yourself to Mina in marriage?"

"I do," Fenris said, sounding a little emotional.

"Excellent," the priest said, smiling at us. "Mina and Fenris, now that you have declared your intentions to marry, please face each other and hold hands so that you may declare your marriage vows."

Fenris and I did as the priest asked, and I felt another swell of happiness as Fenris gently took my hands in his own. "I, Fenris," he said in a clear, strong voice, "offer myself to you as I am, with all my flaws and strengths. I vow to love and cherish you for all time, to raise you up when you are weary, and to take you by the hand when you need someone to guide you through the darkness. I place my heart in your hands today, safe in the knowledge that you complement me perfectly, and that together, as husband and wife, we are unassailable."

He squeezed my hands tighter with those last lines, and I had to blink rapidly to banish the tears blurring my vision. Somehow, I managed to repeat the vow without tripping over my words, or at least I thought I did, because when I was finished, Fenris smiled brightly, and the priest congratulated us both.

"Now that the two of you have exchanged your vows, it is time to seal this pact with the marriage spell," the priest declared. "Best man, bridesmaid, do you have the rings?"

"Yes," Barrla and Iannis said in unison. They handed us the bands, gold with tiny runes inscribed on the insides, and Fenris and I carefully slid them onto each other's left ring finger, then joined our hands once more.

The priest then took our joined hands in his and began to chant the Loranian marriage spell. As the words echoed in the chamber, the air around us began to buzz with power. The hair on my arms rose, and suddenly a flood of emotion swept through me, so intense it nearly knocked me over. Fenris's eyes went wide, and we gripped each other tighter as an invisible bond snapped into place between us. I had to hold back a gasp—suddenly I could feel everything that Fenris was feeling: all the love, joy, fear, and wonder that stormed inside him, twin to my own emotions that raged inside me. I breathed out in mingled wonder and relief—as I understood it, not all couples felt this closeness. Those who did, like Fenris and me, could be certain of the Creator's blessing on their union. And that gave me more comfort than anything else.

"And so it is done," the priest said in Northian, releasing our hands. "Fenris, you may now kiss the bride."

Fenris and I grinned at each other, and then he swept me up into his arms and kissed me soundly. The guests broke out into cheers and whistles, and the string quartet started up a lively, celebratory tune. I clung to Fenris tightly for a long moment as I kissed him back, relishing the feel of his arms around me for the first time as husband and wife.

"We finally did it," he murmured against my mouth as he pulled back. His eyes glowed with a tenderness that took my breath away. "Tamina Marton, you are finally mine."

"Tamina *Shelton*," I corrected him with a teasing smile. We had agreed, for simplicity's sake, to take Shelton as our family name—Fenris was going by it anyway, and neither of us had an objection to the name.

"Yes, that's right. Mrs. Fenris Shelton." Grinning, he offered me his arm. "Now why don't we go and celebrate?"

FENRIS

After the ceremony, we all adjourned to Solantha Palace for an exquisite dinner in one of the private dining rooms. It was a beautiful setting for celebrations in relatively small groups, with a view of the city rooftops and the sea, and tonight, many exotic plants and orchids that evoked a tropical island grove. Sunaya and Iannis could only stay for a short while as the Minister's reception in honor of their own wedding was starting soon, but they toasted our happiness with great enthusiasm.

"I never thought that you would get married before me, Fenris," Sunaya teased as we snacked on appetizers.

"Well I don't think it would have turned out that way if you hadn't taken it upon yourself to orchestrate our wedding," I said with a smile. "Thank you...for all of this, by the way." I looped an arm around Mina and hugged her close. "You and Iannis have made this a wonderful day for us both."

"And for us as well," my mother added—she and my father were seated to my left. "We kept hoping that Polar would settle down and start a family of his own, and while it was not to be, we are happy that at least we have lived to see our grandson get married." She smiled at me, and her eyes gleamed with unshed tears. She'd cried unabashedly at the wedding, and even my father had seemed moved.

"It was our pleasure," Iannis said. "Your grandson is a fine young man, Mrs. ar'Tollis, and I am honored to call him my friend."

My father seemed pleased by that—it was a high compliment coming from a Chief Mage, particularly one so powerful and influential. Iannis and Sunaya stayed for a few minutes longer, then left us, along with Director Chen and Kardanor, regretting they could not stay to enjoy the rest of our feast.

After the last course, Mina and I circulated among the guests. Elnos grinned at us from his seat opposite Elania and came up to congratulate us.

"What an amazing coincidence, that the woman who bought the first set of serapha charms in my shop should end up becoming your wife!" he exclaimed, shaking my hand. "You two look very happy together."

"Thank you," I said, smiling broadly. If he was missing Noria, he manfully suppressed any wistfulness—his eyes were sparkling with his usual good cheer. "And thank you for helping Mina by loaning her that ether owl. It proved invaluable in a recent investigation."

"Oh?" Elnos raised an eyebrow. "I didn't realize you two were in the business of investigating."

Mina laughed. "Well, I *was* posing as a journalist at the time," she said. "I can't tell you what we were looking into, but rest assured that your ether owl was put to very good use."

"I'm very glad to hear that," Elnos said. "Why don't you two keep it as a wedding gift? I've already made two more, so I don't need that one anymore," he added with a broad smile.

"That would be wonderful," Mina said as I bit my tongue. I wasn't certain how I felt about learning that there were more of these out in the world, but considering that it had helped avert certain disaster, I could hardly complain.

Later, after most of the guests had left and I'd bundled my parents into a steamcab and sent them back to their hotel, Mina and I adjourned to one of the east wing parlors with Barrla, Marris, Comenius, and Elania. We finished up the champagne and talked about the future at length—how Mina and I planned on settling down in some beachside town near Solantha, where she could have a surgery and her own pets before the children came along—and, I did not add, where I could teach her everything she needed at our leisure, so she need never undergo a formal apprenticeship.

Elania and Comenius announced that they were pregnant, to our collective delight, though I suspected from the lack of surprise on Mina's face that she'd already known about it. Barrla and Marris then proudly told us that they were getting married.

"We'll have to have the ceremony in Abbsville," Barrla said, "or our families would kill us. But after the wedding, we're thinking about coming back out here."

"Check with Constable Foggart first if it is safe to marry there," I advised, remembering why Marris had to leave his hometown. "If he thinks it's too dangerous, I could help with bringing your families out here for the ceremony." It would be dreadful if Marris went home to marry, only to be arrested by the Mages Guild as he left the temple with his new bride on his arm.

"We'll be careful," Barrla assured us, snuggling against Marris.

"So you like Solantha?" Comenius asked. "It was the same for me, when I first arrived from Pernia. Once you come here, this city feels like home to those of us who like its bustle and energy."

"Yes," Barrla agreed with a smile. "I've also discovered

several out-of-print novels from one of my favorite series in a bookshop in maintown, and rumor has it the author lives in the area. Her identity is a secret, but I am determined to find out who she is," she added eagerly, her eyes lighting up at the prospect of a challenge.

Marris laughed. "She won't stand a chance against you," he said, pecking Barrla on the cheek. "Even without the Watawis mages on my case, I don't think we could stand to spend the rest of our lives in Abbsville after coming to Solantha. There's just so much more to *do* out here. The wages are also much higher here than in Abbsville, and there are more jobs. I should be able to find work easily, and in a year or so Barrla and I can open up some kind of business. Maybe Cobil and Roth will move out here too, once I tell them how great this place is."

"I've already decided it's going to be a bookstore," Barrla declared, though by the way Marris rolled his eyes, I could tell that they weren't agreed on that yet. I could see him more with a hardware store, or perhaps sports equipment.

"What about a photography shop?" Mina suggested. "You have been doing very well with that camera, and I look forward to seeing the pictures you took today before and after the wedding. Doing that would also allow you to get out, do photos of parties, weddings, that sort of thing."

"Hmm," Barrla said, looking intrigued by the idea.

"Elania and I own two different stores, though it is not always easy," Comenius mentioned. "You could go for a book-store and something else too. There are no limitations but your own energy and imagination."

"Has Sunaya found anything out from the Enforcers Guild on that suicide?" Marris asked, by way of changing the subject. "She said she was going to investigate, didn't she?"

"She has interviewed several people, I believe," I said, "but with the wedding and the reception today I don't think she's gotten to the bottom of the issue yet."

"You know..." Barrla trailed off, a thoughtful expression on her face. "Earlier at dinner, I remembered reading a book where a bomb was hidden inside a castle's foundation pillars so nobody could find it. The villain nearly succeeded in blowing the place to smithereens, but the hero—a shifter—managed to sniff out the bomb at the last moment with his superior sense of smell."

The room fell quiet for a moment as we all considered that. "If there was a bomb hidden inside a pillar, even a shifter might not notice, if he wasn't specifically looking for it," Marris said slowly.

"I'm not at all sure that I would scent something walled in," I agreed. "Such a plot would require quite a lot of explosives, but if they were properly isolated from the air, no one would smell them in time."

"Shouldn't we tell Sunaya and Iannis about this possibility?" Mina asked in a worried voice. "The Minister's reception tonight is a prime target—Sunaya and Iannis are there, along with anybody who is anybody in the government."

"Hang on a second," Barrla said, narrowing her eyes. "Isn't the Minister's reception held in that concert hall? Sunaya and Iannis said that was where they were going. Has it been renovated since the quake?"

"Very likely, and that would have been the perfect opportunity for the Resistance to smuggle a bomb in," I admitted, truly worried now. "Sunaya and Iannis would have had the place inspected, but still...there is always the chance something was missed. They would hardly have inspected inside walls or under floors."

"And we know for sure that construction companies were involved in the plot," Elania added. "Nobody would have checked what kind of materials they used while rebuilding, with the whole city in disarray after the quake."

"But they couldn't know that the Minister would hold the Convention here in Solantha and give his reception in that particular building," I objected.

"That was a stroke of luck for them—if we are right," Mina said. "A hall like that is often used for important events. They may have just waited for the right occasion to come along and then offered the venue to the Minister's staff at a very low rent to ensure they picked it."

I scrubbed a hand across my face, torn. Were we just engaged in a bout of collective paranoia, or was there a chance of this nightmare scenario being real?

"The guys I visited earlier today to say goodbye to were still kept in readiness," Marris said. "Nobody has been sent home, though there has been some redeployment. They are expecting a loud bang to signal the start of the fight. I thought their bosses were reluctant to tell them that the attack is off, but maybe the attack is still on."

"Blowing up the concert hall makes a lot more sense than attacking the Convention with guns," I had to concede.

"We can't just sit around here and do nothing," Mina declared, standing up. "We've got to go to the concert hall and warn them. If it's nothing, it's nothing. But if the threat is real, we must act before something terrible happens."

Galvanized into action, the six of us raced over to the Solantha Concert Hall as fast as we could. I pulled the steamcar up in front of the gigantic three-story circular building, where the reception was in full swing. Golden light spilled out of the floor-to-ceiling windows on each floor, and I could hear music and laughter even from here.

Comenius and Elania, with Barrla and Marris in the back-seat of their steamcar, pulled up behind us, and we abandoned our vehicles in the middle of the street—there was no time to try and find parking, which was non-existent in this area anyway. Grabbing Mina's hand, we rushed up the steps to the entrance while the others hung back. A veritable army of guards flanked the large glass doors, along with a tall, dour mage with the Minister's crest stitched on the breast of his dress robes. I vaguely remembered him from previous Conventions in Dara.

"Invitation?" he said in a snooty voice as the others rushed to catch up behind us.

Shit. Mina and I exchanged glances—we *had* been invited to the reception, but we hadn't brought the actual invitations. "My name is Fenris," I said authoritatively. "I'm a close friend of

Lord Iannis. My wife and I are on the guest list." It was the first time I'd been able to refer to Mina like that for real, but there was no time to savor the moment.

"That may be," the mage said coolly, "but due to strict security protocols, no one is allowed in without an invitation."

"Fine," Mina said before I could snarl at him. "Would you please fetch Director Toring, then? We have important information to relay to him regarding a possible attack."

The guards exchanged uneasy glances, but the mage just scoffed. "Director Toring doesn't have time to bother with the likes of you," he said. "Get lost."

"Iannis? Sunaya?" I called as Mina tried to reason with the majordomo and guards. *"I'm outside the concert hall, and the guards won't let me in. I need to speak with you urgently about a possible attack!"*

"Hey, you!" One of the guards had shoved his face into mine. "You heard what the man said. Get lost!"

"Let's go," Mina muttered, taking my hand. Cursing silently, I allowed her to lead me back down the steps to where the others were waiting. I wasn't sure if Iannis and Sunaya were busy, or if the extra-strength wards around the perimeter were interfering with my ability to mindspeak to them, but this was the absolute worst time for them to be out of touch.

"What happened?" Comenius asked, frowning. "They wouldn't let you in?"

"No," I said tightly. "And I wasn't able to reach Iannis or Sunaya using mindspeak, either."

"Where is Barrla?" Mina asked, looking around in puzzlement. "Did she go back to the car?"

"She managed to sneak around to a side entrance," Elania said, sounding faintly impressed. "I think she managed to get in using her journalist credentials."

"I tried to go in with her," Marris groused, "but they wouldn't permit me without a press pass."

"She'll be fine," Elania assured him with a pat on the arm. "Your Barrla has a good head on her shoulders and a knack for getting people to do what she asks. She might very well be able to get a warning to Sunaya or Iannis."

"If she can get in that way, so can I," Mina declared. "I'll go after her—I can use mindspeak to try and contact them once I'm inside."

"Wait." I grabbed her arm as she began to turn away. "Please, let me try one more time to reach them." If there was the slightest possibility of a bomb really being involved, I didn't want Mina any closer than she had to be.

Closing my eyes, I gathered my power, then used it to boost my mindspeak signal. *"Sunaya?"* I shouted down the line. *"Can you hear me?"*

"Fenris? Are you here?"

"Outside," I said, relief rushing through me at the sound of her startled voice, faint though it was. *"I forgot my invitation, and the guards won't let us in. We have a theory that the Resistance may have found a way to smuggle in bombs and are planning to blow up the concert hall tonight."* I quickly explained our reasoning.

"They didn't find anything like that during the security check," Sunaya said, sounding troubled, *"but I'll speak to Iannis and Garrett immediately. We can't evacuate the place based solely on a hunch, but if we find anything suspicious I'll let you know."*

I swallowed my frustration—that might very well be too late. But there was nothing for it; Sunaya couldn't very well evacuate the place on a mere hunch.

"Thanks," I said right before the connection cut—Sunaya must have moved out of range. Raking my hand through my hair

in frustration, I turned back to the others. "Sunaya says she's going to have Garrett look into it, though I don't know what he can do—he can't go around busting holes in the walls or pillars merely on suspicion, and he does not even have shifter senses. I just wish that I could get in to investigate myself." I paced up and down on the sidewalk, frustrated beyond belief at this setback and my inability to check whether we were right, or simply worrying for nothing.

"It's maddening," Comenius agreed, a troubled frown on his face. "Sunaya has come too far to have everything come crashing down right before her wedding."

"I have a bad feeling about this," Elania said, wrapping her arms around herself, her face unusually pale as she looked up at the building. "Something is about to happen."

"Fenris," Mina said in a low voice, tugging on my sleeve. She tilted her head to the left, and I followed her gaze to see a balding man in a suit talking to a cook further down the side-walk. "That journalist calls himself Rubb Slade, and I've met him twice. There's something off about him. What is he doing out here, talking to that cook?"

"Let's follow them," Marris suggested as the odd pair ducked behind a newspaper stall, heads together. "They look fishy to me."

We followed the two men around the building at a discreet distance, toward a service door far from the main entrance. There were guards posted here, too, but the cook showed some credentials, and he was allowed inside. Rubb, on the other hand, waited a bit further up the street out of sight of the guards. He had his hands tucked into his suit pockets and was doing his best to look nonchalant even though it was obvious he was anything but.

"Let's go talk to him," Mina said, tugging at my hand. We stepped out from beneath the shade of the tree we were hiding in, while the others remained behind. "Mr. Slade," she said cheerfully, strolling up to the man. "Fancy seeing you here."

"I'm afraid I don't know who you are," he said brusquely, trying to brush past us.

"Stop right there." Flicking my wrist, I conjured a magical rope and lassoed him around the foot. Even if I hadn't seen the flash of recognition in his eyes when he saw Mina, I could smell his lie a mile off. "Why are you lurking around outside the concert hall?"

I tugged firmly on the rope, and Rubb went down with a yelp. "Unhand me!" he cried as the ropes began to rapidly wrap around his body, binding his legs together and his hands to his sides. I snapped my fingers to engage a privacy bubble around us, but it was too late—one of the guards had heard and was coming our way.

"Hold this," I said to Mina, handing the rope off to her. "Come with me, Marris."

We ran back up the path, toward the concert hall, and met the guard almost immediately. "What's the meaning of this?" he demanded right before I slammed a magical fistful of air into his jaw. He went down instantly, and Marris rushed ahead to incapacitate the other guard while I dragged the first one into a dark corner and put a strong sleeping spell on him.

"I grabbed the credentials on the other guy," Marris said as he trotted back up to meet me. "I think the wards won't let you in without one."

"Good thinking."

We headed back toward Mina and Rubb. The latter was still trussed up on the ground, struggling furiously against the magical rope. "He won't say anything," Mina said flatly, her eyes trained on him. She had her other hand out, facing in his direction, ready to blast him should he try anything. I couldn't help but smile—she had come a long way with her magic since I'd first met her.

"Are you planning on attacking the reception tonight?" I asked. "What did you send that cook in to do?"

"I don't have anything to say to a shifter like you," Rubb sneered. "Go ahead, throw me in the dungeons. I won't tell you anything."

"He's involved," I said to Mina. "That's why he won't talk, because he knows I'll be able to tell if he's lying."

"We need to go after that cook, then," Mina said urgently. "We can't afford to let him complete whatever task he's been sent to do."

"Please." I took Mina's hand and clasped it in both of mine. "Let Marris and me handle this one. I need you to stay with Comenius and guard our prisoner. I have a hunch that he's important—we can't afford to let him escape or be killed."

Mina looked like she wanted to protest, but to my relief, she nodded her agreement. "Come back to me," she said, taking my face between her hands and kissing me. Her sweet scent filled me, and I sucked in a deep breath, savoring the brief moment.

"When this is done," I promised her, "we're going to have a proper wedding night."

I helped Mina escort our new prisoner back to Comenius and Elania, and then gave them a quick update before Marris and I headed in. We bypassed the ward easily with the stolen credentials, and I latched onto the strongest, most recent human male scent and followed it.

"Are you sure you've got the right person?" Marris hissed as we crept through the concert hall. The scent trail led us up a set of stairs to the first floor, then down another to the basement, by the service lavatories that the cook had taken advantage of. Probably nervous, I guessed, and the delay helped us gain on him. We then went up another half flight, and were headed down again.

"Shhh," I whispered, holding up a hand. The scent was getting stronger, and I could hear noises up ahead that sounded suspiciously like drywall breaking. Hurrying down the steps, I opened the door, which led into another section of the basement that was filled with party supplies. Several boxes had been haphazardly thrown aside to uncover the wall on the other end, and the cook was busy swinging a hammer, knocking waist-level holes into the drywall.

"You there!" Marris cried, stalking forward. "What are you doing down here?"

The man ignored him, and my heart jumped in alarm as a large piece of drywall fell away, exposing a light switch that had been hidden behind it. The man reached for the switch, and I quickly snagged his wrist with another magic rope before he could flip it.

"No!" the man yelled angrily as I yanked him back. He went skidding across the floor toward us, and I ducked as he flung the hammer straight at my face. Marris tackled him as he tried to rise, and the two ended up brawling on the floor, rolling around and throwing punches at each other.

"Enough!" I yanked on the rope again, pulling the cook out from underneath Marris, then snapped my fingers. Like with Rubb, the rope rapidly twisted around the cook's body, going all the way up to his neck.

"Are there any more of you?" I snarled.

The man shook his head, trembling with terror—clearly he wasn't as fanatical as Rubb. "N-no, just me," he stammered. "That fellow outside paid me to come in here and flip a switch. He said it was going to activate some kind of trap."

"Blast it," I muttered. *"Iannis, are you there? I need you and*

Garrett to come down to the basement. We've found an intruder."

"I'm on my way," Iannis said immediately—Sunaya must have already talked to him, as he did not sound surprised to hear me. *"Is anyone hurt?"*

"No. But come quickly."

A few minutes later, footsteps thundered down the stairs, and Iannis rushed in. Sunaya and Garrett were on his heels, along with the Minister, who looked red-faced and angry.

"What is the meaning of this?" the Minister demanded, looking at the prisoner and then at the wreckage. "What was this man doing in here?"

"He was paid by the Resistance to come in here and flip that switch," I informed them. "He had just uncovered it in the wall when Marris and I caught up to him. It would seem that the whole contraption was arranged while the concert hall was being renovated."

"A walled-in switch?" Garrett stalked over to the wall, a scowl on his face. "Damn. These wires could be connected to explosives at any place in the building. It will take some time to trace the wire and disarm whatever trap they're connected to."

"Bloody hell," Iannis swore. "We need to evacuate the hall at once."

"Yes," Garrett said in a clipped voice. He looked absolutely thunderous. "I can't believe I missed this. We checked this venue *thoroughly*."

"You're not at fault here," Sunaya said to Garrett. "You had no reason to tear the walls apart looking for bombs, and stuff like that isn't easily visible. I couldn't even scent anything when Fenris warned me just now. I still don't scent anything suspicious here."

"Let's not stand around here, then," the Minister said impatiently. "The last thing I need is for someone to accidentally trip and hit that switch. Let's get on with it!"

After Garrett ordered two of his staff to guard the switch with their lives, and another to take charge of the terrified prisoner, we dispersed. Garrett went to gather a team of specialists while the Minister and Iannis went to inform the guests and evacuate the building. While they ushered the guests out, telling them only that the party was being moved to the Palace, Sunaya, Marris and I went back out with the crowd of revelers to where Mina and the others were waiting. By the time we arrived, a bevy of enforcers and agents were already with them.

"Miss Baine." The enforcer in charge inclined his head. "We're ready to transport the prisoner to a holding cell."

"His name is Rubb Slade," Mina explained to Sunaya. "I met him at the Solantha Press Club."

"Let me have a look at him," Sunaya said. Two of the enforcers dragged Rubb forward, and she leaned in to get a good whiff.

"By Magorah," she said, sounding astonished. "You're not Rubb Slade at all. You're Curian Vanderheim, Thorgana's missing husband."

"I don't know what you're talking about," Rubb said stiffly.

"Don't lie to me," Sunaya snapped. "You might weigh thirty pounds less and wear a different face, but you stink just like before. You should have hired a mage to change your scent. It's a good thing you're not as bright as your late wife was."

"I knew there was something off about him," Mina crowed. "Both times I met him he was always talking about how much he hated mages."

"And now we understand why," I said, crossing my arms over my chest. I had never met Thorgana's husband, so there had been no way for me to detect his true identity. Sunaya, thankfully, had done a few bodyguard jobs for Thorgana back in the day, so she was acquainted with the late Benefactor and her husband.

"Well, now that we've got all this sorted, why don't you come back with us to the Palace?" Sunaya said with a grin. "After all, you're a very important person, Mr. Vanderheim. And we certainly wouldn't want you to mysteriously commit suicide in your prison cell, would we?"

Vanderheim only growled in reply as a dozen enforcers converged about him and roughly put him in manacles. We watched as he was dragged away, and relief swept through me—we'd finally caught the real culprit. I could only hope Garrett and his men identified the trap, and that we did not run across any more danger tonight.

MINA

As we headed back to Solantha Palace, my nerves were buzzing with excitement. "We finally did it!" I exclaimed to Fenris. "Thanks to Barrla's hunch, and our team effort, we managed to catch the bastards before they were able to execute their attack."

"Yes, and thank Resinah for that," Fenris said fervently. "You did great, catching Vanderheim's suspicious behavior. We wouldn't have followed him otherwise, and as it was, we barely arrived in the nick of time."

I shook my head. "I can't believe he changed his appearance so much that nobody recognized him." Mages routinely did that with illusion, but permanently altering your physical appearance was a banned practice. For Mr. Vanderheim to go through with such a thing, with surgery...it was quite a commitment.

Fenris shrugged. "He's a fanatic, just like his late wife. Those types will go to any lengths for their cause."

We got back to the Palace, where the party had already resumed in full swing. Mr. Vanderheim was carted off to a guarded cell, while the rest of us convened in the Mages Guild conference room.

"I'm happy to report that Director Toring and I have successfully located the contraption, thanks to our offices working together," Captain Skonel said. "The parquet floor of the hall had been packed full of explosives, hidden underneath layers of plaster."

"They were presumably stolen from mines," Garrett said. "It seems that many were 'mislaid' during the confusion of the recent earthquake."

"Of course," Iannis murmured. "The quake would have been the perfect opportunity for the Resistance to seize them without anyone being the wiser."

"Thank you both for your vigilance and your help," Garrett said to Fenris and me. "That many explosives would have brought down the entire building and killed everyone, including the patsy who was sent to flip the switch. He was horrified when he realized he'd been about to kill himself along with all the rest of us."

Sunaya shook her head in disgust. "It's amazing what people will do for a bit of coin."

"Indeed," the Minister said darkly.

"Director Toring, Captain Skonel," Iannis asked, "how long will it take to render the concert hall safe again?"

"Days," Captain Skonel said baldly. "Much of the reconstruction will have to be redone once we are finished."

"Better that than to have every Chief Mage in the Federation killed, and many innocents as well," Fenris said, and everyone agreed.

"While we are all here," the Minister said, "I have an announcement that will please you and your new bride, Fenris."

"Oh?" I asked, sitting up straighter in my chair. What kind of favor would a man like the Minister do for us? I glanced at Fenris, but his face was inscrutable.

"To set your marriage off on the right path, and as thanks for your brave service, I am pardoning your father, Polar ar'Tollis, for his past crimes," the Minister said. "Lord Iannis already has the written proclamation."

Fenris smiled, and my mouth dropped open in surprise. "Minister, you have no idea how much that gesture means to me," Fenris said as I stared, stunned. Why would the Minister do such a benevolent thing? It seemed incredibly out of character for him...but I would not look a gift horse in the mouth.

"Thank you so much for your kindness, Minister," I said fervently. "This is the perfect wedding gift." There was no more need for hiding, no fear that my husband, the father of my child, would somehow be discovered and carted off into the night. I felt like dancing with joy, but considering the present company, I restrained myself.

"Minister...are you sure this is wise?" Garrett asked, sounding strained. "I have not closed the investigation yet."

"Well you are closing it now," the Minister said firmly. "This case has gone on far too long—we cannot afford to waste any more time or resources on it. With crafty humans like Vanderheim trying to massacre us and nearly succeeding, we mages cannot be seen to have internal disagreements or infighting. We must present a united front."

"Very well," Garrett said grudgingly. Out of the corner of my eye, I saw Fenris and Iannis exchange a look, and I could have sworn that Iannis winked at him.

"*Fenris,*" I said slowly as a nagging suspicion began to take root in my mind. "*Is there something you haven't told me?*"

"*Iannis used the secret you discovered to blackmail the Minister into pardoning me and anyone who helped me during my escape,*" Fenris said, sounding amused. "*I was there for the conversation, hidden—the Minister was absolutely appalled at the idea, no matter how firmly he espouses it now. But he likes his position far more than he wants to see my head on the chopping block, so here we are, free and clear."*

"Well at least that's one thing he and I can agree on," I said, slipping my hand into his beneath the table.

Suddenly, Fenris stood up, knocking his chair back. "I apologize for the rudeness," he said, bowing to the Minister. "But you will have to excuse my wife and me. We have had a long day, and it is high time that we celebrated our wedding night."

Before the Minister could respond, Fenris swept me up into his arms, bridal style. I squealed as he spun around, and the sound of Sunaya and Iannis's laughter trailed behind us.

"Have fun," Sunaya called as Fenris magically shut the doors. "Try not to keep the entire palace up tonight!"

Laughing, I twined my arms around Fenris's neck and kissed him as he walked us down the hall and up to our suite. The moment the door closed behind us, our clothes vanished, and we fell onto the bed, fully naked.

"Hey!" I squealed, sitting up as he began to trail kisses down the column of my throat. "I plan to keep that dress!"

"Don't worry," Fenris said with a laugh. He nibbled on my collarbone, and the sensation of his teeth on my skin sent little shivers of delight through me. "It's hanging in the closet, safe and sound."

"You'll have to teach me that trick," I purred, settling back down. His hot mouth moved lower, down my chest, and I moaned when he flicked his tongue against one of my nipples. "I have to tell you something," I said breathlessly.

"It isn't something that can wait until *after* we've consummated our marriage?" he asked, slipping his free hand between my legs. His fingers expertly found the bundle of nerves at the apex of my thighs, and my hips came off the bed. "Now that we've tied the knot, I'd like to have a little Mina or Fenris as soon as possible."

I let out a sound that was somewhere between a laugh and a moan and cupped his face between my hands. "But that's exactly it, Mr. Shelton. There *is* another Mina or Fenris coming. Sometime in the next nine months."

Fenris froze, his shifter eyes growing wide. "You're pregnant?" he breathed.

I smiled, guiding his free hand to my belly. "I've known for a couple of days now," I said softly as he splayed his big hand over my abdomen. "I thought it might be a nice wedding present."

"It's the best present I could ask for," Fenris said, his gaze full of tenderness. He kissed me deeply, and I wrapped my arms and legs around his big body, opening for him fully. "I love you, Mrs. Shelton," he growled against my mouth as he slid inside me in one smooth, firm stroke.

"I love you too," I gasped as I arched against him. He covered my mouth with his again, and I abandoned the rest of our conversation. There would be plenty of time to talk about our future...for now, I had everything I wanted here in my arms, and I intended to spend the rest of my night enjoying every single inch of him.

THE END

Want to know why Sunaya and Iannis were missing? Find out in TAKEN BY MAGIC, Book Ten in the Baine Chronicles series! Make sure to join the mailing list so you can be notified of future release dates, and to receive special updates, freebies and giveaways!

Did you enjoy this book? Please consider leaving a review. Reviews help us authors sell books so we can afford to write more of them. Writing a review is the best way to ensure that the author writes the next one as it lets them know readers are enjoying their work and want more. Plus, it makes the author feel warm and fuzzy inside, and who doesn't want that? ;)

GLOSSARY

Abbsville: a small town in the state of Watawis, population ca. 800 including the surrounding farms.

Abbsville Book Club: popular with the local ladies. Among its members are Mina Hollin, Barrla Kelling, Mrs. Cattin, Mrs. Vamas, Mrs. Tamil, Mrs. Bartow, Mrs. Staffer, Mrs. Canterbew and ancient Mrs. Harpton.

Ackleberry Farm: a farm outside Abbsville that Fenris has bought from the Ackleberry family, sight unseen, under the name of J.F. Shelton.

Annia: see under Melcott, Annia.

Apprenticeship: all mages are expected to complete an apprenticeship with some master mage, that usually lasts from age fifteen to about twenty-five. Only after the final exam may they use colorful robes, and are considered legally of age. Otherwise they only attain their majority at age thirty.

ar': suffix in some mages' family names, that denotes they are of noble birth, and can trace their descent to one of Resinah's twelve disciples.

Baine, Mafiela: Chieftain of the Jaguar Clan and Sunaya's aunt.

Baine, Rylan: Sunaya Baine's cousin, and like her, a panther shifter. An active member of the Resistance, with the rank of Captain, he was captured and imprisoned during the uprising in Solantha, but ultimately pardoned.

Baine, Sunaya: a half-panther shifter, half-mage who used to hate mages and has a passion for justice. Because magic is forbidden to all but the mage families, Sunaya was forced to keep her abilities a secret until she accidentally used them to defend herself in front of witnesses. Rather than condemn her to death, the Chief Mage, Iannis ar'Sannin, chose to take her on as his apprentice, and eventually his fiancée. Their wedding will be very grand, and is rapidly approaching.

Barrla, see under Kelling, Barrla.

Benefactor: the anonymous, principal source of financial support to the Resistance, who was eventually unmasked as the socialite Thorgana Mills (now deceased).

Bilam: a country on the north coast of Faricia, facing the Central Continent.

Black Market: an area in Solantha where illegal items can be purchased, by night, at the buyer's risk.

Calmias, Father Monor: a charismatic preacher in Ur-God temples, with many fanatic followers all over Northia. He was imprisoned in Prison Isle outside Solantha City for preaching genocide against mages and shifters, but later freed after the Chief Mage "adjusted" his views on racial harmony.

Canalo: one of the fifty states making up the Northia Federation, located on the West Coast of the Northia Continent.

Canter: an elderly mage often manning the reception at Solantha Palace.

Central Continent: the largest of the continents on Recca, spanning from Garai in the east to Castalis in the west.

Chen, Lalia: the current Director of the Canalo Mages Guild in Solantha. She immigrated to the Northia Federation from Garai after her apprenticeship, and serves as deputy to Iannis ar'Sannin, the Chief Mage.

Chief Mage: head of one of the fifty states of the Northia Federation, usually addressed as "Lord Firstname". The Chief Mages come together as the Convention every other year, usually in the capital Dara.

Chieftain: a title used to distinguish the head of a shifter clan.

Cobil: childhood friend and co-conspirator of Marris Dolan and Rotharius.

Comenius: see Genhard, Comenius.

Convention: the assembly of all Chief Mages and highest authority in the Federation.

Creator: the ultimate deity, worshipped by all three races under different names.

Croialis: a poison made from the seed of a tropical plant, popular for assassinations as it is not susceptible to magical healing.

Dara: capital of the Northia Federation, located on the east coast of the Northia Continent.

Dira: Lord Iannis's principal secretary in the Mages Guild offices in Solantha.

Dolan, Marris: a young Abbsville farmer who has spent some time fighting for the Resistance. Friend and neighbor to Fenris.

Dorax, Gelisia: an ambitious and corrupt mage official, formerly Finance Secretary in Nebara, and later in Innarta.

Downtown: the seamy area of Maintown, especially at

night, when the Black Market is operating there. Full of brothels and gaming dens.

Elania Tarrignal: girlfriend and later wife of Comenius Genhard, she is a witch specializing in potions, with a shop in Witches' End, The Black Curtain.

Elnos: see under Ragga, Elnos.

Enforcer: a bounty hunter employed by the government to seek out and capture wanted criminals. They operate under strict rules and are traditionally paid bounties for each head, although Sunaya is trying to reform this system. While the majority of them are human, there is a strong minority of shifters, and even the occasional mage.

Enforcers' Guild: the administrative organization in charge of the enforcers, led by Captain Wellmore Skonel. Also, the building from which the various enforcer crews work under their respective foremen.

Faricia: a large continent that straddles the North and South hemispheres, located south of the Central Continent's western region. Inhabited by many different nations and tribes; partly inaccessible to foreign travelers.

Federation: see Northia Federation.

Fenris aka "Jalen Fenris Shelton": a clanless wolf shifter of unusual antecedents, close friend and confidant of Chief Mage Iannis ar'Sannin and Sunaya Baine. After striking out on his own to evade the scrutiny of the Federal authorities, he has lately become engaged to Mina, a young mage and veterinarian.

Secretary: in each state, the Chief Mages are assisted by Secretaries (Finance, Reconstruction, Legal, Agriculture, etc.), some of whom may eventually achieve the rank of Chief Mage themselves.

Firegate Bridge: Solantha's best-known structure, a

large red bridge spanning the length of Solantha Bay. It is accessible via **Firegate Road**, adjacent to **Firegate Park**.

Foggart, Davin: Constable in Abbsville, the only local law enforcement officer.

Forrane: a large, prosperous country in the western Central Continent.

Garai: the largest and most populated country on the Eastern Continent. Garaians are known for slanted eyes and ivory skin as well as their complicated, rune-like alphabet.

Genhard, Comenius: a hedgewitch from Pernia, owner of the shop Over the Hedge at Witches' End. Close friend of Sunaya Baine, father of Rusalia Genhard, former employer of Noria Melcott, and husband of the witch Elania.

Genhard, Rusalia: daughter of Comenius Genhard. Came from Pernia to Solantha to live with her father after her mother's sudden death.

Graning, Zavian: mage, currently Minister of the Northia Federation. Elected by the Convention for an indefinite term, he is charged with coordination of governmental business and particularly foreign affairs, between the biannual Convention sessions that he prepares and presides.

Great Accord: a treaty struck by the ruling mages centuries ago, which brought an end to a devastating war known as the Conflict. It is still the basis upon which mages rule their countries and territories. All new laws passed must be in accordance with the provisions of the Great Accord.

Gulaya: a star-shaped charm, usually made of metal, that is anchored to a specific location and can take its wearer back there at need. They are rare, and difficult to recharge.

Haralis: a port city on the east coast and capital of Innarta, one of the most prosperous states in the Northia Federation.

Hawk Hill: near Solantha, on the other side of Firegate Bridge; the location of the mages' hidden Temple.

Hedgewitch: a variety of mage specialized in earth-based magic.

Iannis: see ar'Sannin, Iannis.

Innarta: one of the fifty states of the Northia Federation, where Mina's family hails from.

Janta Urama: mage and scholar, head librarian in the Solantha Mages Guild, and foster mother of a young girl whose human family rejected her for having magic.

Kardanor: see under Makis, Kardanor.

Kelling, Barrla: Mina's best friend in Abbsville, who works in her parents' general store and loves shifter romances.

Kelling, Mr. and **Mrs. Sallia:** Barrla's parents, owners of Abbsville's general store.

Lady, the: mages refer to the First Mage, Resinah, as the Lady, most often in the phrase "by the Lady!"

Lakin, Boon: a jaguar shifter, currently the Shiftertown Inspector, friend and ally of Sunaya.

League of Justice: a secret society to combat injustice. Members are Marris, Cobil, Roth, Fenris and later Mina and Barrla.

Loranian: the difficult, secret language of magic that all mages are required to master.

ar'Lutis, Fennias: pseudonym Fenris used among the Watawis mages.

Mages Guild: the governmental organization that rules the mages in each state, and supervises the other races. The headquarters are usually in the same building as the Palace of the local Chief Mage, to whom the Guild is subordinate.

Magitech: devices that are powered by both magic and technology.

Magorah: the god of the shifters, associated with the moon.

Makis, Kardanor: a human architect specialized in public buildings and safety, who was rewarded for his whistle-blowing with his appointment as Canalo's Secretary for Building and Reconstruction. Lover of Director Chen.

Manuc: an island country off the west coast of the Central Continent, where Chief Mage Iannis ar'Sannin was born and educated.

Manucan: the language of Manuc, an island country northwest of the Central Continent.

Marris, see Dolan, Marris.

Marton, Soran and **Monissa:** Mina's late parents, who died in an airship accident.

Marton, Tamina: Mina's original name.

Marwale, the: a luxurious hotel on the west coast, about an hour from Solantha, the capital of Canalo. It caters to mages and rich humans.

Melcott, Annia: a human enforcer, close friend of Sunaya. After Annia's younger sister Noria was sentenced to hard labor in the Mines and disappeared during the great earthquake, Annia set off to find her sibling and has not yet returned.

Melcott, Noria: Annia Melcott's younger sister. A gifted inventor who used to work part-time in the shop Over the Hedge, belonging to Comenius Genhard. She had a mage boyfriend, Elnos, but left him to join the Resistance, and was sentenced to hard labor in the mines.

Mills, Thorgana: socialite and former owner of a news media conglomerate as well as numerous other companies. After being exposed as the Benefactor, she was imprisoned. She managed to escape during a prison fire, but later died around the time of the Solantha earthquake.

Mina, aka **Tamina Marton,** aka **Mina Hollin,** aka **Tuala Harmon,** aka **Mina Shelton:** Mina's original name is Tamina Marton, and from childhood she was called "Mina" by her friends and family. After running away as a teenager, she used the name Mina Hollin and eventually, various other pseudonyms as needed.

Mindspeak: shifters' telepathic way to communicate over short distances, especially useful when in animal form. A few mages also share this ability.

Minister, the: the mage who presides the Convention of Chief Mages, and coordinates the affairs of the Northia Federation between sessions, particularly foreign relations. The office is currently held by Zavian Graning.

Nebara: one of the fifty states making up the Northia Federation, located north of Canalo, and Fenris's home state.

Noria: see under Melcott, Noria.

Northia Federation: a federation consisting of fifty states that cover almost the entire northern half and middle of the Western Continent.

Northian: the main language spoken in the Northia Federation.

Osero: one of the fifty states of the Northia Federation, located north of Canalo on the continent's west coast.

Over the Hedge: a shop at Witches' End selling magical charms and herbal remedies, belonging to Comenius Genhard.

Pandanum: a base metal used, inter alia, for less valuable coins.

Pernia: a country on the Central Continent, from which Sunaya's friend Comenius Genhard hails.

Polar: see under ar'Tollis, Polar.

Ragga, Elnos: mage and inventor, formerly Noria

Melcott's boyfriend. He and Noria worked together to develop new magitech devices.

Recca: the world of humans, mages and shifters.

Resinah: the first mage, whose teachings are of paramount spiritual importance for the mages. Her statue can be found in the mage temples, which are off-limits to non-mages and magically hidden from outsiders.

Resistance: a movement of revolutionaries planning to overthrow the mages and take control of the Northia Federation, financially backed by the Benefactor. Over time they became bolder and more aggressive, using terrorist attacks with civilian casualties, as well as assassination. The discovery that the Benefactor and the human leaders of the Resistance were planning to turn on the shifters once the mages were defeated dealt a blow to the unity of the movement, but its human component is far from completely defeated.

Roor, Ilain: a young farmer in Abbsville, son of Mrs. Roor. He pestered Mina with unwanted attentions, while his jealous mother accused her of witchcraft.

Rotharius aka **Roth:** together with Cobil, friend and companion of Marris Dolan.

Rusalia, see under Genhard, Rusalia.

Rylan: see under Baine, Rylan.

ar'Sannin, Iannis: Chief Mage of Canalo, and close friend of Fenris. He resides in the capital city of Solantha, from which he runs Canalo as well as the Mages Guild with the help of his deputy and Secretaries. Originally a native of Manuc, a country located across the Eastern Sea. His impending wedding to the half-shifter Sunaya Baine has drawn great media attention.

Serapha charms: paired amulets that allow two people, usually a couple, to find each other via twinned stones imbued with a small part of their essence. Normally, only the wearer can take a serapha charm off.

Shelton: the false family name under which Fenris has bought Ackleberry farm in Abbsville.

Shifter: a human who can change into animal form and back by magic; they originally resulted from illegal experiments by mages on ordinary humans.

Shiftertown: the part of Solantha where the official shifter clans live.

Shiftertown Inspector: a shifter chosen by the Shifter-town Council to police shifter-related crime. The position is currently held by Boon Lakin, a jaguar shifter.

Silver: the metal is toxic to shifters, and burns their skin when they touch it. It is nevertheless used for coins in the Federation.

Skonel, Wellmore: human; since the retirement of his predecessor, Captain of Solantha's Enforcers.

Solantha: the capital of Canalo State, a port city on the west coast of the Northia continent. Seat of Chief Mage Iannis ar'Sannin and the Canalo Mages Guild, and home of Sunaya Baine.

Solantha Bay: spanned by the Firegate Bridge, the bay gave its name to the city and port that became the capital of Canalo.

Solantha Palace: the seat of power in Canalo, where both the Chief Mage and the Mages Guild reside. It is located near the coast of Solantha Bay.

Solantha Press Club: an institution dedicated to supporting the press, known for its well-stocked bar.

Sunaya: see under Baine, Sunaya.

Thorgana: see under Mills, Thorgana.

Thrase, Nelia: a young human, Sunaya's social secretary.

ar'Tollis, Polar: former Chief Mage of Nebara, who was condemned to death in absentia for a crime against the Great Accord.

ar'Tollis, Rotho and Balina: Polar ar'Tollis's aged parents.

Toring, Garrett: mage, Federal Director of Security, former Federal Secretary of Justice. An ambitious high official in the Federal government, determined to expand his power, and catch the fugitive former Chief Mage Polar ar'Tollis.

Trouble: a non-corporeal ether parrot that resulted when Sunaya tried the ether pigeon spell on her own. He appears whenever Sunaya pronounces his name in any context.

Tua: a legendary and highly dangerous race of very long-lived beings with powerful magic, who sometimes cross from their own world into Recca, most frequently in Manuc.

Ur-God: the name the humans call the Creator by.

Vanderheim, Curian: human millionaire and business-man, husband to the late Thorgana Mills. After his wife's arrest, he managed to flee the country with some of his vast fortune.

Watawis: one of the fifty states of the Northia Federation, landlocked, in the mountainous northwest. It is one of the least populated and poorest of the fifty states.

Willowdale: capital of the state of Watawis, seat of its Chief Mage and government.

Witches' End: a pier in Solantha City, part of the Port, where immigrant magic users sell their wares and services.

Words: Loranian formulas used by mages for almost all standard spells.

Zavian Graning: see under Graning, Zavian.

ABOUT THE AUTHOR

New York Times and USA Today Bestselling Author Jasmine Walt is a big fan of books, chocolate, and sharp, pointy objects. Somehow, those three things melded together in her head and transformed into a desire to write, usually fantastical stuff with a healthy dose of action and romance. Her characters are a little (okay, a lot) on the snarky side, and they swear, but they mean well. Even the villains sometimes.

She also writes under Jada Storm (reverse harem romance).

When Jasmine isn't chained to her keyboard, you can find her working on her triangle choke, spending time with her family, or binge-watching Supernatural on Netflix.

Want to connect with Jasmine? You can find her at www.jasminewalt.com. She loves to hear from readers, so feel free to drop her a line at any time at jasmine@jasminewalt.com.

Secret of the Dragon

The Dragon's Gift Trilogy

Written under Jada Storm

Dragon's Gift

Dragon's Blood

Dragon's Curse

Her Dark Protectors

Written under Jada Storm, with Emily Goodwin

Cursed by Night

Kissed by Night

Hidden by Night

Broken by Night